S0-CAA-347

UNFORGETTABLE NOVELS
OF THE WEST
BY JACK BALLAS ...

TOMAHAWK CANYON

Cole Mason came to New Mexico Territory looking for a good graze—and found a bloody range war instead ...

DURANGO GUNFIGHT

Quint Cantrell wants to bury his past. But the Hardester clan wants to bury *him* ...

MAVERICK GUNS

Clay Mason's brother has been marked for death by a sly killer—but when you take on one of the Mason clan, you take on *all* of the Mason clan ...

MONTANA BREED

Young Rafe Gunn wanted to look into his family's past. But first he had to look death square in the face ...

Jove titles by Jack Ballas

DURANGO GUNFIGHT
MAVERICK GUNS
MONTANA BREED
TOMAHAWK CANYON

APACHE BLANCO

JACK BALLAS

JOVE BOOKS, NEW YORK

APACHE BLANCO

A Jove Book / published by arrangement with
the author

PRINTING HISTORY
Jove edition / September 1994

ISBN: 0-515-11452-9

A JOVE BOOK®
Jove Books are published by The Berkley Publishing Group,
200 Madison Avenue, New York, New York 10016.
JOVE and the "J" design are trademarks
belonging to Jove Publications, Inc.

PRINTED IN THE UNITED STATES OF AMERICA

10 9 8 7 6 5 4 3 2 1

APACHE BLANCO

CHAPTER
1

Gundy pressed flat against the adobe wall. Fire lanced at him from the corner of the alley, and bullets chipped chunks from the wall next to him. His gut tightened. He pulled the trigger of his .44 and heard a curse—or a prayer. "*Madre de Dios . . . el cabron . . . bastardo*, he shoots straight."

Gundy fired another shot. He had no friends here in Ciudad Juárez, and no one to come to his aid, except perhaps the man, Kelly, who had sent him the message, and Kelly had no way of knowing Gundy was here. More shots came his way.

A building across the street had a galleria with a low-hanging wooden roof. Gundy figured the building would butt up against Kelly's hacienda. He holstered his Colt and sprinted toward it. Fire lanced at him from both sides.

He ran under a beam, grabbed it, swung forward, and then back enough to bring his leg up and lever himself to its top. He stood and, bent almost double, ran to the front of the building, catapulted himself over the top of the facade, and lay there panting, tasting the brass of fear in his throat, smelling his own sweat, and feeling his gut muscles loosen. The cool roof tile under his cheek and hands soothed a little of the tension.

His enemies would stay where they were, not daring to chance climbing in the face of his deadly fire.

He took only a moment to get his breath. Staying low, he

ran to the rear and went belly down, looking for a place to go to ground. He peered into the courtyard of a hacienda, hopefully the one he looked for. The garden area below, enclosed on two sides by high, thick adobe walls and in the front by the hacienda itself, looked safe—maybe too safe.

He searched the area. Ferocious dogs might be as bad as those who hunted him; he had been recognized by one of the men as the Apache Blanco.

His look found nothing to worry him on the ground. The garden area looked deserted. It was dimly lighted with two lanterns. He jumped, cushioned his fall with his hands, and stood.

A wrought-iron gate, set into the thick walls close to the house, looked like his best escape route. He hesitated, then knowing he could not stay there, stepped toward the heavy steel bars.

"*Señor*, do not make a move for your gun or you die. And hold your hands high above your head so I can see them."

Gundy's hand stopped, frozen halfway to his holster. He slowly raised both hands over his head. The knot was back in his stomach. "I wish you no harm, *señor*. I am here only to try and save my own hide."

"Don't turn until I relieve you of your weapons."

Gundy felt the weight removed from his right side; then the handle of his big bowie knife rubbed his back while being pulled from its sheath. Hands patted him for more weapons— and missed finding the slim, deadly throwing knife between his shoulder blades. If it became necessary, he could at least go out fighting.

"Turn around—carefully."

Gundy turned expecting to find a Spaniard, or a middle- to upper-class Mexican, facing him. Instead, the face that looked back at him could have been the map of Ireland. Red hair, green eyes, pugnacious chin. Gundy realized he had estimated the whereabouts of Kelly's house correctly. With this hair and face the guy had to be Irish, and probably Kelly.

"Who are you, and why are you here?" the man asked.

"Trace Gundy, and if you heard the shots, they were aimed at me. Hanker to keep my hide in one piece." They had been speaking English. He had expected to be addressed in Spanish.

His captor chuckled, but the heavy pistol he held in his right hand didn't waver. "You sound like a Texian."

"Been there more'n anywhere else, so reckon I'd be right in makin' that claim." Gundy glanced upward to his hands. If he could lower them to shoulder level, his throwing knife would be in reach. "Mind if I lower them a little?"

"Keep them where they are. We'll go in my hacienda while I decide what to do with you." He pointed toward a door next to a large gardenia bush. "In there."

Gundy walked ahead of the big redheaded man. When he reached for the handle, the man said, "Open it and step through all the way. I don't need to catch an oak panel in my face."

Gundy looked over his shoulder and grinned. "Careful, aren't you." If he could cause his captor to relax, just a little, he could bring his throwing knife into play.

"Do it."

When Gundy pushed the door open and walked in, even though he'd been expecting comfortable furnishings, he was surprised at the luxury. Chairs and settees were massive in the Mexican style, and all were leather-upholstered; a grand piano was in one corner, and two crystal chandeliers, with at least a hundred tapers each, lighted the huge room.

Gundy walked to the middle of the room and faced his captor. "All right, we're here. What you figure on doin' with me?"

"Sit over there. We're going to talk. I want to know all about you."

Gundy sat, his hands still held high.

The big man said, "Lower them, but keep 'em where I can see them. Now start talking."

Gundy lowered his hands and curled his fingers around the curved ends of the chair's arms. "First off, I'd like to know who *you* are."

Laugh wrinkles broke the smooth ruddy complexion at the corners of the big man's eyes, and a slight smile crinkled the corners of his lips. He nodded his head in one snappy jerk. "Alejandro Kelly, half Irish, half Spanish, and one hundred percent tarantula."

"All right, Mr. Kelly. I'm Trace Gundy, don't know what nationality, but there are them who ought to know figure I can be meaner'n hell too. An' besides, you sent for me."

"You still haven't told me who you are. I sent no Trace Gundy a message."

"I told you who I am, an' 'less they's two Alejandro Kellys, you sent for me or somebody pulled a helluva joke. 'Bout to get me killed."

"All right. You won't tell me, so I'm gonna tell you." The diameter of the .44 pointed at Gundy seemed to have grown a couple of inches, and it had not wavered a hair.

"The people in West Texas, New Mexico Territory, and here in Mexico call you the White Apache." He nodded. "And I'm one of those who figure you to be meaner'n hell. Yeah, I sent for you."

Gundy stared at the Irishman a moment. "Why?"

Kelly shook his head. "We're gonna talk before I let you know that. First there are always two sides to any yarn. I want to know yours." The gun still held steady, but Gundy began to relax—a little. The man wanted to talk, and he didn't show fear for having a known savage in his home. Gundy decided to push his luck.

"Before I tell you my story, and maybe I won't tell you nothin', I'll tell you why I'm here, and that answering your invitation was somethin' I figured wouldn't hurt, seein' as how I was gonna be here anyway."

Kelly settled deeper into his chair and nodded.

Gundy wondered how much to tell Kelly, then thought it couldn't hurt anything if he told the truth. "Come down here to try an' round up ten or twelve of these *vaqueros* you folks got so many of."

The muzzle of the .44 dropped a fraction. "What the hell you want with them, gonna start yourself a band of Comancheros?"

The blood rushed into Gundy's neck. His reputation was bad, and he had earned every bit of it, but to have it thrown back into his face made him almost forget the gun in Kelly's hand.

"Don't look like you're willin' to b'lieve there's two sides to every story," Gundy said. "Hell, no, I don't want them to be Comancheros. I want them *vaqueros* to help round up some of them unbranded mavericks down yonder in Tejas. Gonna start myself a ranch. Reckon I'm—"

"Papa, would you and your guest like a cool drink?"

Gundy's look snapped toward the voice. A girl—or woman—stood inside the doorway. Black hair, green eyes, skin a golden hue, and from toe to head the most beautiful woman he'd ever laid eyes on. He grabbed for his hat. "Ma'am, sorry to barge in like this, but reckon your father wouldn't have it no other way. At any rate, I ain't a guest."

"Gundy, this is my daughter, Dolores, and a string of other names her mama pinned on her. *Niña*, this is Mr. Gundy, Trace Gundy, and no, thank you. We are not on drinkin' terms—yet."

Gundy breathed easier. The hand that held the gun now rested on Kelly's leg—plenty of leeway for Gundy to get his throwing knife into action—but he wouldn't jeopardize the girl.

He nodded to her and turned his eyes back to Kelly. "You made up your mind whether to tell me why you want to see me?"

Kelly stared at him a moment, nodded, and tossed Gundy his Colt and knife. "Yeah, but I'm gonna ask you to come back tomorrow night. If you can get back here alive I'll have a proposition for you." He stood. "Think you can get back across the border without gettin' killed?"

"Don't know, but I know one damned thing—excuse me, *señorita*—gettin' killed sure is possible."

Kelly shook his head. "If you can get back here, I figure you may be able to do the job I have in mind."

"Ain't lookin' for no job."

A slight smile creased the corners of Kelly's lips. "What I have in mind might interest you. It could make you a good bit of money."

Gundy stood and shook his head. "No, sir. I got a bad reputation, but I ain't doin' nothin dishonest—never have, never will."

"This is honest, although many would say it's against the law, and dangerous as hell. You think about it. Now you'd better see if you can get back to Texas."

Gundy had been holding his .44 and knife. He shoved them back in their holsters, and tipped his hat to Dolores. "Tomorrow night, *señorita*, I *will* be a guest."

He went out the front door. As he left, Kelly said those who hunted him would think he was a late-night visitor. But whatever Kelly's belief, it didn't fool Gundy's enemies very long.

He'd gone only a block when shots came at him from two directions, one behind and one to his left.

CHAPTER
2

Gundy crouched. His .44 came smoothly into his hand. He thumbed off a shot at the spot to his left, twisted, and fired blindly to his rear. The stench of street garbage filled his nostrils.

He sprinted toward the corner, directly toward the gunman who had fired from his left. Another red blossom stabbed at him—he flinched when the bullet tore through his vest. The building's wall stopped his dash.

Gundy glanced to his rear in time to see that attacker running toward him pistol leveled. He squeezed off a round. The bullet stopped the slim Mexican in his tracks—then he stumbled toward Gundy, falling. Gundy wouldn't have to worry about that gun again, but the shots would bring others.

He stood close to the wall. His other adversary waited just around the tan adobe corner from him. The one who moved first in this kind of situation usually had the advantage. He sucked in a breath, pulled his bowie, crouched low to the street, and launched himself to face the man there.

He fired up into the man's gut and swung his knife at the same time. The sharp blade cut across the hand lowering the pistol to shoot into him. The gun, and fingers, fell to the street at his feet.

The Mexican facing him opened his mouth to say something, but his tongue pushed a thin black stream from the cor-

ners of his mouth. Blood. It looked black in the night. Blanco
relaxed the pressure on the trigger.

He scooped up the dead man's gun and ran toward the next
corner, hoping to get to the edge of town, out in the open
where he could run, out where neither they nor he could hide.

He didn't slow when he crossed the street, now little more
than a dirt path. Still running, he gained the cover of the
hovel across the dirt track, but bullets whined so close their
noise caused his gut muscles to tighten and brace against the
impact of a bullet.

From the sounds of the shots, he now had five or six guns
pointed his way. At the back side of the shack, sagebrush,
creosote bush, and cactus loomed stark and black against the
night sky. The Rio Grande was only two or three hundred
yards away.

For the first time he thought ahead far enough to figure he
would make it. He avoided running for the bridge, knowing
his enemies would shut off that means of escape.

The danger one of the deadly Spanish daggers, or yucca
spears, would cripple him didn't slow his pace, but his boots
were a hindrance. Moccasins would have been better.

A look over his shoulder cost him a couple of yards. The
shots seeking his hide did not come close. If one of his enemies stopped and aimed . . . Gundy pushed the thought from
his mind. He brushed past a prickly pear and the pain of a
hundred needles burned him.

His side felt like a hot knife pushed into it—his breath, or
lack of it, caused that—but he could run as long as the others
could. The river must be close, had to be—and then the thin
silvery sheen of the Rio Grande stretched before him. He had
almost run over the bank. Gundy slid down it to the stream's
edge. Abruptly, he turned at right angles to the flowing,
murky water. Crossing now would make him a prime target,
dark though it was.

About fifty yards upstream he slid into the water, and
stretched out so only his head showed, holding his gun out of
the water. His breath caught in his throat. The water was
frigid. If they got close enough to identify him, they'd be too
close. They, or he, would die.

The pack of men ran cursing to the river's edge, blindly fired into the muddy surface, continued cursing, and searched along the bank. Two of them came within ten feet of where Gundy lay. He slowly sucked in a breath, brought his .44 into position to fire, and waited.

The two fired into the river again. It seemed the powder flash lighted up the entire riverbank. After firing they grumbled that he'd had time to reach the Texas side and they were damned if they'd pursue him there. Cursing again, they turned back to their companions.

Gundy let his breath out slowly, and at the same time became aware that the cold was bleeding his strength, even though it was late spring. He still didn't dare move to cross the river. He lay there until he began to feel warm and comfortable. He'd heard a person got this way when he was about to freeze to death. His teeth chattering, he pushed the thought out of his mind. Cold or bullets—he'd still be dead. The voices of his pursuers faded, grumbling into the distance.

He had to chance they hadn't left anyone behind. El Paso, and safety, lay just the other side of the narrow stretch of water.

An inch at a time he pulled his legs under him. His cramped muscles protested, and when he moved, fire seemed to shoot through every nerve-end.

By the time he reached the other side he was able to walk more freely. When finally he stood, drenched, shivering, and wishing his horse was closer than the livery across town, he wondered why he had left the impression with Kelly that he would see him the next night.

What kind of job awaited him? If some would look on it as illegal, and if it wasn't stealing, what could it be? Dangerous as hell, he figured, simply from the fact that Kelly had wanted him to run that death gauntlet again in order to see if he was up to it. Still, Gundy needed money.

He walked toward the livery while he thought out the problem. He'd either saddle and head for San Antonio and try to find riders there, or he'd gather his bedroll, find a hotel room, take a bath, and sleep until it was time to try and work his way back to Kelly's place. The money almost clinched it for him, and then the thought of Dolores made up his mind.

A damned fool was born every minute, he thought, and then he grinned into the night. Every gun in the New Mexico Territory was against him, and now he could include Mexico. And he had never found a way of clearing his name. But he would do it if it killed him—and it just might do that.

While walking about town the next day Gundy planned how to get to Kelly's without getting shot to rags. Night would be the best time, and he had to have a disguise—but what? His height was against him. He stood six feet one in his stockings. But he was slim; that was in his favor. He had black hair, but blue eyes, and was tanned almost as dark as an Indian. He decided to try what had been in the back of his mind. His border Mexican was as fluent as any native. He'd learned that while with the Mescalero Apaches. He'd dress as a *peon*.

His plan pretty well in place, he looked for a store and found the one he wanted. It was far from the riverfront, but ideal in order to avoid much of the Mexican trade.

"What can I do for you, *señor*?" the clerk said.

"Need somethin' to wear to one of them parties where everybody dresses up like somethin' they ain't."

"Ah, you are going to a masquerade party?"

"Yeah, reckon that's what you call it."

"What did you have in mind? A Spanish grandee, a bullfighter—or perhaps an Easterner?"

"Sort of figured goin' dressed like a *peon*."

The clerk's face showed disappointment. He would not make as much money on this purchase. He frowned a moment, nodded, and said, "Let me suggest something better."

Gundy unconsciously covered the pocket holding his money. This guy was gonna try to sell him the store. "All right, you tell me, but I tell you right now—I ain't got much money."

The clerk studied him from head to foot and nodded. "I think it would fit you. Tell you what; I have a suit, the beautiful suit of a gentleman. I will rent it to you."

"Let's see it."

The clerk brought the suit out. Gundy looked it over. Dressed like this he could ride his horse, and wear his boots rather than the sandals he'd have to wear as a *peon.* "Better see if it fits."

"Dressing room's there in the back."

That night, well after dark, Gundy crossed the border. People afoot stared at him. When he'd looked at himself in the mirror before leaving his room, a slim, young Spanish grandee had stared back at him.

Every muscle taut, he kept his eyes straight ahead. He didn't think anyone would recognize him, but there might be some little thing he'd forgotten that might give him away. His horse and saddle were not decked out as elaborately as he'd wished. He'd had to use his old work saddle and bridle—no silver conchos—but maybe at night like this no one would notice.

When he left the bridge, the border guard looked at him a moment and waved him by.

Gundy nudged his horse to a faster pace.

He rode to the rail in front of Kelly's hacienda and tied the buckskin.

There was only a short wait after rapping, and then Kelly opened the door. "Made it, huh? Didn't hear any gunfire."

"No, but you might if I don't get this Texas-branded horse out of sight."

Kelly called over his shoulder, "Juan, take the gentleman's horse to the stable." He stood aside and beckoned Gundy to enter. "Wondered if you'd come dressed like you were last night." He ran his hands through his hair. "You got some brains anyway. That's one thing I was hoping for. Come on in and have a seat. What do you drink?"

"Beer."

This time a small Mexican girl brought the drinks. Gundy felt a pang of disappointment that Dolores had not done so.

When they were seated with their drinks at hand, Kelly studied Gundy with a steady gaze that caused him to want to fidget. Instead he stared back. The Irishman would get down to business in his own good time.

Finally, Kelly held his drink out for a toast. "Here's to you getting the job done."

"Ain't took no job—yet. You better tell me what I'm gettin' into, and what I'm gonna get out of it." Kelly's assumption that he would take the job irked him.

Abruptly Kelly called, "Dolores, you need to hear all of this. Come on in."

She was as beautiful as Gundy remembered, with hair so black it looked midnight blue. And those green eyes seemed to swallow him. He stood, nodded, and said, *"Señorita."*

"Mr. Gundy."

As soon as she was seated, Gundy sat.

"Now, Gundy, we can get down to business," Kelly said. "My daughter is as interested in this as I am. It involves her brother's life."

Gundy glanced at Dolores. She sat in a straight-backed chair, her hands folded in her lap, yet she looked relaxed, and her look was that of a woman interested in a man. He sat a little straighter.

"As you may have guessed," Kelly continued, "I'm not a poor man. I have holdings on both sides of the border."

Gundy nodded.

Kelly continued. "None of my holdings are as much to me as my son and daughter. They have taken my son from me and I want you to get him back. They have taken him and are asking a great deal of money for his return."

Gundy took a swallow of his beer. "You just said you got a lot of money. Why don't you pay 'em?"

"Because they'll get my last peso—and then they'll kill him. They have no intention of letting him go."

"You keep talkin' 'bout 'they.' Who's 'they'?

"The *policía*. He gave some guns to the Yaqui—"

"The police? You gotta be crazy. You told me this was not illegal."

"Mr. Gundy, I believe my father told you that it was not dishonest." Dolores's voice was soft but firm. "I think you had better hear what he has to say."

Gundy felt like a small boy who had been scolded. "I'm
listenin'."

Dolores continued. "Mr. Gundy . . ."

"Call me Trace, *por favor*?"

"All right, Trace. We've tried to get him brought to trial,
but that doesn't serve their purpose. They want the money my
father can give them, and we know how that ends. He will try
to escape and they will shoot him. It has happened to others."

Gundy drank the last of his beer and sat staring at the wall.
Many of the Yaquis were his friends, and to a certain degree
they were still free to fight. And then there was Dolores. He
felt like a money-grabbing thief doing something like this for
her, but he wanted his own ranch. "Why have you picked me
for this job, *señor, señorita*? You don't know nothin' 'bout
me."

"Gundy, I know as much about you as you know yourself.
I tried to find you for over six months, but nobody here or in
the Territory knew where to find you. I sent my most trusted
employee into Texas—didn't think you'd be in the Territory
under the circumstances. He found you, but didn't know why
I wanted to see you."

"How much will you pay for this?"

"Five thousand American dollars," Kelly said, as though he
knew Gundy would not turn it down.

"Ten thousand—five now and five when I bring 'im to
you."

"Seven."

Gundy stood.

"All right. Ten thousand."

"Papa, I'm ashamed of you. Negotiating for your son's life
as though he was a bag of oats."

"Ah, *niña*, I suppose I never forget that I was once a very
poor man. I'm sorry."

She looked at Gundy's empty glass and stood. He nodded,
and she brought him another beer.

"Now, Trace, I'll draw you a map of where he is being
held," she said.

Before you do that, *señorita*, where am I to take your

brother when I get 'im out? This side of the border and
they'll simply take him again."

"We have a ranch northwest of Las Cruces. Once we get
him across the border, he'll be safe. But where he's held is
about a hundred miles south of here. It is a small town, and
the entire town is in on holding him." She looked Gundy in
the eye. "You have a very hard and dangerous job ahead of
you."

Gundy shifted his eyes to Kelly. "Reckon we ain't through
negotiating yet. You want me to deliver him into New Mexico Territory. They ain't a soldier or a lawman there what
wouldn't give a year's pay to collect my scalp. That'll cost
you twenty-five hundred more—and I want four of the best
horses you got, plus provisions, an' one of them horses saddled and bridled for your brother. *I'll* use my own. An' in
case I forget it, your son's gonna need a good rifle and pistol.
Take it all to that livery stable north of El Paso. Meet you
there tomorrow 'bout daylight."

Gundy stood to take his leave, and Dolores came to him.
She gazed into his eyes a moment. "Bring my brother back
to me, Trace. Papa and I'll meet you in the morning at the
livery, and the extra money is no problem." She placed her
hand on his arm. "*Vaya con Dios, mi amigo;* be careful."

When Gundy rode toward the border he thought he'd
found a friend. He wasn't sure about Kelly, but he felt Dolores was a woman who would stand by him. He shrugged.
Hell, he had a lot of work to do before he could think of a
woman—any woman.

Crossing into the States again went smoothly. He went to
the hotel, gathered his gear, and went to the livery stable.
He'd decided to sleep there, figuring it would be safer than a
room in the middle of town.

CHAPTER
3

By noon the next day, Gundy was several miles up the Rio Grande. He wanted to be well away from El Paso and Juárez when he crossed the border. He dressed as an Apache: baggy britches, leather leggings, headband. If he ran into any Yaquis, he wanted them to recognize him as a friend. He also wore his guns.

The sun beat down. Sweat streamed down his chest and back, but his headband stopped the salty fluid short of his eyes, which he kept squinted against the brightness. He'd gotten used to his old floppy-brimmed hat shading his eyes, but now it was wadded up in his bedroll. Dressed as he was, he had more to fear from whites than Mexicans.

The heat cooked into the desert, giving the air a scorched, dusty smell, and the earth shimmered with heat waves. Heat and cold had been a part of his life for longer than he could remember. If he sweated, or shivered, that was how it was—he ignored it.

For several minutes Gundy had the feeling he was under someone's gaze. A cold knot formed between his shoulders. He didn't turn his head, but used his eyes to search every arroyo, every land-swell, the trunk of every yucca, even the ground behind the scrubby creosote bushes. It paid off.

A faded red shirtsleeve showed from behind a yucca trunk. It could be a friend—or an enemy. He needed to see more.

He rode another hundred yards while keeping the yucca in sight. His observer finally had to move around the trunk or be in the open. Gundy recognized the clothes, but not the man. He reined his horse in.

"Come out, *amigo*. I mean you no harm." He spoke in Spanish.

"Ah, Blanco, you have not forgotten the things we taught you." A reed-thin Apache stepped from behind the yucca. Gundy didn't know him, but he certainly knew Gundy. Otherwise he would not have called him the name all Apaches had finally substituted for his Indian name, Man Who Fights the Big Bear.

"*Hola, hermano*, I am glad you remember me. It has been many summers since I sat at the People's fire."

"The People still talk of you, Blanco. You were one of us when we held our heads high among all warriors."

Blanco nodded. "Those were good days, brother. Now I do not ride in the land of the Mescalero. The chief in the big house in Santa Fe has said he will pay many dollars for my scalp. I never come into the New Mexico Territory now. I have been running for fourteen years. Those years the Mescalero have been free while I alone have not been allowed peace. I was eighteen summers when I left the land of the People."

The young Apache walked toward him, his gaze fastened on Gundy's. If he was alone he would be wary, his eyes constantly searching. Gundy knew he had warriors with him.

"Tell your warriors to come on in, brother."

"I am called Little Coyote, and not many would know I have others with me."

"Well, Little Coyote, why do you track me? Have I done something to offend the People?"

Little Coyote gave a signal with his hand. Five more warriors appeared as if by magic.

"Blanco, we did not know you until we were close. We trailed you for your horses. *Madre de Dios*, they are beautiful animals. Now we know it is you . . ." He shrugged. "We will find horses elsewhere." He peered closely at the four animals. "Why do you travel with so many?"

Gundy thought to avoid answering, but changed his mind. These men would be sympathetic to his mission. "I go to Villa Ahumada to meet with a friend. When we leave there we will ride like the wind." Little Coyote's band pressed closer to hear his every word.

"Why must you be in such a hurry, Blanco?"

Gundy smiled into Little Coyote's dark face. "There will be many who wish me to leave my friend where he is, in the *calabozo*."

"Ah-ha! Do you wish to keep all this fun for yourself? Must your friends beg to share it with you?"

Gundy led his horses to the meager shade of a large yucca and squatted. "Little Coyote, it would be an honor to travel in your company." He spread his hands in a futile gesture. "But such a party would only draw attention, and that is something I don't want."

Little Coyote motioned his men to relax. He squatted next to Gundy. "Blanco, as much as we want to go with you, I know you are right. We would only bring trouble down on you. If you still fight like you once did, that whole town will be no match for you."

Gundy smiled, knowing his eyes were hard. "I've had fourteen more years' experience fighting, but the Texians don't bother me so I spend most of my time there."

Little Coyote stood. "We will go now, my brother. *Vaya con Dios.*"

Gundy watched them ride off wishing he dared keep them with him. But he would only get them killed. He had told the truth. Even with four extra horses he would not draw as much attention as would a band of Apaches.

The afternoon passed. Gundy felt that a large patch of hell had been moved and put smack in the middle of the trail. The wind had hidden, not one dust devil stirred the landscape. Rattlesnakes, scorpions, and Gila monsters hid in the shades of rocks showing no interest in causing him trouble.

When the sun sank below the western horizon, Gundy made a dry camp in the lee of a pile of boulders. He had hoped to make it to the Laguna de Guzman, but guessed he was still fifteen or twenty miles short of it as the sky turned from blue to a fiery orange and shades of pink and turquoise.

A small smokeless fire boiled his coffee. The rest of his supper consisted of hardtack and beans. After scrubbing his pots with sand, Gundy lay back against his saddle, wondering if he'd ever be able to convince Governor Lew Wallace that he had never been on a raid in the fourteen years since he left the Mescaleros.

The Chiricahuas under Cochise had made peace, but renegade bands and small groups still caused trouble. The most powerful were those under Geronimo, along with his lieutenant, Victorio.

The latest of Geronimo's raids had been against Las Lunitas on May 18, 1880, only three days ago. Gundy had read the story in the El Paso paper, and it claimed the Apache Blanco had taken part in the attack. Hell, like all the others he was supposed to have taken part in, he'd been several hundred miles from the action. He could stay in Texas since the Rangers weren't looking for him, but he wanted to start his ranch over by the Capitan Mountains, slam in the middle of New Mexico Territory.

He could surrender and go on trial, and if acquitted he could ranch wherever he wanted. But if found guilty . . . Angry bile boiled into his throat. He tossed away a yucca spear with which he had been toying, turned on his side, and went to sleep.

The desert cooled during the night, but the sun rose in a brassy, clear sky. Gundy cast a sour look at the blue expanse, grunted, and rode on.

Mid-morning he topped a rise and looked down on Laguna de Guzman. The water looked cool and inviting, but Gundy threw his leg up and hooked it around his saddlehorn. He sat still and carefully studied the shoreline for movement. Being a patient man he took his time, and after about thirty minutes he straightened and urged his horse down the gentle slope. He had seen only a shepherd with his flock.

"Hola, amigo, buenos dias."

"Hola, amigo," the shepherd said, and glanced at the remuda Gundy had in tow. "With so many beautiful animals

you must be wary of the *soldados*. There are many around
here, and they will accuse you of stealing them."

"I did not steal them, *amigo*, but I know how that goes. I
will be guilty without having a chance to defend myself."

"*Sí*, so you must refresh yourself with the water and leave.
The *soldados* spend much time here."

Gundy knew the old man spoke the truth, but he would
take time to fill his canteens and bathe in the lake. If he had
to, he'd fight for the right.

His canteens full and the horses watered, Gundy waded
into the lake and sank to his neck in the water, feeling the
heat flow from his parched body.

Even though he was immersed in comfort, his eyes never
stopped searching. He had swept the skyline twice when he
saw them come over a land swell. There were four of them,
and they were close enough to identify—soldiers.

Not wanting to appear hurried, he casually waded to shore
and strapped on his guns. He didn't bother with his rifle. The
four would be in handgun range as soon as they rode to him,
and they had already reined their horses in his direction.

The one in charge of the detail opened his mouth to speak,
then closed it. He examined Gundy from head to toe. "You're
not Apache or Yaqui." His glance slid to the horses. "Where
did you get the horses, *hombre*?"

"They are mine, *señor*. Why do you ask?"

The captain smiled, but his eyes never softened, and he
gave an almost imperceptible signal to his men with his left
hand. They reined their horses a few feet apart.

Gundy's .44 appeared in his hand. He had not thought
about drawing it—but it was there. "*Señor*, you had better
have your men close ranks, like right damn now, or I'm
gonna blow your head all the way to Chihuahua." He had forgotten and spoken in English. Maybe they didn't understand
his words, but the big bore of his .44 spoke a language they
understood well. They again sat their saddles shoulder to
shoulder, eyes wide.

The captain, his voice failing to hide his admiration, said,
"*Jesus Christos*, I have never seen a gun appear so fast. You
must be a man much sought after, *hombre*."

Gundy nodded. "*Sí*, there are those who look for me, but never with only four men."

The captain looked at his men, and with some silent command they dismounted and stood at ease. For the moment, the threat of danger eased. Gundy thought the captain wouldn't try him alone, but the verbal sparring continued.

"What do those who look for you want you for?" the captain asked.

"They want to hang me for killing so many white men."

"Como se llama?"

Gundy kept his face devoid of any expression, but he laughed inside. He might as well spread it on thick. "If I tell you what I am called, then you too will hunt me, only with many more men. *Sí?*"

"What you have done in your country is no concern of the Mexican Government. You need not hold that big *pistola* on me. We are friends. Now, *como se llama?*"

Yeah, like hell, Gundy thought. But there was a slim chance that his name would be known down here so he said, "There are many in Nuevo Mejico who call me the Apache Blanco." He knew as soon as he answered that he had been wrong. The captain *did* know the name, because he stepped back a step with Gundy's answer.

The captain turned to his men. "*Hombres*, you can tell your children, when you return to your *casas*, that you have met the great Apache warrior Blanco." A slight smile creased the corners of his mouth when he again looked at Gundy. "If what I hear is true, there have not been many who have met you and been able to tell anyone of the event."

Gundy felt his eyes go flat and mean. "Yeah, there have been a few—the smart ones. Let's quit the sparring, Captain. You going to try and take me right here, or are you going to wait for a better time?"

The captain saluted Gundy. "There will be another time."

Gundy led his horses away, never turning his back to the Mexican soldiers until he'd put a rise in the land between them. Only then did he mount and urge his horse to a lope.

He rode west, thinking to fool the soldiers. Villa Ahumada lay to the southeast.

CHAPTER
4

Kelly and Dolores stayed in El Paso only long enough to watch Gundy ride out. Sitting atop his horse, a tall, slim, square-shouldered man, he looked capable of doing any job. As soon as he was out of sight, they rode back to the hacienda.

Again in the large sitting room, Dolores looked at her father. "Papa, is Trace tough enough to break Paul out of that hellhole? He seemed such a likeable man, almost gentle when he looked at me."

Kelly stared at his daughter a moment before answering. "*Niña*, if there is a man in the world who could get Paul out, it's Gundy. Tough? I'd say he's the toughest sonuvagun I've ever met. The Territorial Governor of New Mexico still hunts him, but only with many soldiers. The Texians leave him alone. They walk a wide path around him." He picked up a small bell on the table at his side and shook it once.

A maid looked through the arch from the *cocina*. "*Sí?*"

"Carmen, bring me a beer, *por favor*." He looked at Dolores. "Drink, *niña*?"

"Coffee, *por favor*."

Kelly leaned forward in his big chair, which Dolores often likened to a throne. "Now, back to Gundy. You say he seemed gentle, and I agree, but around women only. I deliberately left him with a throwing knife that I'm convinced he would've used if you hadn't been in the room.

"While trying to find someone to break Paul out, I collected a pretty thick sheaf of papers on Gundy. As far as I could find, he hasn't done anything outside the law since he left the Mescaleros. The newspapers have credited him with leading, or being in on, many raids. I have not been able to disprove that—yet.

"The Apaches killed his folks when he was six years old, took him to their mountain hideout, and raised him as one of them. He became the Apache Blanco, one of the most feared of all Apache warriors. He stayed with them until the government began to herd their tribes onto reservations.

"He told Black Elk, the old chief who raised him, he would never adhere to anything the government tried to make him do. Then he left. Gundy lives by his own code, but as far as I can find out, he's never done anything dishonorable, and yeah, he's tough enough to take on any job and get it done."

Carmen brought their drinks, and father and daughter sipped on them a few moments before Dolores said, "I still like him. And I couldn't respect a man who wasn't tough, but gentle with the right people."

They sat there in a comfortable silence for a few moments. Dolores wondered how to bring the next subject up, and decided that head-on and honest was the best. They had never skirted any issue with each other. "Papa, you have influence in the capital, haven't you?"

Kelly stared at her, a slight smile crinkling the corners of his eyes. "Yeah. Some. Why?"

"If it's as you say, and Trace hasn't done anything wrong, and you can prove he didn't take part in all those raids, and you can convince Lew Wallace of that, why shouldn't he deserve a full pardon?"

Kelly wondered if he should tell her he had already started some action along those lines despite thinking that it was a futile effort. At the same time he wondered if he shouldn't stop trying. He had never seen her interested in any man before. And, he admitted to himself, he felt a small pang of jealousy because of it. He countered her question with one of his own. "Why, Dee?" He used the name the ranch hands called her by. "Why should it make a difference to you what happens to him?"

Dolores gave him that devilish little smile she seemed to save for when she wanted to torment him. "Jealous, Papa?" She stood and came to the side of his chair. "I only want justice served. He's a handsome man, perhaps the most handsome I've ever seen, and as you say, he is tough as bullhide. But no, I don't think I'm interested in him that way. I'll have to know him much better than I do before I can consider the idea."

Kelly nodded, still not satisfied that he could get much done. He would think on it awhile. But, he admitted, he hated to see any good man wasted, and Gundy had impressed him as one of the best.

Gundy knew what he was about to do would test how good an Apache he was. He was certain the captain would fall back and get more *soldados*, and probably a Yaqui warrior to track for him.

He continued west for two days, days that were hot enough to paper hell a mile. Early in the afternoon of the second day clouds showed to the northwest. He eyed them with hope. Perhaps they would bring rain, but even if they didn't, wind would be almost as good.

The soldiers were probably at least a day behind him, allowing for the time he figured it would take the captain to get reinforcements. It was late afternoon when he felt a breeze freshen against his bare chest.

Still Gundy held his westward course until wind began to pick sand up in little swirls. Then he turned to the southeast. By the time the captain got this far, Gundy's tracks would have been obliterated by the blowing sand. Energy surged through him. He had gotten lucky.

Three and a half days later, Gundy looked down on Villa Ahumada, a haphazard collection of adobe hovels gathered around three or four more pretentious structures. The sun had cooked them to a light tan. The *calabozo* had to be in one of the larger buildings.

Gundy led the horses into the cover of an arroyo and pondered the problem: how to break Paul from jail. The one thing he was sure of was that he had to wait until night.

There would be few people out after dark. The early part of the evening would have the most, those going to and from the *cantina*. He didn't want to encounter them, and there was a chance a rider might stumble across his horses. He decided that after midnight would be the best. But again, how would he break Paul out? He'd gone over the whole thing in his mind a hundred times while on the trail, but he had to see the lay of the town and the surrounding land before making his plan.

Taking a strip of jerky from his bedroll, he chewed on it, thinking. Then he tethered the horses and sat, waiting. He now had a good idea how he would try to get the job done—except for watering the horses. That might be the most dangerous part of the mission, but they would have to have water before heading into the desert again. It never occurred to him that he might not be successful.

Occasionally, Gundy cast a glance at the Big Dipper to find the time. Finally, after about four hours, he opened his bedroll and changed into range garb. He wished he had a widebrimmed sombrero, but no matter. He'd have to make do with what he had.

Finally, he checked the tether on the horses, took the spare belt with handgun, and slung it over his shoulder. Then, his guts tied in knots, he walked down the hill.

Close to town, he came up behind a lone scraggly yucca, and stood there several minutes searching every building for movement—and lantern or candle light. The town stood dark and still, a stillness that could breed death with one mistake.

He pulled a strip of jerky from his pocket. If a nosy dog made noise, and most of these towns were full of them, the deer meat might quiet him.

He moved from the yucca as a shadow, blending with the landscape, making no more sound than a vagrant breeze. He skirted one of the hovels, ducked under the lone window, and ghosted his way to a larger building about fifty feet from it.

Circling to the back of it, he looked for the next one. This one had no bars on the windows and doors.

Not a single mangy cur barked. Some of the tension flowed from his muscles.

The second building had what he looked for: bars down the windows. At the first back window, he stretched to get his mouth even with the opening. "Pablo Kelly," he whispered. No answer. Two windows to go.

The next window brought the same results. Damn, maybe he's asleep and not hearing me, Gundy thought. But he didn't dare whisper louder. One window to go. If there was no response, he'd start with the first window again.

About halfway between the second and third windows he came upon a wooden box, glanced at it, started around it, then stopped and picked it up. He felt the heft of it. It might hold him so he could look into the cells.

At the third window he placed the box snug against the wall and eased himself onto it. It held him.

He peered through into the dimly lighted cell. Only one bunk was occupied. "Pablo—Pablo Kelly." The form on the bunk stirred and groaned.

"Pablo—Pablo Kelly," Gundy whispered louder, his look shifting to the door that went into the office. If the jailer heard him he'd have to shoot. The whole town would come awake. The dark form rolled to sit on the edge of the narrow bed. "Yeah?" The voice was no louder than Gundy's.

"Come to the window," Gundy said in English, thinking it might give Kelly more trust. He was sure he was talking to Paul now, because Kelly's reaction had been in English.

"You Paul Kelly?"

The shadowy form lurched upright and came to the window. "Who are you? What do you want with me?"

"Want you out of there. Your father hired me to break you out. How many you figure are in the office?"

"One, and he keeps the door locked and barred."

"Damn. Don't want no noise."

"If you're figuring on that, better let me wake him. He drinks enough *mescal* after he locks that door to knock him out till morning."

Gundy thought about it a moment. He had no other choice. "Give it a try, *amigo*. If it doesn't work, I'll break the door down."

He waited, then heard Kelly curse and call to the guard. "Hey, *amigo*, I need a drink of water, *por favor*."

"*Madre de Dios, gringo*, you want something always. Now that you wake me *I'll* have a drink myself."

From where he stood on the box, Gundy heard the cork pop from the bottle the guard must have kept close to him. Then the Mexican cursed and said, "Ah, now that I take care of myself, I feel like being good to you. Now I bring you the water."

As soon as he heard the gourd ring against the side of the bucket, Gundy sprinted for the front door—and didn't slow down. His shoulder hit the door, almost causing him to fall on his face when it swung inward, knocking over a chair and the pail of water the *soldado* had left sitting on the floor.

He drew his Colt and headed for the cell block, meeting the fat Mexican, in his underwear, running toward the front.

"*Señor*," Gundy said, "you are very lucky you do not have a gun with you or you might have made a very foolish move. Turn around."

As soon as the guard showed him his back, Gundy swung his .44 against his head. With a long sigh the man slumped to the floor.

Gundy raced back to the door, closed it, and placed a chair against it. A glance about the room in the murky light showed no key ring. He went to the old desk, its top almost black with cigarette burns, and opened the middle drawer. In the half light his hand failed to find anything that felt like keys. He opened the right-hand-side drawer.

"Officer, you all right? I thought I hear noise from in there," said a voice in Spanish from outside the front door.

Gundy, holding his voice to a muffled grunt, hoping to fool the man outside, said, "*Sí*, I made noise. I got up to relieve myself and fell over a chair. It's all right, *amigo*. Go back to bed."

"*Sí, gracias.*"

The sound of retreating footsteps brought a silent whistle

to Gundy's lips. His fingers searched the drawer. Still no keys, but there was an old newspaper there. Gundy threw it to the floor, dragged his fingers around the drawer again, and found what he wanted.

The third key he tried turned easily in the cell door. When he pulled it open Kelly slipped through the opening, trying to tie a knot in the rope that served as a belt for the rags he wore for trousers. Gundy looped the gunbelt and handgun over Kelly's shoulder. "Hope you don't need it, but we both know better. It's got all six loads. Treat it careful-like."

"Where you got the horses?"

"In a arroyo west of town, an' we gotta water them 'fore we leave here."

Kelly stared at Gundy a moment. "Friend, I don't know who you are, but I have a feeling you an' me're going to travel a lot farther together than just away from here. Let's get the horses."

While climbing the hill, Gundy said, "We'll talk about who I am after we shake the dust of this town."

They worked silently pulling the picket pins and leading the horses down the hill. Only the muted clop of hooves in the soft dust and the soft jangle of bit rings broke the silence.

"You fill the canteens while I water the horses," Gundy said, taking the reins and lead ropes of the four horses.

They came around the corner of a shack—and dogs came to life. Every cur in the province seemed to bark. Gundy's guts turned to water. "Just keep walking like we got nothin' to worry about," he told Kelly under his breath. "We'll bluff our way through if we can. Don't want no shootin' 'less we have to."

The windlass screeched like the demons of hell when Kelly lowered the bucket into the well. Gundy didn't hesitate. He led the horses to the trough and watched them dip their muzzles into the water.

A door close by opened and a tall thin Mexican walked toward them shrugging galluses over his left shoulder. He carried a rifle in his right hand. "Hey, *hombre*, you ride late to come to our town, eh?"

If the rifle barrel tilted a fraction of an inch to point toward

him or Kelly, Gundy would kill the man. "No, just passin'
through. We ride at night to enjoy the cool. Headed for
Saltillo, gonna have a little *mescal*—an' some nice warm
women when we get there."

Others now walked into the street, all armed. Gundy
glanced at Kelly. He was knocking the cork into the top of
the last canteen, but Gundy wanted the horses to take on as
much water as they could hold. He let them drink. Another
man walked up, said something innocent to Gundy, and
glanced at Kelly. Then he took another look.

"Hey—this is the prisoner—"

Gundy pulled his .44 and yelled, "Hold it, all of you."
They froze. "I don't want to kill any of you, but I sure as hell
will if anybody tilts one o' them guns in our direction. Stay
right where you are till my horses get a bellyful; then we
gonna ride out peaceful-like. You 'bout finished, Kelly?"

"Yeah, waiting for you, friend."

Gundy led the horses around the townspeople, saw that
Kelly also had his handgun out, handed him the reins to his
horse, and said, "Let's get out of here."

They rode at a dead run due north. The only choice they
had was to put as much distance as possible between them
and the Mexicans before they could saddle their horses. This
time, heading in the wrong direction would only fool them
for a few minutes. It wasn't worth the gamble.

After about thirty minutes, Gundy reined down to a steady
lope, looked across his shoulder at Kelly, and said, "Now I'll
tell you what name to call me by. Trace Gundy's the name.
Your pa knows me by it as well as another. We'll talk about
that when I get you back to him."

"Gundy, I don't care what they call you. To me you'll always be 'friend.' Tell you something right now, though. If
they catch us, you do what you want. I'm not ever going back
to that hellhole."

Gundy smiled, and knew it was only a grimace. "*Amigo*, I
never figured to go anywhere but back to the States. Glad we
understand each other. Dead ain't so bad if you got to give up
freedom instead."

They held a steady pace until the sky in the east lightened

and the desert plants turned from ghostly black to browns and
greens.

Gundy slowed the pace. "Ain't gonna stop to eat. Figure
they will, or they'll give up and go home." He handed Kelly
a strip of jerky. "What I ain't told you yet is that a bunch of
soldiers been trackin' me for about four days now. Don't
know where they are, but figure on seein' them before we get
to the border. It ain't gonna be friendly."

They topped a rise, and Gundy stopped to study their back-
trail. He narrowed his lids and peered from the horizon down
toward where he sat his horse, then did it again. He couldn't
be sure, but thought he saw a thin veil of dust hanging in the
distance.

"They ain't give up." He nudged his horse back to a fast
walk. "An' I'll tell you something else, Kelly. I reckon not
too far behind that town bunch them soldiers are closin' in.
We might have a fight on our hands yet."

Kelly glanced at Gundy, pulled his Winchester from its
scabbard, checked its loads, and shoved it back in the scabbard.

Gundy watched with approval, then checked his own rifle.

Noon came and went while Gundy shared another strip of
jerky with Kelly. It didn't seem the dust cloud drew any
closer, but Gundy continued to search the desert ahead, behind, and to the sides. That captain didn't have to be behind
him. He could have cut cross-country. The soldiers could not
have guessed what he was about, but knowing who he was,
the captain might figure he had to get back to the border and
would try to cut him off.

Every hour or so they changed horses. Gundy didn't think
the pursuers would have brought extra horses, simply because
they were poor people and most of them would not have extra horses to bring.

About two hours after noon, another dust cloud appeared to
the northwest. "Think them soldier boys done figured where
we are." He was talking more to himself than to Kelly, but
Kelly heard him, because he pulled his rifle from its scabbard
and held it across the saddle in front of him.

To gain a little time and a chance to find a place they could defend, Gundy veered to his right, still heading toward the border, but also hoping to find water.

Another mile and they topped a rise. This time there was no doubt the soldiers were closing in from the west, nor was there a hint of water. Gundy searched for a thin line or splotch of green, anything that might suggest a sump of any kind—nothing. But they had a *little* luck. Tumbled boulders surrounded the spot where they sat their horses. A good place to defend.

"You any good with that long gun, Kelly?"

"I usually hit what I'm lookin' at."

Gundy nodded. "I'm gonna stay here, see if I can keep them off you. You ride like hell for the border. It ought to be 'bout fifty miles."

"Like hell. You stay, I stay."

"Promised your pa an' your sister I was gonna get you back. Now get goin'."

"Not leavin' you."

Gundy studied Kelly a long moment, pulled his rifle from its scabbard, and found himself a place to lie behind the boulders. A large one lay on top of two flat ones, leaving him a hole to fire through. Then he took one of the canteens and gave the horses a little water.

"This ain't no gentleman's fight," he said over his shoulder. "When they get close enough for sure aim, cut 'em down—no warnin'. Only way we can even the odds a little."

They lay there with no shade. The sun baked through what clothes they had on. Sweat evaporated as fast as it dampened their shirts. The dust drew closer.

Gundy turned on his side to look at the canteens. "We better wet our mouths a little. Then, so's a stray bullet don't puncture one of them canteens, let's put one by each of us an' cover the rest over with sand. We might be here awhile."

CHAPTER
5

The dust cloud drew closer, and hazy human forms took shape in it. Then each soldier stood out plainly. Looking down his sights, Gundy said, "Pick a target and put your sights on the center of his chest—no head shots. Don't fire till I do. I'll take the one on the far right."

Gundy didn't worry about himself. The tight knot in his gut was for Kelly. He had taken on the job of getting him back to his family safely, but with the number of men they faced there was little chance he would do it.

The soldiers drew closer. Kelly growled, "Damn, Gundy, you gonna wait until they get astraddle us?" Gundy fired and everything went to hell. Horses reared; soldiers grabbed for weapons, some already firing. Gundy fired as fast as he could jack shells into the chamber. Men spilled from their saddles. Kelly's rifle took its toll also. The soldiers obviously had not expected to run into them so soon.

Bullets chipped chunks off the boulders around them. One found the hole Gundy fired through and peppered his face and eyes with rock fragments. He wiped them clear and fired again.

He had counted fourteen troops coming at them when the fight started. Now there were eight. They fell back out of range and gathered around one man Gundy guessed was the captain he had faced at the lake.

"Hold your fire, Kelly. They gonna talk, then they'll come again." He twisted to look to the south. The people from town were coming, although still several miles away. Hope we don't have to kill none of them, he thought. Poor bastards ain't got much to live for, but reckon life's as sweet to them as ours is to us. He again looked toward the soldiers. The one obviously in charge waved one arm in a circle and three of the men broke off and headed toward the northeast. Gundy watched until they began to circle, then split again.

Uh-huh, they're gonna try and surround us with eight men. They got a bigger job than they think. A glance back showed the five remaining soldiers heading in the opposite direction.

"We got a little bigger job than we had when they were bunched. You watch to the west and south of us; I'll take the north," Gundy said, pushing his hat back and wiping his brow.

He glanced at the horses. They were all right, and he thanked the Everywhere Spirit they were gun-broke. His gaze swept the area he'd staked out as his responsibility. Nothing moved. A dust devil started, swirled, and died away. He'd seen some swirling winds strong enough to pick up small rocks.

A soldier stood—and fell, as though something had knocked him down. Strange he went to ground like that, Gundy thought, as if he'd been fired at. He shrugged it off. Maybe that's the way they teach 'em to fight down here. Then another of them did the same thing.

When that one fell, a flash of red showed behind a yucca. Hope swelled Gundy's chest. Did he dare wish for so much? It was not impossible. They were down here four days ago. Maybe they'd found enough mischief to keep them busy until now.

"Kelly, I may have some friends coming in from the north. Don't fire at anything you ain't sure of. These friends are Mescaleros. You know how they dress, so don't fire at anyone dressed like an Apache."

Kelly grinned. "*Amigo*, you have strange friends, but if that's the way you figure it, I'll be the last to mess it up. Let's hope you're right, because our friends to the south have just joined up with the soldiers. We're gonna need all the help we can get."

Gundy looked over Kelly's shoulder. "How far off you figure they are?"

"About a mile and a half, and now there are maybe ten of them since they joined up."

Gundy nodded. " 'Bout the way I got it figured. I'm of a mind to head out an' try to outrun 'em. Being we got two horses each an' they only got one apiece, their broncs oughtta be gettin' pretty tired."

"Sounds good to me."

Gundy glanced to the north again, then shook his head. "Can't do it. Them friends of mine are afoot. Can't leave 'em to fight ten men. You go ahead. I'll stay."

"Told you, I'm not going anywhere 'less you're with me."

Gundy smiled. His chest tightened with pride in this young man he'd begun to think of as a friend. "You ain't helpin' me get you back to your pa safe, but hell, I'm right proud of you for stickin'."

He looked to the north again. One of the Mescaleros ran about twenty feet and crouched behind a yucca. He peered from behind it, and Gundy waved him to come on in. The Apache gave a hand signal to his men and headed in alone. Gundy soon identified him as Little Coyote.

"*Hola*, Blanco. I hate to break into all the fun you so much wanted to keep all to yourself, but it looked like you were having too good a time for my men and me to stay out of it." Little Coyote spoke Spanish and Gundy, knowing the Mescaleros were more comfortable with it than English, answered him in the same language.

"*Hola*, Little Coyote, I was just thinking how selfish I was to keep all this to myself knowing how much you and my brothers would enjoy it. Welcome, brother." He grinned. "Reckon you know how glad I am to see you."

"Ah, the great Apache Blanco could have taken care of twice this many without my help, but *gracias*, we thank you for letting us have part of the fun."

As soon as Coyote called him by his nickname, Gundy

looked for Kelly's reaction, and was disappointed. Kelly wore
a smug smile and slowly shook his head.

"Didn't think my pa would hire just any old cowpoke to
get me out of that stink-hole. He went right to the top,
though, hired the best." Kelly stuck out his hand. "Honored
to meet you, Blanco."

"Don't know 'bout all that stuff you were sayin', but we
got one hell of a lot o' fightin' to do before we begin to feel
good." Gundy looked at Little Coyote. "You gonna leave
your men out there, or you want them here with us?"

"I'll go back out there with them and fight like only the
Apache knows." He headed back the way he'd come.

Now the soldiers were all gathered about the captain again.
"Hope he decides to try and circle us again," Gundy said.
"Little Coyote and his band'll cut 'em down to size, an'
what's left you an' me can take care of."

The captain soon made the same circular motion with his
hand, and the group headed toward the east, and then bore to
the north. Every fifty yards or so one of the group would split
off and take up station. The rest continued until all of them
were in the position they wanted. Gundy spoke. "If you an'
me want to get our share of them varmints, we better get the
job done, or Little Coyote's gonna hog all the fun for the
Mescaleros."

Kelly's gun spoke before Gundy finished his sentence.
Gundy shifted his sights to a different sector. One of the soldiers crouched and ran to the backside of a clump of prickly
pear. Gundy fired where he figured the man was hunkered,
then bracketed his first shot with two more. His target ran
from behind the cactus, heading for a small boulder. Gundy
led him about a foot and sqeezed the trigger. The man fell
and did not move. The Mexicans now all started firing. The
rock fortress Gundy had chosen abruptly filled with rock
fragments and whining slugs.

"Get flat, Kelly, and stay there." Gundy looked over his
shoulder. Kelly stretched out on his stomach, a raw gash
alongside his head and blood welling from a hole in his
shoulder. The rag Kelly wore for a shirt had no sleeves. The
hole in his shoulder showed plainly. Gundy stared at it a mo-

ment, stood, ripped his shirt off, and bolted from the boulder, and from his throat came a yell he had not uttered since leaving the Mescalero. He ran directly into the fire of his assailants.

He zigzagged toward them, bullets creasing his naked hide, some whining and whirring past his head. A solid hit in the thigh knocked him down. He rolled, came to his feet, and saw his first soldier close up. His rifle in his left hand, his right spewed death from the end of his .44. He changed course, and in a running hop went down the line the captain's men had formed. Two more went down before his handgun. Coming on another, he shoved his pistol into his waistband and pulled his bowie knife. The khaki-clad figure, terror in his eyes, fired point-blank at Gundy, and missed. Gundy's bowie swung—and the man had no head. Blood spewed as from a fountain from the stump of his neck. Then the body fell at his feet. Gundy ran on. Another man still on his feet stood directly in front of him. Gundy raised his knife to swing again—and realized he faced one of Little Coyote's men. He brought his arm slowly back to his side.

"Madre de Dios, you are truly the Apache Blanco. Never have I seen such a warrior. Now I believe the stories of you. It is all over, Blanco. You killed the last of them. We got the rest."

Gundy looked at him a moment, then pointed to the pile of boulders he had left only moments before. "My friend is in those rocks. He is hurt—perhaps badly. *He* too is a warrior. Call the others in. We've got to save him."

When they got to the rock fortress, Kelly sat at its edge staring as in a daze at the line of combat. His gaze traveled its length. Then he focused on Gundy. "My God, you *are* the White Apache, aren't you. I had some doubts about it until you took on the whole bunch. I believe if Little Coyote and his band had not gotten them all, you would have."

"Sí, hombre, you can believe it," said Little Coyote. "Stories are told of Blanco around every campfire, and now that I have seen, I too believe."

Gundy felt uncomfortable with this sort of talk. They didn't realize that this story would get to the capital in Santa

Fe and Lew Wallace would have even more reason to hunt
him like a dog.

Little Coyote checked their wounds, went to some scrubby
plants, pulled the roots from them, ground them into a
gummy mess, and bandaged it to the bullet holes in each of
them. "There," he grunted. "They will heal in a few days."

Gundy checked his guns, cleaned and loaded them, then
shoved the rifle in its scabbard, holstered his six-shooter, and
climbed aboard his horse.

"Where you going? We might as well cook some grub,"
Kelly said.

"No, for two reasons. Them corpses gonna begin to ripen
right soon and I don't want to have to smell 'em. Second, if
another patrol comes by here, I don't want to have to fight
again today. Let's go. We'll put another four, five hours behind us 'fore we eat."

"Blanco is right, *amigo*," Little Coyote said. "Four, five
more hours of hard riding and we can make a run for the border if we have to."

"We gonna make camp then?" Kelly looked hopefully at
Gundy.

Gundy nodded. "If you want to, but I was thinkin' a nice
night ride would put us across the Rio Grande. Then our
friends can head for the mountains and you an' me can get a
good night's sleep."

About three hours after they had eaten, the first hot meal
Gundy had eaten in a couple of days, they crossed the river.
He said to Kelly, "You're free, Mr. Paul Kelly. We'll make
camp here, and I'll see you delivered to your pa an' sister in
a couple of days—if I don't run into any troops or law officers." To Little Coyote, he said, "*Muchas gracias, amigo*.
Sure don't know what we'd of done without you."

"*De nada*, Blanco. We are the ones who owe you thanks.
You shared your fun with us—and gave us another story to
tell at our campfires. We thank you."

Gundy boiled a pot of coffee and shared it with the Mescaleros. Then they rode out with promises they would see
him again.

The middle of the second day, Gundy and Kelly stopped for their nooning, and were about to clean up when Kelly said, "Riders coming in."

"Yeah, saw 'em a while ago. If they're the law, or troops, act like we been saddle pards a long time an' just been to Las Cruces for a little spree after payday. Hope they don't know me from some old picture."

The two riders approached the fire that Gundy hadn't had a chance to cover with dirt. "We'd ask you to rest your saddles and set," Gundy said, "but we just now finished what coffee we had an' was ready to ride on." His hand stayed close to his holster. These two had lawman stamped all over them. If he had to kill them, he would never get a pardon.

"We already et," the older of the two said, peering closely at the rags, now bloodstained and dirty, tied around Gundy's and Kelly's wounds. "You boys had some trouble?"

"Nothin' we couldn't handle," Gundy said, his face feeling stiff, his muscles pulled tight as a watch spring. Any move out of either of the two and he'd draw and fire. A New Mexico trial with a biased jury, and maybe prison or a hangman's rope, wasn't one of his druthers.

"Run into a little trouble in Las Cruces—whipped the guys what brung it to us, then they jumped us on the trail. Took care of that trouble too."

The older of the two sidestepped away from his partner. "Don't do that, mister," Gundy said. "Might figure you as bein' unfriendy. Just close it back up and tell us who you are."

A slight, cold smile touched the corners of the man's mouth, but he did as Gundy told him. He speared Gundy with a look sharp as a stiletto. "I'm Jake Munson, deputy United States marshal, an' this's my partner, Bob Daily. We're lookin' for renegade Apaches who jumped the reservation. You seen any?"

Kelly shook his head. "Seen nobody, and don't hope to until we get to my pa's ranch, the Circle AK up northwest of here."

The officer's attitude changed abruptly. "You Alejandro

Kelly's boy? Well, I'll be damned. Heard you was being held down in Mexico somewhere."

"Yeah, but that was a while back. Me and Jim here just went in town for a little fun three, four days ago."

"All right, you boys get along. We'll use what fire you got left and make some coffee."

Gundy relaxed a bit, but kept his face to the lawmen while he mounted. And when he and Kelly rode off, a hard knot stayed between his shoulders until they were out of rifle range.

"Whew, I was afraid you were gonna kill those two," Kelly said. "You were ready to do just that, weren't you?"

Gundy glanced at Kelly. "I was ready. But I'm still hoping for a pardon someday."

The sun sank slowly behind the Mimbres Mountains, throwing red spears into the cloudless sky in a last futile effort to stop the encroaching darkness, and then night settled in. The stillness was broken only by the soft, measured strides of the horses.

"We close enough to ride on, or you want to make camp?" Gundy asked.

"Gundy, even if we were still twenty miles out I'd ride on. But by my guess we'll be home in less than an hour. Should see lights soon as we top that rise."

CHAPTER
6

They had not gotten to the arch that opened into the ranch yard when a voice rang out. "Who is it that rides in the night?"

"*Hola*, Chico, is that you? It is I, Pablo. Are my parents and sister at the hacienda?"

"*I-yi-yi*, Pablo . . ."

That was all Gundy heard before an old *vaquero* launched himself at Kelly and hugged and beat him about the shoulders. "*Sí, su mama y papa y hermana* are all in the hacienda. Go, go now, boy, and let them see you."

Paul cast Gundy an embarrassed glance. "Chico practically raised me since I was a baby. He still thinks of me as a little boy."

Gundy laughed. "Yeah, an' how're you gonna explain all the huggin' an' kissin' that'll be goin' on when you get to the house? Go on, boy. I'll put the horses away an' be there in a minute."

"You will like hell. You're coming with me—and I'll bet you get your share of all that mush too."

Kelly was dead right. Gundy began to wonder who they were more glad to see, him or Paul. And then Dolores, who had been hanging back while her mother and father greeted him, walked to stand squarely in front of him. She looked him straight in the eyes. "Trace Gundy, God bless you. I don't know who I'm more happy to see, you or Paul." Then she put her arms around him and kissed him soundly. When she stepped back, she smiled and said, "Part of that was for getting Paul out of Mexico, and a good bit of it was for you coming back safely. You're quite a man, Trace Gundy."

Gundy stared back into her eyes. "Dolores, some day I'm gonna want you to say them things to me again. 'Tween now an' then I gotta earn the right."

Her face turned the prettiest pink Gundy thought he had ever seen, and he wasn't at all sorry he had caused her some slight embarrassment.

"*Señor?*" A young Mexican girl stood at Gundy's side with a tray of drinks. He glanced questioningly at Dolores. She nodded and said, "White wine, *por favor.*"

Gundy took a beer and wine from the tray, handed Dolores her drink, and turned toward Paul's parents. When he did, Dolores placed her hand in the crook of his arm, and with that small gesture seemed to Gundy that she laid claim to him. Even though he was dirty and sweaty, he felt like that guy Galahad he'd once read about.

They stood and talked awhile. Then Mrs. Kelly, who'd told Gundy to call her Maria, said that he would sleep in the guest bedroom, that she'd had bathwater prepared for both him and Paul, and that she would clean and dress their wounds.

After his bath, and after his wound was dressed, Gundy lay in bed and stared at the ceiling. Tired though he was, he had a lot of thinking to do. He wanted to head for Texas and start the roundup of longhorns for the ranch he didn't yet have. He had to have men, land, and most of all freedom to go where he pleased.

He had saved some money through the years, but not enough. He could sell the mavericks he gathered in order to buy land. Then he could gather more longhorns to stock his ranch. Land was cheap.

It was during breakfast the next morning that Paul's father told Gundy to call him Alex, and Gundy shortened Dolores to Dee, just as Paul did. Alex also told Gundy that after breakfast, if he'd come to his office, they could settle up on the balance of what he owed him.

"Alex, reckon *I* owe *you*, not the other way round," Gundy said. "I'll get the other five thousand back to you soon's I get back to where I stashed it." Gundy stared into the bottom of his coffee cup a moment. What he was doing tied his gut in knots. It set his plans for a ranch back, but no further back than before he'd met Kelly. He looked up and locked eyes with him. "Don't reckon I can take money for somethin' I would've done anyway if I'd knowed Paul an' you folks was gonna be my friends."

Shocked silence settled over the room. Gundy felt every eye there looking at him. He squirmed, then said, "That's how I feel, an' that's how it's gonna be."

"Like hell. Son, we made an agreement. I'll stick to it, and you will too. You can't afford to put your plans back."

"Papa." Dolores stood. "I told you the day we took the horses to Trace what kind of man I thought he was. This proves it, but he *will* take the money. I'll see to it."

Gundy, forgetting his manners, went to the stove and poured himself a cup of coffee, put the pot back on the stove, then picked it up and poured coffee for them all. The little maid, Chiquita, looked as though he had hurt her feelings. After all, he had done *her* job.

He stared around the table. "Y'all been talkin' like I was somewhere else, not even here. Now I'm gonna tell you how it is. I ain't takin' the money. An' even though you folks have made me feel like family here in your home, I gotta cut out after breakfast. Got some cows to gather and start myself a ranch. Looks like it's gonna have to be in Texas. 'Cordin' to the governor I'm still an outlaw. But I promise you one thing. Leave the latchstring out 'cause I'm comin' back." He'd ended up looking into Dee's eyes when he said those last words. She again turned that pretty pink color.

Paul said his first words since sitting down, partly because he was catching up on eating good food. "What's this about going after some of those wild Texas cows?"

Gundy told him his plans, and noticed they all listened as closely as did Paul. When he finished, Paul looked at his family. "If Gundy needs another cow nurse, I'm going with him."

"Hell, boy, you just now got home."

"Yeah, I know, Pa, but I noticed on the way up through Mexico Gundy needs somebody to take care of him. I elected myself—if he'll have me."

"Of course I want you along, but this ain't doin' your family right. You need to spend some time with them." Gundy felt like he was betraying the whole family by admitting he wanted Paul to come with him.

"Trace," Dolores said, "if he's with you, I'll feel he's safe. If he's not with you, he'll leave anyway on some scatter-brained trip, and then we'll all worry ourselves sick."

Alex spoke to Gundy for the first time since decreeing that he would take the money. "Tell you what. Both of you stay here for a week, rest up, eat up—and then you can have a couple of my best men to help on the gather. Hell, you're gonna have to have men from somewhere, and the two I let you have'll give you a start—and most importantly, you can trust them." Then, just like his daughter, he blushed. "Besides, you're both hell-raisers, and I'll feel better with two stable *vaqueros* along."

The week he and Paul stayed proved invaluable. Gundy and Alex finally agreed to splitting the ten thousand dollars if Gundy would let Alex outfit the four with a remuda, chuck wagon, and food supply for two months. Gundy figured he would have enough cattle to make up a good-sized trail herd in that time.

When they were ready to ride out on the morning of the seventh day, there must have been a hundred cowhands, along with Alex, Maria, and Dolores, gathered to wish them safety and success.

Before he mounted, Dolores threw her arms around him and whispered, "You better come back to see me, Trace Gundy."

"You can bet your best cow pony on that, Dee. I'll be back soon's we get the gather sold, probably by early October."

"That's a long time, Trace, but I'll settle for that if you promise to come back."

He stared into those green eyes. "I promise, Dee, if the

Territorial police don't stop me. If they figure on trying it, they better have a whole bunch with 'em."

The small party rode out, and from the top of the hill Gundy looked back. Dolores still stood where he'd left her, and she still held her arm high. He raised his, and rode ahead.

"Looks like you and my little sister like each other pretty much," Paul said, looking at him with the most serious expression Gundy had seen.

"*Amigo*, reckon the day I headed down into Mexico to try an' get you free of them *policía*, I knowed I wanted to be more than just a friend to your sister. Figured I must be crazy. Ain't no woman fine as your sister gonna look at the likes of me. But she does seem to sort of like me, don't she?"

"Gundy, if she'd made that any more obvious, my daddy might've shot you." He frowned. "Damn, that's sort of strange too. She kissed you when you brought me back, and when we left awhile ago, she gave you a hug which I thought was a chunk more than friendly—and Pa never even scowled. I know, because I looked to see how he'd take it."

The next couple of days their small party wended its way down a trail of grama grass, circling clumps of prickly pear, yucca, and desert brush, all the while keeping an eye peeled for strangers.

Gundy thought he could talk with any Apaches they might encounter, but white men might be a problem. It was on the morning of the third day that Emilio pointed to the northwest.

Gundy peered into the distance. A dust cloud gathered there. Wild horses? He continued gazing at one spot for a point of reference, and saw that the dust tracked in their direction and would cross their trail in maybe another hour.

"If them riders are Mescaleros, let me do the talkin'. If they're soldiers, or a posse of some sort, you do the talkin', Kelly. If they don't know you, they'll know your pa."

Kelly nodded, and they held their course. True to Gundy's guess, in a little over an hour a band of riders was close enough to recognize as Apaches.

"Don't do anything, but hold your long guns ready," Gundy said. While he talked, he stripped his shirt off and tied

a headband in place. Then, ready for the Apaches, he held his
hand out palm forward.

"*Hola*, brothers. Why do you ride so far from the People
today?"

"You call us brothers," a short, stubby Indian said. "You
are white. By what reason are we your brothers?"

There were twelve of them, and if they wanted a fight,
Gundy figured to take as many as he could with him. But it
was a hopeless thing he thought on. He would get Kelly and
the others killed.

"You call me white, as do my brothers who know me. That
is how I got the name Apache Blanco. Have you not heard of
me, brother?"

"*Sí*, I have heard much of Apache Blanco. How do I know
you are Blanco?"

"Do you know Little Coyote? He and I rode together in a
fight no more than ten and four suns ago."

"*Sí*, I know Little Coyote. How many were in that fight
with you?"

"My brother Pablo, Little Coyote, and four warriors."

The Apache then asked more questions, and Gundy answered them to his apparent satisfaction. Then the Indian
said, "When we eat?"

"Climb down and rest your horses. We'll have our nooning
now."

The Indians went about preparing the fire and starting the
food cooking as though it was their camp. Their leader, Geronimo, one of the meanest-looking men Gundy thought he'd
ever seen, continued talking.

"The white men in Santa Fe want you dead, Blanco. Why
don't you come with me? You and me, aaah, we could make
men fear us all the way to the big waters where Father Sun
rises above Mother Earth."

Gundy dumped another couple of spoons of grounds in the
coffeepot. "No, brother. I still hope for the right to travel in
the land of the Mescalero as a free man. If I join you I'll give
up that right and must fight forever. I want to be able to
choose the enemies I fight. With you, all men would be my
enemy."

Geronimo nodded. "*Sí*, you are right, Blanco. I will not win this fight with the white man, but I must fight. After what they did to my family, it would not be honorable to do other."

They had their nooning, and Geronimo and his party left. Gundy wished he could have kept them with him through the Lipan country. Even though the Lipans claimed the territory, the Comanches encroached on it whenever they pleased. He didn't know of anyone in his right mind who didn't fear Comanches.

They watched the Apaches ride away. Kelly took a swallow of coffee, frowned, and spit it out. "Too thick."

Only a couple of hours had passed when Gundy spotted another thin dust trail. Damn, he thought, we're only four, five hours from crossing into Texas. Wish we could've made it.

He pointed. "Country's gettin' mighty crowded. Seen less folks durin' roundup. Keep your guns ready."

He changed course to veer more southward, hoping to make the border before meeting the riders. Then he saw it would make no difference where they met. These were Comancheros—and he knew their leader, Manuel Santos, who he figured he would have to kill someday.

CHAPTER
7

"If they want a fight, that front one hunched over the saddlehorn is mine," Gundy said. He reined his horse so his right side showed to the four approaching riders, his hand close to his .44.

He kept a tight rein on his horse, his gut muscles tight, as the Comancheros drew near. He tried to push his hate for them aside, but the blood pressed into his neck and head despite his effort.

When they were close enough he hurled his challenge. "What are you doing riding around in the sunshine, droppings from a dog? I thought the likes of you hid under rocks and only crawled out at night." He'd pressed hard, hoping for one of them to make a move for his gun.

"Ah, Blanco, you do not like me, eh?" Manuel replied. "You think to make me mad so I fight you? Blanco, I do not want a fight. You are my friend." He was smiling that greasy smile Gundy remembered from Fort Bliss when Manuel had tried to have the army arrest him. The colonel had said there were no charges against him in Texas, and had let him go.

Gundy pushed harder. "You sayin' you're my friend makes me feel about as filthy as you, Manuel. 'Bout the only thing I want outta you is distance." Gundy didn't want to leave them alive, or Comancheros would be after his outfit farther down the trail. "You ain't leavin' this meetin' straddle your horse, so make up your mind, pull that handgun, take your chances—or run an' I'll shoot you in the back."

"Blanco, you would not shoot me in the back." While talking Manuel reined his horse as though to ride away.

Manuel turned his horse to shield his gun hand from sight, but his shoulder on that side dipped. Gundy drew and fired, then turned his gun on the other three—but they were already falling from their saddles, one with blood spurting from his neck, the other two with holes in the middle of their chest.

Manuel, bleeding from a shoulder wound, spurred his horse into a hard run. The three now on the ground had weapons out, but had not had a chance to fire them. Manuel twisted and fired across his shoulder.

A pall of smoke still hung over them. Paul, Emilio, and Fernando sat their saddles staring at him. Gundy looked from them to the departing Comanchero with narrowed lids.

"You deliberately goaded them into a fight, Gundy. Why?" Paul asked.

"When a rattler's done hit you once, you kill 'im when you got the chance," Gundy said. "I had the chance an' missed. We gonna have trouble with him, or some of his friends, before we get to the Big Bend country. Count on it." He opened the cylinder of his handgun, punched spent shells from it and reloaded, then looked up from his task. "You got to read people a lot better'n you did just now. You was 'bout a second away from gettin' shot outta your saddles. You got your guns limbered up just in time."

Paul sighed. "All right, let's bury them."

"Ain't gonna bury 'em. Let the coyotes and javelinas have them—they gotta eat too."

"Hell, Gundy, you can't just let them lie there."

He stared at Paul, knowing his eyes were hard as agates, then said, "The hell I can't. Let's ride."

A few more hours and they were in Texas by his best reckon. Now all they had to worry about were Comanches *and* Comancheros. The Comanches, the fiercest fighters and best horsemen of the plains, and Comancheros, the vilest and most treacherous of men. They stole women and sold them into brothels south of the border, and killed from ambush or from the back. He would not give any of their kind a break.

They rode, every eye searching the hills, arroyos, and desert growth for movement. And Gundy felt the searching, questioning stares of those who rode behind him when their flicking glances touched on him. He didn't care. As their leader he would keep them safe—if he could.

They made camp that night in a shallow canyon. The men deserved a hot meal, and the shoulders of the gully shielded the fire from hostile eyes.

After eating and helping clean up camp, Gundy lay in his blankets, staring at the velvet blackness of the sky, the stars hovering just beyond his fingertips. Dee forced her way past thoughts of Indians and bandits. He had no right to even think of taking her from the luxury she had known all her life. At first, his ranch would be only a shelter thrown together from whatever he could find on the desert floor. He had to build his crew, his herd, his remuda before thinking of finer things.

He didn't doubt her feelings for him, although they had never spoken of it. Maria and Alex had done nothing to indicate they were opposed to the idea. But did any of them know what his being tagged as an outlaw in the New Mexico Territory would do to a marriage, when every time he took her to visit her folks he put her life in jeopardy?

He thought about getting set up in Texas and then submitting to trial, but that idea didn't make much sense either. He worried the idea to a frazzle before sleep overtook him.

The next morning it was more of the same: heat, sweat, ride awhile, and change horses, always with the scorched, dusty smell of the desert in their nostrils.

They headed more to the southeast now, and occasionally spotted and sometimes gathered in a lean, mean longhorn. By nightfall the small herd had grown to eighteen, and that number would grow to many more when they got farther south.

Although his riders had experience with the wild Spanish cattle, some with horns six feet and more from tip to tip, Gundy never ceased to warn them of the danger to both themselves and their horses. An old brindle bull had taken the lead, and Gundy's small herd seemed satisfied to follow him.

They skirted Fort Bliss and headed for the Cornudas Mountains, not much of a range by Gundy's thinking, but still enough to create deep ravines and hard going for the horses. The good thing about it, there was more cover from hostiles.

Four days had passed since tangling with Manuel Santos, plenty of time for the bandit to get more of his kind and come seeking him—and there was no doubt he would come with more men than he'd had the last time.

"You know where we're headed, Gundy?" Paul asked.

"Yeah, they's a trader by the name of Reiley 'bout ten miles ahead. Got a little post hunkered down in a narrow valley, sells cheap whiskey to the Comancheros an' buys and sells most anything they got. We'll get his woman to cook up a hunk of beef for us. Santos might've headed for his place. If he did, might save us a bunch of misery to get rid of him now, before he can get more men."

Paul muttered, "Another gunfight."

When they were about a quarter of a mile from Reiley's place, Gundy told his men, "The light's gonna be dim in there. Go in, put your backs to the wall until your eyes get used to it. Keep the whole inside where you can see it. Don't trust nobody what's there. I'll go in first."

They made no effort to ride quietly. Gundy figured Reiley knew they were coming before they got within a mile.

Dismounting outside the post, he told Fernando to stay with the cattle until they got through inside. Then he'd have his chance to eat and get a beer.

They stepped to the wooden veranda, stomped the dust from their boots, and shouldered through the open doorway into the smell of stale alcohol and dirty, sweaty bodies. Only the owner was in the room.

"No need to put yore backs to the wall like that," he said. "This here's a friendly place." From behind the bar, a rough board slab, Reiley stared squint-eyed at Gundy. "What you doin' in these parts, Blanco?"

"Just come to see you, Reiley. Ain't you glad to see me?"

"Yeah, 'bout as much as I'd like to see a good dose o' cholera walk through my front door. What you want?"

Gundy walked to the bar and leaned across it. The smell of Reiley's unwashed body caused him to shut down his breathing to only what he had to have in order to talk. "First, I want some straight answers. Manuel Santos been in here?"

Reiley's glance shifted to a door at the side and quickly came back to Gundy. "Naw, ain't seen hide nor hair of that Mex for 'bout three weeks. What you want with him?"

Gundy shook his head. "Not much. Just gonna kill 'im." Reiley's glance had told him what he wanted to know. Santos was in that side room, and Gundy had answered the question loud enough so Santos would be warned—he'd give him that much chance. To his men he said, "Keep Reiley here till I get through."

He walked to the side of the doorway the storekeeper had looked at, drew his handgun, and, bent low to the floor, stepped through the opening. A slug tore splinters from the frame above his head. His gut tightened. Another shot knocked his hat from his head. He fired a quick shot into the pile of blankets and dodged to the side, a brassy taste in the back of his throat. That last shot at his head had been close to putting him down. A slug tugged at his shirtsleeve, but his gun rolled out three more shots that sounded as one. The lump on the bed jerked, jerked, and bounced as though being pulled by puppet strings.

Gundy walked to the bed, a wisp of smoke still curling from the end of his pistol barrel. He gripped the sheet and peeled it away from what had been Santos. "Thought you woulda knowed better'n to try a head shot—miss too often with those." Santos had three holes in his chest close enough together to be covered by the palm of Gundy's hand. His first shot had caught Santos just above his navel.

Gundy straightened and went back to the bar. "Now, Reiley, I want your woman to cook us up some steaks, big ones, an' I want spuds, beans, an' tortillas with that steak. She can throw one on the fire for my rider outside after she feeds us. While she's doin' that, pour us a beer and take one to Fernando out yonder."

The look Reiley threw at him was pure poison, but he went about doing as told.

When they had eaten and paid, they headed for the door.

"What you gonna do about buryin' Santos?" Reiley asked.

"Nothin'. You do it—you took the bastard in." Gundy got another one of those looks.

Outside, Kelly stared at Gundy across his saddle. "You're a hard man, *amigo*. You could've let that man in there live. He couldn't hurt us before we got where we're going."

Gundy mounted and looked him in the eye. "Kelly, I been taught by them what raised me to stomp out trouble afore it gets started. Figured Santos was gonna bring it to us whenever he could." He shifted his look to Fernando, who hadn't had a chance to eat. "Go ahead and eat. Reiley's woman's already got it fixed. We'll wait here."

Watching Fernando head into the shack, Gundy thought Alex had picked his two best riders to send with him. Both of them knew cows, and Gundy had never seen many who could ride better.

After they had all eaten and had the small herd strung out, Gundy removed his guns, one at a time, and cleaned, oiled, and reloaded them while riding.

That night, while lying in his blankets, Gundy stared at the sky, not seeing the stars. He thought about what Kelly had said. Was he really a hard man? Since leaving the Mescalero, he thought he'd had as deep feelings for those he considered friends as any man. Yet when confronted with those who were a danger to him or those he cared about, he seemed to revert to all the savagery he'd learned as an Apache. When he'd worried the thought as long as he could without making a decision, he closed his eyes. To hell with it, he thought. A man don't live long out here 'less he gets rid of his enemies when and where he can.

The days turned into weeks. What had been a small herd and a small crew when they left Reiley's was now a herd of about seven hundred ornery longhorns with a crew of twelve men pushing them. Gundy had hired the rest of his crew in Van Horn. He'd picked them for gun-smart and cow-savvy. And not least, he'd talked to each of them to make sure he could trust them. He felt comfortable about all but one, Nance Yount. He'd been anxious to get back into the chaparral and had taken Yount on to fill out his crew. He had told them all when he hired them there would be no payday until they sold the herd.

He had not yet made up his mind whether to sell the herd in New Orleans or trail them north to Kansas, but he was leaning toward Kansas. Might get a better price for them in Dodge City.

When he took the trail, for whatever market, he wanted at least twenty-five hundred head.

They held the gather in a pocket of the Davis Mountains north of Marfa. That he'd found such a place caused him surprise. It had ample water from spring-fed streams, and the grass was lush enough to put meat on the cows. Each day the herd grew, some days by only ten or fifteen head. Most days those numbers tripled.

A month into the roundup, Gundy looked at the men gathered around him after breakfast. The sky had not yet turned light in the east. "Men, I found seven head of branded stuff in yesterday's gather. I cut 'em out and drove 'em off. Tell you again. Don't bring in anything with a brand; it'll only give somebody an excuse for a fight. We don't need that."

"What's the matter, Gundy?" Yount said. "A cow's a cow. You can get as much in those trail towns for them with or without a brand—if you slip the brand inspector a little cash under the table. You afraid of a little fight?"

Gundy stared at him a moment, every muscle tight as dried rawhide. "Yount, gonna let that pass this time. But if you ever again say anything like that, say it with that Navy Colt you got strapped to your leg." He sucked in a deep breath. "Fact is—say it now."

Yount stood there, fidgeted a moment, then laughed. "Hell, Boss, I wasn't saying you're scared. Just figuring that any cow will make money on the other end of this deal."

Gundy relaxed. Looking into Yount's eyes, he knew the man hadn't backed down from fear. There was something else there that caused Gundy to wonder, and to decide to keep a closer watch on him. It was almost as if Yount looked at the profits made from the herd as his.

They worked and sweated, cursed and bled for two weeks without a break. Then Gundy told six of the men to take two days, go into Marfa, get drunk, find a woman, and come back ready to work. "You go with them, Kelly. When you come back, the rest of us'll go." He kept Yount in the bunch he would go with.

Keeping the cattle from straying proved easy. Grass and water aplenty gave them no reason to look for better pastures. Two riders held the herd, and the remaining three searched the brush for more cows.

When Paul brought the five riders back from town, Gundy led his bunch out. He didn't figure the next day would be too good a day for the bunch that came in. They looked like they'd been stewed, wrung out, and thrown out.

Once Gundy's riders got to town, the others stopped at the first saloon while he rode a little farther down the street and tied his horse to a hitch rack in front of a general store. He sat in the shade on a bench outside and waited.

He'd not been there over thirty minutes when Yount walked out of the saloon, stood by its batwing doors, and searched the street both ways. Apparently satisfied, he walked down the street and pushed through the doors of another saloon. Before long two other men came out of that saloon, each going hurriedly in opposite directions. In less than ten minutes they both came back, each with three men in tow.

Gundy stood, crossed the street, and went in the same saloon. Going from bright sunlight into semi-darkness, he slipped to the side of the room and stood there long enough to adjust to the light. Then, careful to keep his eyes focused on the room, he went to the end of the bar. "Beer," he told the bartender, while studying each person at the tables. He didn't notice Yount the first time around, failing to see him under the smoke that hung like a sheet over the room. But in the second sweep of the room he found his man, sitting with his back to the other tables. Gathered around him were the men Gundy had seen come back with the two who had left.

Yount held their attention. He sketched with his finger on

the top of the table, while they stared at the finger, which was apparently drawing them an imaginary picture. Gundy would have given fifty head of cows to hear what Yount was saying.

He studied the face of every man around that table and didn't remember seeing any of them before. One thing he did know. Yount knew them, and they weren't planning their evening's fun. Gundy was as careful while leaving as he'd been when he came in.

Outside again, he leaned against the side of the building next to the saloon. With nothing to go on except a gut feel, he figured Yount planned to take the herd. When and how was the question.

He pushed away from the store front and walked down the street thinking of what he'd witnessed. He passed several stores and a couple of saloons. He decided to go somewhere quiet, somewhere to think. He wouldn't be welcome in the good part of town. That was where the town's citizens went. So he walked back to the last saloon he'd passed and went in, ordered a beer, and took it to a table in the back against the wall.

One of the house girls, swinging her hips in a way Gundy was sure she thought was seductive, said, "Buy me a drink, good-looking?"

He shook his head. "Not now."

He wasn't really aware she'd asked, or that he'd said no. He was staring at his beer when two huge hands grasped the edge of the table and upended it in front of him.

"What you mean insultin' my woman?"

Gundy raised his look to see a massive redheaded man, unshaven and filthy, standing in front of him. "Ain't insulted nobody," Gundy said. "Just told the lady I wasn't of a mind to buy her a drink."

Sitting was a disadvantage. This puncher was looking for trouble, and whether with guns or fists, Gundy knew the man would lose. Abruptly, he leaned forward and peered around the lout. "What was that?" he asked, and when the filthy bastard twisted to see who Gundy had addressed, Gundy came to his feet swinging.

His fist connected with Red's ribs. A gust of breath left his lips and he staggered backward. Gundy hit him again, once in the ribs and a shot to his nose. It spurted blood. Gundy bored in, not giving Red a chance to set his feet for a swing.

He hooked a right and left to the body, a left hook to the chin, and a right cross to Red's already splattered nose.

The huge hunk of beef took another step backward, tripped over a chair, fell—and grabbed for his gun. His .44 only halfway out of its holster, he froze.

"Go ahead. Ain't gonna bother me a damned bit to blow your stupid head off." Gundy's handgun had cleared its holster with a flicker of movement.

CHAPTER
8

Red's hand slowly uncurled from his gun's grip. "You an' me, cowboy, we got somethin' to settle," he said. "Put that gun back in the holster an' we'll start over."

Gundy glared. "You filthy bastard, you need killin', an' the way you're goin' somebody'll do it for me. Let it drop."

A voice spoke from the bar. "If you have good sense, Red, you won't take it any further. You're facing Blanco. He can beat you with guns, fists, or knives—using his left hand. Get up and get outta here."

Red's face turned a whitish gray color. He eased his hand back to his pistol, pushed it hard into its holster, crawled to his feet, and scooted for the door.

"Reckon that old boy was kinda glad to get outta here, Blanco. How you doin'?"

Gundy watched Red skitter through the batwings, then looked to see who was talking. A glance showed Clay Allison standing at the end of the bar, a bottle and glass on the counter in front of him, the bottle about half full. Allison had the reputation of being one of the meanest gunmen in the West when drinking, and Gundy didn't want to stay long enough to test the truth of that.

"Howdy, Clay. What you doin' over this way?"

"Come over to Pecos for supplies. About the closest place to Colfax County. Got me a ranch over that way."

56

"You're lucky. If I go into that territory, gotta be ready to fight the army, state police, an' damned near anybody else wants to take a shot at me."

Expressionless, Allison said, "Figure you'd win most o' them fights. You got no give in you, Blanco. A man with no give is gonna have trouble. Come on over. I'll help you out."

Gundy shook his head. "Like to, Allison, but I got me a herd north of town. Figure to head 'em for Kansas soon's I get a few more cows. Thanks for keepin' me from having to kill that redhead." He tipped his hat and walked out. Before nightfall, his altercation with Red would be blown into a full-fledged brawl. He hated that. It would add to his reputation.

He finally found a saloon where he could get a beer and think about Yount. Again, he picked a table against the back wall, out of the flow of traffic.

He figured Yount to have friends around there because of where he'd hired him, but on the way into town, Yount had said nothing about wanting to meet anybody. And he had waited until the rest of Gundy's men were settled in a bar before leaving. Usually a puncher on a night's spree in town stayed and caroused with the men he worked with. Strange, Gundy thought. But then again, maybe not so strange.

He finished his beer, and outside on the boardwalk found a bench from which he could see the string of saloons across the street. He sat there an hour before Yount emerged from the saloon along with his eight buddies.

Without hesitation, they went to the hitch rack and climbed aboard their horses. Maybe they had only decided to change drinking places. Gundy watched, waiting for them stop at another saloon. They didn't.

With Yount in the lead, they rode down the dusty street and out of town. Gundy glanced at the sun and figured it to be about five o'clock. He frowned. Nobody left town just before time to really start drinking and raising hell. He stood, went to his horse, and headed the same way the riders had taken.

Letting them get out of sight, Gundy studied the tracks their horses made until he knew them like a book. They could go wherever they wanted; he'd find them.

He thought to leave his horse tethered to a scrub oak and

track them on foot, but discarded the idea. They might go another mile—or ten. He didn't cotton to the idea of walking
ten miles.

Riding slowly, he studied the ground, looking up frequently
to make certain he didn't close on them. From the way they'd
left, they seemed to know exactly where they were going, and
he was willing to bet they wouldn't stay there. They would
do whatever it was they had ridden out for, and come back to
spend the remainder of the night in saloons and brothels.

After about an hour, with only a couple hours of daylight
left, Gundy decided maybe he should leave his horse. Close
to the ground made tracking easier.

He reined off the trail. About fifty feet into the chaparral,
he tethered the buckskin and went back. He'd not trailed
them but another quarter of a mile when the tracks led to the
left, at a right angle to the trail, along a narrow path that
wound between and around the thorny growth on all sides.

Gundy slowed. He might walk right into the middle of
them. The odds weren't right, but he wanted to know what
they were up to.

They held to the path for another half hour. Gundy was
downwind of them and thought, it being supper time, there
would be a cookfire wherever they headed. He tested the air
every few feet. His efforts soon paid off. Smoke. He faded
into the brush at his side, and gently breathing through his
nostrils again, checked for smell. The pungent smell of burning mesquite was stronger.

Staying off the path, he worked his way ahead. A thorn
grabbed his shirt. He carefully picked it out and placed the
twig back to its natural bent.

He moved now with deliberate, fluid movements. A jerk,
or fast motion of any kind, could give him away. Even with
that, he almost walked into their camp. They were lying
around a fire while Yount talked. Gundy lowered himself to
the ground and lay there, straining to catch the words.

"Toss me that bottle," Yount said. One of his men sitting
to the side jammed the cork in the bottle's neck and passed
it to the guy next to him, who handed it to Yount. After taking a long swig, Yount passed it to one of the others. "Now,

like I was sayin'. Gundy's gonna have all the cows he can handle in another two weeks. We'll hit 'em before they git out o' the bowl where they're holdin' 'em. We'll keep our camp here. Don't want to go stumblin' up on any of his hands. Them brush-poppers been gettin' cows outta places nobody with any sense would go into." Yount called for the bottle again, and after drinking said, "You men stay close to camp starting a week from now. I'll come get you when the time's ready. The boss is countin' on this herd."

Gundy counted Yount's men again. The number had doubled. Seventeen men, counting Yount. Gundy's troubles weren't getting any better. He backed out of his hiding place and, staying low to the ground, worked his way back to the path. He straightened and, hitting a fast trot, went to his horse and headed for town.

The dim glow of lanterns and a glance at his watch showed him it had taken a full hour less to come back than it had to find Yount's camp. He got a hotel room, went to the barbershop for a bath and a shave, and then went back to his room to lie down to think.

His first impulse was to fire Yount when he came back. Then he checked his money and found what he already knew. He couldn't pay Yount off unless he wanted to head north with short supplies. He didn't have a penny to waste. Then he grinned. If he waited until the bandits made their move, he'd not have to pay him at all—a corpse didn't need money. And unless he'd heard wrong, Yount had said something about a boss. Gundy wondered about that.

He thought about the best way to handle the situation, made his decision, and then went looking for his men. He wanted a beer.

Figuring they had stayed where he'd last seen them, he went to the first saloon.

"Hey, Boss, c'mon over. Grab yourself one o' these pretty ladies an' a drink," Emilio shouted.

Gundy ordered a beer and, ignoring the invitation of one of the girls, went to the table where his punchers sat. He twisted a chair around and straddled it. He would not let on about any of the afternoon's happenings. They might let something slip to warn Yount.

Another of his men, Bob Slidell, squinted bleary-eyed at Gundy and said, "Done heered you scared the dawg crap outta some puncher down the way. He was in here braggin' he done had a fight with the Apache Blanco an' lived to tell about it. Sounded right proud to be walkin' around."

Gundy took a swallow of his beer. "Wasn't nothing. He'd had a whole bunch to drink. Anybody coulda whipped 'im." He wished it hadn't happened at all. "Clay Allison was there. He broke it up. That redhead was afraid of Allison, not me."

"Git yourself a woman an' join the party. We only got 'nother night an' day to raise a little hell."

Gundy shook his head. "Not now. Might after a while." He wanted a woman, all right, but not one of these. There was only one woman for him and he stood a long way from getting her. Until then he'd do without.

He had another beer and put the empty mug on the table. "Gonna see what's in them other saloons."

Gundy had barely cleared the batwings when Ben Darcy stopped him in the street outside. "Hear you had a little trouble this afternoon, Blanco."

Gundy raked the man with a glance and homed in on the star on his chest. "Last I seen of you, Darcy, you was wearin' a Ranger's badge. You give up Rangerin' for marshalin'?"

"Yeah, hankered to stay in one place for a while." Darcy cast a glance in both directions and said, "Been lookin' for you. Got somethin' to tell you."

When Darcy said he'd been looking for him, Gundy's gut had tightened. Now he grinned. "You scared me for a minute, Darcy. Wondered why you was lookin' for me."

Darcy's face, looking like it was chiseled from granite, cracked a bit when he smiled. "No, Blanco. If I was lookin' for you that way, I'd have a dozen men with me." He again glanced down the street and nodded to the jail across the street. "Let's go to my office and I'll tell you about it."

They walked around a sleeping dog in the middle of the street, stopped to let a buckboard pass, then stepped to the opposite boardwalk.

Inside the office, Darcy trimmed the lantern's wick and sat behind his desk. "Pour yourself a cup o' that coffee yonder on the stove. Pour me one too while you're at it."

Gundy did, and remained standing. "What you got to tell me, Marshal? Ain't never had much truck with the law."

"Sit down—relax. I got no deputies hid around here to cause you trouble."

Gundy sat across the desk from him, and Darcy continued. "Hear tell you're pure hell on any Comancheros you run into. Don't know how many of 'em you've sent over the divide, but a whole bunch from what I hear."

Gundy nodded. "One or two."

Darcy chuckled. "Yeah, one or two *dozen*, and what I want to talk about is them. 'Fore I left the Rangers, a rumor was going around there's one man who controls most o' them. Sends 'em out and takes care of the goods they bring back. Women, cattle, gold, silver—whatever. Hear he pays 'em in cash, and then he sells to an open market in Mexico and the States. He's rolling in money, and is also the bull o' the woods wherever and whoever he is. You hear anything like this?"

Gundy nodded. "Yep. Most folks have heard the story, but nobody puts much truck in it. What's that got to do with me?"

Darcy packed his pipe and lighted it, all the while staring at the wall frowning. He shook his head. "Probably nothin'. But the way you roam this country, thought if you see or hear anything we could put our teeth into, you'd let me know."

"Sounds like you're still Rangerin'."

He nodded. "If I can help them find that bag o' cow dung, I'll do it. Yeah, far as that scum goes, you could figure me still a Ranger. Once a Texas Ranger, a man don't never lose it."

Gundy stood. "I'll let you know, but I ain't got a damn thing right now you can use."

The marshal came around the desk and shook Gundy's hand. "Thanks, Blanco, figured you'd help if you could." His face cracked in that hard smile again. "Promise you won't try to clean 'em up by your lonesome?"

"That old chief what brung me up didn't raise a idiot."
Gundy stepped toward the door.

"Nearly forgot somethin', Blanco. The rumors also say the
guy who runs them has promised a thousand dollars to the
man who kills you. Watch your back-trail."

"Just wasted them words, Marshal. I always watch where
I'm comin' from." He left.

He walked down the street, and through the normal smells
of dust, horse droppings, and the faint scent of mountain ce-
dar wafted on the breeze, Gundy caught the aroma of coffee
and frying steak. He hadn't eaten since breakfast.

He followed the smells to a small restaurant down the
street. While eating, he pondered the marshal's request. He
had always thought Comancheros operated in independent
bands. Even when he'd heard the rumors of them having one
leader, one brain, he'd refused to believe it. But if the Rangers were putting some credence to it, then maybe he'd look
into it after he got back from Kansas. If somebody didn't collect that thousand dollars first.

He thought back to Ben Darcy, who had been a gunfighter
with a reputation. One that stacked up with Hickok, Luke
Short, Bill Longley, and most of the others he'd heard of.
Funny how the Rangers could take a young hell-raiser, put a
badge on him, and save him from turning outlaw.

Gundy smiled to himself. There had been several times
he'd worked with the Rangers and had felt right good about
it. He decided the best time to find out what he could about
the Comanchero operation was when he started building his
ranch. He would be right in the middle of where they operated, and he'd be doing himself a favor by doing his part in
ridding Texas of the trash.

After eating, Gundy wandered up and down the street. He
wasn't ready to go to bed, and he didn't want a drink, but
what the hell could he do? He couldn't just walk up and
down the street the rest of the night. Maybe a small-stakes
poker game would be good. He went in the next saloon he
came to.

There was only one table with stakes he could afford, so he

stood there long enough for a seat to open and pulled up a chair.

The dealer glanced at him. "Two-bit limit, dime ante, fifty cents on the last card, three raises, dealer's choice." His eyes swept the rest of the players. "Five-card stud."

Gundy nodded.

He sat through three hands, won two of them, and dragged in his money. But he couldn't get his mind into the game. It kept jumping back to Yount. He stood and pocketed his money.

"What's the matter, big spender? Make enough for a few drinks and now you gonna quit?"

Gundy lowered his gaze to the puncher putting out the crap. "You talkin' to me?" His voice was soft, almost gentle. The young cowboy was drunk, losing, and looking for trouble.

"Yeah, you. Sit down an' let me get my money back. You ain't quittin' now."

Gundy stared at him a moment. He didn't want trouble with this kid—and that's all he was, maybe nineteen years old. "Cowboy, I'm tired, sober, an' gonna hit the sack. Leave me alone."

"You got trouble," the puncher said, and stood.

CHAPTER
9

Gundy swung back-handed, palmed his .44, and thumbed back the hammer. "Cowboy, told you, don't want no trouble." He stared into a face that was cold sober, eyes wide and full of fear.

The kid stood, hands held wide of his holsters. "Don't reckon I want any either, sir. Just let my mouth overload my ass."

Gundy holstered his handgun and held out his hand. The kid shook it. " 'Stead of blowin' my money in here I better save what I got left," the kid said.

"You lookin' for a job?"

The puncher nodded. "Yeah, an' I better find one right soon, or I ain't gonna be eatin' regular."

"This is your lucky day, kid." Gundy smiled. "I didn't kill you, an' now you got a job—if you want it."

"You hirin'?"

"Uh-huh, if you'll wait'll I sell my herd to get paid."

The lanky young man grinned. "Heck, yeah, I can wait, long's you feed reg'lar."

Gundy groped in his pocket a moment and pulled out a silver dollar. "Here's something to feed you until day after to-morrow mornin'. Meet me in front of the hotel—sunup."

Gundy headed to his room. He wanted to get off the street. Here he was, in a town where he had no reason to have trouble, and he'd already had to avoid killing two men—and he'd been able to do so only because of his quick gun. If he'd been any slower, both men would have tried for theirs. He shook his head, thinking a fast draw had some good things going for it.

Only then did he begin to wonder who had put a price on his hide. He didn't wonder why the Comancheros wanted him out of the way. He hurt them wherever he found them. His hatred of those who killed women and children, robbed and terrorized whole communities, always seethed barely under control. He hadn't learned that set of values from the Apache. Again he shook his head. It must have been something he'd gotten from the mother and father he'd never known.

Early the morning of the third day, Gundy stood by his horse in front of the hotel. His punchers wandered up one by one, bleary-eyed, smelling of stale alcohol, tobacco smoke, and cheap perfume, looking like it would take a full week for them to round back into shape. The third man to join up with his party was the kid from the saloon two nights before—and he didn't look like he'd had a drink since Gundy left him.

"You gonna work for me, need to know your handle," Gundy said.

"Cale Madison, sir. Shore am happy to be joinin' your crew."

"Glad to have you. Figure on bein' a mite short-handed soon."

Madison slanted him a puzzled look.

Gundy covered his slip by explaining he would need more men for the trail drive. When all of his men had ridden up, they headed toward the roundup camp.

On the way, he pondered how to tell his men what he'd found out about Yount. He didn't want Yount warned by word or action, and decided to have Kelly do it when he could talk with each man in private.

Four days later, Kelly told him they had about twenty-two hundred head. "I figure another five, maybe six days and we can start the drive."

"You tell the men about Yount?"

At Kelly's nod, Gundy said, "Good. I'll watch him. You keep the men pullin' them cows into the herd." He had been drinking coffee, and tossed the dregs to the ground when the drumbeat of several horses broke the stillness.

He pulled his Winchester from its scabbard. "Kelly, get into the brush with with these men. Take rifles." He waited by the fire.

A tall, rawboned old man, leading six riders, rode toward him. Gundy studied them. They were as salty as any crew he'd seen. They were bone-lean, leathery skinned, and clean-shaven except for the handlebar mustaches they all sported. And though it was unusual for this part of the country where water was scarce, these men wore clean clothes and looked as if they'd had a bath in the not too distant past. Even if they brought him trouble, they had his grudging admiration.

The old man had the coldest ice-blue eyes Gundy had ever stared into. His words were as rough as he looked. "Who's in charge here?" He didn't bother with a greeting.

"Me." Gundy bit his word off.

"What're you doin' rounding up my cows?"

"Ain't your cows. An' 'fore you get any notions about them guns you're wearin', they's a whole pile of Winchesters trained on you. So climb down from your horse and set. We'll talk a spell."

The old man flicked a glance at the surrounding brush, nodded, and told his men to stay put. He dismounted and Gundy handed him a cup of coffee. "Set."

The six others who'd ridden in sat their horses, hands hooked in their gunbelts not too far from their six-guns. It would take only a signal from their boss to start them shoot-ing. The grizzled old man sat cross-legged across the fire. Gundy stared at him a moment. "Not one cow in that herd wears another's brand. You're welcome to have your men take a look."

"Don't have to look. You got 'em off my range—they're mine."

Gundy allowed a slight smile. "And, sir, I figure you got your range *and* your cows the same way I'm gettin' these. In about another week, I'm startin' these cows toward Kansas.

You can try to stop me, but if you do, you better know where you can hire a whole bunch o' more riders. You gonna lose a passel o' them you got."

The hard eyes bored into Gundy's for what seemed forever. Then the old man asked, "What's yore name?"

"Trace Gundy, sir, an' I don't want to fight you—but I will. *Como se llama?*"

"I'm Rance Senegal"—he said it like the world should know who he was—"and the land from here to San'tone, Marfa, Van Horn, an' El Paso b'longs to me. Now you git yore men an' make tracks."

Gundy pulled a sack of Durham from his shirt pocket and offered it to Senegal, who shook his head. Gundy took his time in building his cigarette, looked up after putting fire to it, and asked, "Why don't you claim the rest of Texas? Seems like you ain't left much for nobody else."

Ignoring Gundy's sarcasm, Senegal took a swallow of coffee. "Son, I got fifty riders. You won't get off my range before every man you got will be dead, and these cows you done worked so hard to gather will be scattered from hell to breakfast—and they'll still be on my land."

What the man said was true. Gundy stared into the fire, thinking. There had to be a way out of this, and it had to be a way where they both would profit. Finally, he thought he had an argument that might stand.

"Mr. Senegal, you're probably right, but we'd both lose, me more'n you." Killing time, he poured them each another cup of coffee. "I got a offer to make you.

"Gatherin' these cows, I figure it's been one helluva long time since you made a gather of your own, an' them mavericks o' yourn need harvestin'."

A glint of amusement flickered in the old man's eyes. "Ah, so you're doing me a favor by thinning my herd down. Is that it?"

Gundy shook his head. "Wait'll you hear me out, then have your say. First off, reckon you have 'bout as much trouble with the Comancheros as everbody else. I'm known by another name here and in the New Mexico Territory, and them *banditos* hate me, mostly 'cause I done killed a bunch of them."

Gundy studied Senegal a moment to see if he was listening. Satisfied he wasn't being ignored, he continued. "Figure if you left to drive a herd to railhead you'd lose cows, men, and maybe even some of your ranch. I got word they're better organized than anybody would believe.

"I'll toss my men in the pot, we'll help you round up whatever you need to get rid of, then you give me some of your men and I'll drive the whole kit and kaboodle up there—but I keep my cows."

Senegal looked into the fire a long time, then turned those hard eyes back to Gundy. "Son, what you say about the Comancheros being well organized may be true, but you trail-drivin' my cows ain't gonna help that situation any."

"Yes, sir, it will, 'cause when I get back, I figure to find who their leader is and kill 'im. Without his leadership, an' the folks he sells the stuff to, they gonna have to find another trade."

The old man grinned. It looked like it hurt his face to do so, but he did it. "Gundy, you'd have to have an army with you to rout him, whoever he is, out of his stronghold, wherever it is. Reckon you're gonna ask me for some o' my men to help you do that job too?"

"No, sir, gonna do it alone."

Senegal had just taken a swallow of coffee. At Gundy's statement he spit the coffee out, and pinned Gundy with a look like an eagle. "What the hell do you mean? You're either crazy as hell or you ain't never tangled with even one Comanchero."

Gundy stood and looked down at Senegal. "Sir, like I told you, I already killed a passel of them and they want my hide a whole lot worse'n you do. That other name I told you about? Well, there's them what call me the Apache Blanco, an' the only way to get the man runnin' that show is alone. Figure I'm the one to do it."

Senegal pointed to Gundy's shirt pocket. "Give me a smoke, *por favor*."

Gundy handed the hard old man his sack of Durham and

watched while he built a smoke. This is almost the same rit-
ual the People go through, he thought. Now that we are going
to smoke together, we probably ain't gonna have no fight.

"Tell your men to climb down an' have some coffee,"
Gundy said.

Senegal nodded, and without further words his men swung
from their saddles. Gundy still didn't signal his men to come
to the fire.

Senegal smoked almost his whole cigarette before he said
another word. Finally he speared Gundy with another look.
"You're Blanco? Somehow I expected a man ten feet tall and
about six hundred pounds. Shows even I can be wrong sometimes. When you want to get started on my roundup?"

Gundy's neck hair tingled. There were times being the
Apache Blanco paid off. This was one of them. Then, thinking of Yount and his men, he frowned. "Mr. Senegal, I have
a job to finish before we get started. There's a bunch what
figures to take these cows from me. I gotta get rid of them
first. Where can I find your place?"

"I'll leave a couple of men with you. They'll show you."
Senegal turned to his men. *"Vamanos."*

CHAPTER
10

Dee intercepted the rider who had gone to town for the mail, and riffled through it before taking it to her father. One thick envelope, heavily bound in brown manila paper, had the wax seal of the Territorial Governor. She again looked to make sure there was no letter from Paul or Trace. They had been gone over a month, and even though she really didn't expect to hear from either of them, she felt a pang of disappointment. Oh, why don't you admit it, she thought, you really wanted a letter from Trace. At the same time she wondered why it made so much difference. He had never given any indication how he felt about her.

She handed the package to her father, and asked, "Are you trying to get Trace pardoned, Papa?"

"Why do you want to know, Dee?"

Her face warmed and her chest tightened. She was being forced to answer the question she'd asked herself many times. "Because I care. To me he's a good man, and on *anybody's* scale he's a *man*, with everything the word means."

Kelly ripped the thick envelope open and gave her a slightly worried look. "I wish you didn't care, honey. He's all you say, but chances are, I'll not be able to influence Lew Wallace. Yes, I'm trying, but there are many in the territory who carry as much weight as I, and few of them believe Gundy innocent."

He took out pages of data from the envelope and leafed through them. Frowning, he pulled several from the stack. "These may help. Wallace refused to consider my request again, but he may have done us a small favor. He's listed the raids Gundy is accused of taking part in, and the dates." Kelly placed two sheets side by side and studied them. "Why, hell, if they had any sense, they could see from this the impossibility of the whole thing. They accuse him of being in on both these raids on the same day and four hundred miles apart."

Dee leaned over and kissed her father on the cheek. "Papa, I knew you'd help. You like Trace as much as I do, and you are a fair man."

Kelly cast her an amused glance. "Somehow, Daughter, I doubt that I like Trace as much as you."

She blushed again. "Oh, I don't know. I've asked myself why it makes so much difference. I don't dare admit I'm in love with him. I don't even know how he feels. But I do know this. He's a lot more the kind of man I want someday for my own than anyone I've ever met. Since the night we met him in Juárez, he's been in my thoughts constantly."

Her father looked into her eyes. He was much more serious than she was accustomed to seeing him. "Dee, if you are in love with him and we can't get him a pardon, what would you do?"

"If he'll have me, I'll go wherever it takes for us to be together."

Kelly stacked the papers, filed them in the top drawer of his massive wooden desk, and stood. "Let's find the coffeepot and talk about this."

They found Maria Kelly in the kitchen harassing Juanita, the cook, who had been with them since Dee was a baby. And ever since, Maria had been giving Juanita unwanted advice.

Kelly poured them each a cup of coffee, put the cups on the table, and sat.

"Looks like we're going to have a family meeting," Maria said. "Every time you tromp into my territory, draw coffee, and sit so regally, I figure the *king* wants a meeting."

"This's no joking matter, *querida mia*. Tell Dee how a rancher's wife has to live when he's first getting started in the cow business."

"Now why in the world do you want me to do that?"

Kelly swiped his hand through the air. "Because I think our daughter's in love with a penniless outlaw, and I don't believe she has any idea of the hardships she'd have to endure."

Maria threw her head back and laughed. "Well, dear me, what a terrible thing." Then she pinned Kelly with a look that Dee would have bet penetrated his very soul. "Alex Kelly, with the exception of being an outlaw, have you forgotten how we started?"

"Hell, no, my love. That's why I want you to tell her about it. If *I* tell her, she'll think I'm being over-protective, like she does every time we go to a fandango and she dances with the same man too many times."

Maria dusted biscuit flour from her hands and sat across from her daughter. "Regardless of what you think about your father's degree of protectiveness, he's right," Maria said. She took a swallow of her coffee. "You've never wanted for anything. Your father has been a good provider. None of it has come easy, but you don't remember those days. While he built his herd, we lived in a small shack. I made what clothes we had and your father stitched moccasins, and made buffalo robes and hats to keep us warm. I grew vegetables and canned them so we'd eat in the winter."

Alex sat there nodding, putting emphasis to each word she said. Maria swung her attention from Dee to him. "That what you wanted her to hear, Alex?"

"Yep. Figure that ought to do it."

"Not quite." Maria's voice was firm. "Now I'm going to show her the other side of the coin." She stood, walked around the table to Dee, and hugged her to her still attractive, petite figure.

"*Niña*, your grandparents, my parents, were well-to-do. I too had been reared with everything I wanted; clothes, nice home, jewelry. But when I met your father, I would have followed him to the ends of the earth—still would. So when you get your man's attention, don't worry about anything. Saddle that wild mustang you've cut out for yourself and ride the wind." She tightened her arm on Dee's shoulders. "Trace Gundy is a man to ride any trail with. Grab your dream, *niña*. You'll never be sorry."

Alex's face had gotten redder with each word Maria spoke. "Well, by damn! You ain't helped matters one damned bit."

"You hush, Alejandro Kelly. You *are* too protective. Admit it. You can't bear the thought of anyone taking your place in your daughter's heart." Maria rushed around the table and hugged Alex, then kissed him. "My love, no one will ever take your place in her heart. She'll just make room for another."

Alex stared across the kitchen, seeing nothing, thinking. His face softened. He tilted his head to look into Maria's eyes. "As always, my love, you're right. Our boy cub has left the den, and now it looks like our little girl has grown up, and the same man is taking them both. We can't hold her back." He stood. "But by damn, she's not going to marry an outlaw. I got a lot of letters to write—see if I can make our hard-headed governor see daylight."

After Senegal left, Gundy waved his riders to the fire. "Boy, I thought for a good while there we were gonna have a shoot-out," Kelly said. "That's one rawhide-tough old man."

Absently, Gundy nodded. Senegal was tough, all right, but somehow he had the feeling the old man liked him. He thought he'd made a friend. Now he had to measure up. But first he had to do something about Yount. He didn't know whether to wait until they strung the cattle out on the trail, and then try to repulse an attack by Yount and his men, or try to slip up on their camp and wipe them out. And he'd better make up his mind soon, because after a couple of hundred more longhorns he and his men had to help Senegal with his roundup. He had to think on it.

The next few days Gundy kept half his crew branding. He'd decided on the AB Connected brand. At the same time they trail-branded them with a large S. In the meantime, he'd decided to hit the bandits where they camped.

Every time he caught one of his men alone, he told him

how he figured to stop Yount. At supper one night he pulled
Kelly aside. "Pablo, I want you to set a watch on Yount, two
hours for each man. When he gets up and slips out of camp,
wake me. We'll follow him. If I knew when he planned to
take our herd, I'd station men around his camp ahead of
time." He kicked at a cow chip. "Don't know, so we'll follow
him."

Three nights later, Gundy felt a tug on his arm. He sat up,
put on his hat, pulled on his boots, and stood. Most of the
crew were up and strapping on weapons. Then each man
checked his rifle.

"Don't make no more noise than a snake," Gundy cautioned. He worried about how to start the attack. It wasn't his
way to open fire on a man while he was in his blankets, but
how the hell could he do otherwise?

While they grabbed a swallow of coffee, Gundy had
Fernando go out to the herd to tell the night riders they would
have to stay until the rest got back. Meanwhile, Gundy swept
his men with a glance. "Don't any of you take more chances
than you have to. Don't wait for me to open fire, but make
sure of where you put your lead. Let's go."

They ghosted out of camp on foot since Yount had also left
on foot. Gundy kept them close-packed for almost an hour
until they turned off the trail onto the path where he'd previ-
ously followed Yount and his men. He gathered his own men
around. "Men," he whispered, "we'll scatter here. You five
go to the other side of their fire. We'll circle from this side.
Be careful."

Within seconds Gundy stood alone with only the sound of
the wind rustling the leaves in the scrub oak. He still worried
about drygulching the bandits.

His men moved through the brush. None but an Apache
could tell the difference between the man sounds Gundy
heard and those of the wind. He worked his way to almost
the same spot in which he'd hidden the other time he'd been
there. From his hiding place he counted seventeen men
around the fire. They were all there, talking in low tones.
Gundy still could not bring himself to fire into the outlaws.
Abruptly, the decision was out of his hands.

A loud crashing in the brush on the other side of the fire brought every man in the camp to his feet, rifles or handguns swinging wildly, firing at targets they had not identified. His AB hands opened up. Bullets whipped through the brush, cutting branches from the trunks and ricocheting into the night. Gundy used his six-gun at this range. On the balls of his feet he cat-footed into their midst, firing methodically. A man directly in front of him went down, a blue hole above his left eye. Gundy searched for Yount. He wanted him for himself. Another man went down in front of him. His men poured shots into the firelit circle. Men fell, yelling their life's breath out as they died. Then Yount stood alone, across the fire from Gundy. Gundy walked in on him, spacing his shots. Three times he fired, and each time a hole centered in Yount's chest blossomed red in the firelight. Yount stood there, a wild, insane look in his eyes, pulling the trigger. He wouldn't fall. Gundy triggered another shot into him—this time in the gut.

Yount sank to his knees. He pulled the trigger of his .44 time after time, seemingly unaware that the hammer fell on spent shells, his eyes blazing. "Who told you—you white Indian, you traitor?" He started to topple, and threw his empty gun at Gundy, but never saw where it went. His eyes went wide and glazed over.

Gundy stood in the center of the circle next to the fire. The utter silence screamed at him. Even the wind seemed to have stilled. A pall of gunsmoke hung over the site, its acrid odor biting his nostrils. Silently, his men slipped into the light.

"You're hit, Boss. Bleedin' pretty good."

"Ain't bad or I wouldn't be standin'." Gundy swept his men with a searching look, counting them at the same time. They were all there. "Any of you hit?"

"Only a scratch here and there, *señor*," Fernando answered. "Looks like Madison got a crease across his shoulder. We'll fix it back in camp."

Gundy looked at the kid. "Can you make it that far?"

Madison grinned. "Hell, Boss, we get worse'n what I got every day out in the brush. What we gonna do with these hombres?"

Gundy walked to each of Yount's men and toed them over so he could see both sides of them. They were all dead. Without looking up he said, "Pete, find a arroyo close by. We'll drop 'em in it an' push some dirt over them.

"Emilio, find their horses; we'll add 'em to our remuda. Kelly, take a couple men and gather the guns, money, and anything else we can use. They ain't gonna have no need for it where they've gone. If they's a letter or anythin' on any of 'em to tell where he's from, keep his stuff separate. We'll mail it to his family."

Before carrying out his orders, Kelly studied him a moment. "You have no feelings for these men, do you, Blanco?"

Gundy pierced him with a look. "Kelly, gonna tell you somethin'. If we'd waited a couple o' hours, they'da been a bunch of dead on the ground in our camp—an' we'd of been them. Now I'm gonna answer your question. Yeah, I got feelin's for every one of this trash. I got puredee joy at seein' 'em lay here. They been ridin' toward this endin' for a long time. If it hadn't of been our lead what got 'em, it woulda been somebody's noose swung over a cottonwood limb."

Paul shook his head and went about helping the men gather weapons and whatever else looked to be of use.

Gundy walked off to the side, and back in the shadow he swallowed several times to keep the bitter bile from his throat. Hell, yes, it bothered him that they'd had to kill this many men. Even when he rode with the Apache it had affected him, and he'd had to prove himself over and over again—and most of the time he knew the proving was to himself. The Apache already knew the kind of warrior that rode with them.

Back in his own camp the crew threw the loot from the raid into the chuck wagon. "Find anything to tell us who any of them were?"

Kelly answered for them all. "Nothing, Boss. Sort of wish there was, though."

Gundy went to his bedroll and dropped his guns and gunbelt by it.

"All right, Kelly. You and Emilio divide up the money between the rest of the crew. Sure as hell ain't gonna throw it away." Gundy sat, then slid down to rest his head on his saddle. "Don't cut me in on the divvy."

For a long time Gundy lay there after the rest of the crew turned in. Like most nights, he thought of Dee, and as usual he thought to write her a letter when time allowed. Hell, he would make time—but like before, he didn't know when. From Dee his thoughts shifted to the ranch he wanted to build. Only now he had more reason for building it. Tomorrow they would have to start the gather for Senegal. He went to sleep.

CHAPTER
11

The men Senegal had left behind showed Gundy and his riders to the R-Bar-S headquarters. Gundy left four men with his herd, so he had a generous offering of manpower with him. Senegal met him at the front door.

"Howdy, Gundy, c'mon in. Tell your riders to head for the cookshack. Bell just rung for dinner. You and me'll go down after a while. Have a drink first."

Gundy shook the calloused old hand Senegal offered, and stepped into the kind of room he dreamed of having someday. The walls were about three feet thick, which made for a comfortable temperature the year round, and the room itself had marble floors, probably freighted in from Mexico. The furniture was Southwest style, massive, with a heavy Mexican influence.

Senegal poured tequila, and offered a plate of sliced lemon and a shaker of salt. Gundy put a little salt on the back of his hand, licked it, took a bite of the lemon, held his drink up in a toast, said *"Salud,"* and tossed his drink down.

"Brung thirteen brush-poppers with me, countin' myself," Gundy said. "We work for you till the roundup's over. Then I take charge till I bring back your money from the drive. That okay? Reason I say that is 'cause I already been on two trail drives 'fore this."

Senegal's face creased in an effort to smile. "Way I had it

figured. No need for you to work along with them now, though."

"Mr. Senegal, I pull my weight wherever I go. I'll chouse them cows outta the brush right along with the rest of the men. You or your *segundo* are in charge. Show us the area you want to hold your cows an' we'll do our part in gettin' 'em there."

Senegal nodded. "We start in the mornin'. Tonight I expect a guest. Want you to meet 'im. My closest neighbor, says he lives the other side of Marfa. Never been to his place. Come in here right after the War Between the States an' set himself up in ranchin'. Name's Matt Ross."

Finished with their drink, they went to the cookshack and ate with the crew. Twenty of Senegal's men were there. "Keep 'bout this many riders around here most of the time," Senegal said. "The rest come in sometimes on weekends and payday. These here I figure protect against Comanches—or Comancheros."

Gundy looked Senegal's men over. They had the stamp of fighting men on them. He nodded. "Reckon I wouldn't want to tangle with any of them." At Senegal's amused look, Gundy leaned closer and said, " 'Preciate it if you'd sort of forget that other name I'm called by. Might keep me from havin' to live up to it."

"My word on it."

After dinner, Gundy's men went about mending gear, while the regular crew tended to chores they'd started that morning. Gundy noticed with approval that the first thing most of his men did was to take a bath. He cleaned up with the rest of them, but apologized to his host that he had no better than range garb to wear that night.

"Don't fret about it, son. If Ross don't like what we wear around here, he can pull freight." That was the first indication Gundy had that Senegal didn't like his neighbor.

Gundy and Senegal sat and talked the afternoon through. In answer to some pointed questions, Gundy told Senegal his plans and how he figured to accomplish them.

"You got a woman, Gundy?" Senegal asked. Then his voice softened. "Tell you, son, every man should ought to

have himself a woman. Mine died 'bout twenty year ago.
Ain't never seen one since that I wanted. Probably none of
'em woulda had me no way."

Gundy was surprised Senegal talked of family, and after
studying on it a moment, figured the old man was lonesome.
"Yes, sir," Gundy said. "I figure to get married someday, but
I got to get a start first. Got a lot to do." He stood and went
to look at a large oil painting of a nice-looking woman sitting
between two young men.

"Them's my younguns, with my wife," Senegal said. "The
oldest was killed at Shiloh. The youngest got gored and
didn't live long enough for us to find him. Got nobody no
more, Gundy. When you get in double harness have a whole
passel o' kids, somebody to visit with in the evenings, somebody to carry on after you're gone."

"Yes, sir, figure on it, but like I say. I got a lot to do 'fore
I dare ask the one I picked out if she'll have me."

Senegal looked hard at Gundy. "Way I got you figured,
son, any woman what would turn you down would be missin'
a few brains."

The fat motherly-looking Mexican woman who cooked,
kept house, and ran the hacienda in general came in. She told
Senegal that one of the hands had told her Ross and his
daughter were only a half mile away. "Thank you, Teresa,"
Senegal said. Then under his breath added, "Damn! He
brought his witch with him."

He looked at Gundy. "Boy, that woman you're about to
meet's got a tongue that'll scald the hair off a fat hawg. Less
you have to say to her the better."

Gundy couldn't help laughing. "Partner, seems like you
don't much give a damn for her."

"Don't, nor her pa neither."

They had only a short while to wait until the jangle of harness sounded out front. Senegal and Gundy met Ross and his
daughter at the door.

On first look, Gundy would have said Ross's daughter was
a really good-looking woman, with blond hair, big blue eyes,
and a figure that would cause a cowhand to lose many a
night's sleep. Senegal introduced them both to Gundy. Hillary

was Ross's daughter's name. "Glad to know you, ma'am," Gundy said.

She looked at Gundy's scuffed boots, faded jeans, patched buckskin shirt, his face—and dismissed him without acknowledging him.

Gundy felt his face flush, and his tongue fixed itself to change "ma'am" to "bitch." He choked off the impulse and locked eyes with Senegal, who for once, showed him a real smile.

During supper and the visiting afterward, Gundy might as well have been part of the furniture. He sat without contributing anything to the conversation. None was pointed his way. He used the time to study Ross.

Smooth, Gundy thought, too damned smooth. Everything Ross did was deliberate. Not a chance for anything he said or any of his actions to be misunderstood. For the most part he was the epitome of an Eastern gentleman, but under the surface Gundy pegged him as hard and calculating. He deserved Hillary.

Ross was talking, and Gundy started paying attention. ". . . got a few neighbors up there above Marfa, small-fry mostly, with under a hundred thousand acres. I'd run them off, but I intend to get elected to the legislature and can't afford to make enemies right now. Once I get in, it'll be a different story." He stood and walked over to stand in front of Senegal. "That's what I want to talk to you about. You have friends in Austin. I expect you to support me with them."

He said it as though it was a mandate that Senegal would not dare refuse. But Gundy had sat there all evening, chafing at the way they'd treated him, and even though he was a guest, with no interest in the area once he got his cattle on the trail, he said softly, "Personally, I'd see you in hell before supporting you for anything."

The three snapped their eyes in his direction. Senegal stared at him poker-faced. Hillary stuck her nose up in the air as though she smelled something bad, and her father sucked air like a fish out of water.

"Just what are your stakes in this game, young man?" Ross said. "I don't believe you own property, nor would I in my wildest dreams think of you as a man of influence. I would appreciate you sitting quietly, as you've done all evening, and let us discuss things of import, things of which I'm certain you would have no knowledge."

Gundy stabbed him with a look. "First place, mister, you'd be surprised at the things I have knowledge of. Secondly, I don't have to play at being a gentleman. I was born one. And third, I reckon any who judge a man by what he's wearin' ain't much more'n trash. And last, I'm a guest in Mr. Senegal's home and won't take advantage of that. Otherwise, I'd run you and that cold bitch you call a daughter slam back to Marfa." He stood. "Mr. Senegal, I'll sleep with the crew. See you in the mornin'."

Senegal looked as though he'd not seen anything more enjoyable in his life. "Son, you're welcome to stay anywhere on my place you feel most comfortable. You and I'll have a drink 'fore you turn in." He walked Gundy to the door.

When he came back into the room, Ross stood facing him. "I must say, Senegal, you have strange, and I'll add, unsavory friends. I should have called him out. Had it not been that Hillary was here, I would have."

The smile had never left Senegal. "You know what, Ross? You're the luckiest sunuvabitch I ever seen. You better be glad your daughter *was* here. That man would have chewed you up, spit you out, an' never knowed he'd been in a fight— guns, fists, or knives." He chuckled. "That boy is 'bout as good with words as them weapons I mentioned too. Didn't know that till just now." He laughed and slapped his thighs in sheer delight.

These people were his guests, and Senegal would never let it be said that he was inhospitable to anyone, so his civility the rest of the evening was everything it should have been, but no more than what he thought was required.

As soon as Teresa showed the Rosses to their rooms, Senegal picked up a bottle of tequila and headed for the bunkhouse. His thoughts centered on Gundy.

If his boys had lived, he reckoned there wasn't anyone he'd rather they'd be like more than Gundy. He hadn't beaten around the bush in setting Ross straight. Senegal decided he liked Gundy. It never occurred to him that this was the first time in years he had admitted to liking anyone.

Outside the bunkhouse door, he yelled, "Gundy, c'mon out. We'll have that drink now."

They sat there in the dark, drinking from the bottle, getting to know each other.

"Mr. Senegal, I want you to know I never intended to start a rukshun in your home. They—well, they treated me like some sort of dirt all night, an' reckon it sort o' got under my skin."

"Pshaw now, boy, don't worry 'bout it. Hell, I got a kick outta the whole thing. Fact is, was beginning to wonder how long you was gonna stand still for the way they acted."

"Well, just wanted you to know."

They sat in silence awhile. Then Gundy said, "Sort of figured on comin' back by Austin after the drive and seein' what land might be handy up yonder north of Marfa. Don't want to come in on any land you might claim. That is, if you can hold off on me bringin' your money till then."

Senegal took a swig of tequila, wiped his mouth on his sleeve, and handed Gundy the bottle. "Hell, son, I ain't hurtin' for that money. Take care o' your business, then bring it on down." He chuckled and cocked his head to slant Gundy a look. "When you decide to try for some land up yonder? 'Bout the time you figured it would put a burr under Ross's saddle?"

Gundy laughed. "Senegal, I'd be lying if I said different. Reckon I let that bastard and his daughter get to me more'n I thought. An' too, can't see the likes of him sittin' in the State House."

"I don't figure on lettin' nothing like that happen," Senegal said, and tilted the bottle again.

Gundy took another drink and said he thought they ought to get to bed. Tomorrow would start many days of hard work.

Senegal knocked the cork back in the bottle with the butt of his hand and stood. "You're right, but want you to know I ain't enjoyed just sittin', drinkin', an' talking to anybody like I have you in a long time."

"Thank you, sir. I've enjoyed it too."

• • •

Sweat, blood, and bone-tiredness marked the days, four weeks of them, in which thirty-three men choused cows out of the brush and branded, road-branded, and gathered them into a trail herd. The men rolled into their blankets at night too tired to think of the next day, and crawled out of them the next morning before daylight to do it all over again. Then they brought the two great herds together to start the drive.

CHAPTER
12

Gundy looked up from cleaning his guns while the rest of the crew checked their gear. Senegal rode to the fire, dismounted, poured a cup of coffee, and sat across from him.

Without looking up from his task, Gundy said, "Gonna head 'em out in the mornin'. Countin' your men we got twenty-eight; twenty-five drovers, one cook, and two wranglers—plus myself."

Senegal nodded. "That gonna be enough?"

"Enough. Each man's takin' his pick of ten horses—from your remuda. I'm takin' fifteen—gotta cover more ground. Gonna be drivin' near to three hundred head of horseflesh is the reason for two wranglers."

Senegal finished his coffee and threw the dregs to the side. "What trail you takin'?"

Gundy ran a rag down the barrel of his Colt, pointed the barrel at the fire and peered through it, and satisfied there was no dust, shoved the gun in its holster and reached for his rifle. He glanced at Senegal. "Figure to drive east to meet up with the Western Trail, then head toward Dodge City. Gonna drive 'em hard the first two or three days. Twenty, twenty-five miles a day—enough to get trail-broke. Then we'll settle in to driftin' 'em ten, fifteen miles a day."

Senegal nodded. "Sounds good. Reckon I'd be wastin' talk

to say be careful, son. 'Spect you been that most o' your life."

Gundy grinned. "You got that right, sir. The trails I come over don't allow for not. With luck, we won't lose a man, cow, or horse. In '74, I went up the Chisholm Trail with the XT brand. A hailstorm hit us, froze our horses to death, an' we lost men and cattle. Don't want nothin' like that on this drive. On another drive, though, we didn't lose man or animal." He shrugged. "Matter of luck."

They sat there, and occasionally one of them stood and poured coffee. Talk was sparse. Every man in camp enjoyed the last peace and quiet they'd see for a couple of months. Gundy took a swallow of coffee and said, "Senegal, we got a late start, but that ain't all bad. Spring thunderstorms are ended, but should be enough grass and water along the way. I'll take as good care of your animals an' men as I can."

"Know you will." Senegal glanced at the sun. "Reckon I'll get back to the house 'fore dark sets in." He stood, climbed aboard his horse, waved, and said, "See you in the fall."

Senegal rode off, his back stiff and straight. Ain't much give in that old man, Gundy thought, but he's sure as hell one to ride the trail with. Then he wondered at the trust, friendship, and acceptance Senegal showed him.

By the time the herd stirred the next morning, Gundy and the cook had been on the trail more than two hours. Gundy knew where the water holes were until he hit the Western Trail. After that he had to scout ahead to find places for nooning, as well as where they would bed the herd at night.

The chuck wagon stayed far enough ahead so meals would be ready when the outfit caught up at noon and night.

Once the cattle were trail-broke they would graze along the trail and fill up on water and grass during the nooning. Gundy tried to impress the drovers that after the first few days they would be no more than drifting the cows, keeping them headed north strung out in a long fore and aft line. They didn't want the cows to walk off more weight than necessary. A herd in good shape could command as much as fifty cents a head more. That was money in Gundy's pocket as well as Senegal's.

The first two weeks went quietly. A big brown and white steer took command and led his charges at the pace Gundy wanted. Coming to the bed grounds in time for supper, Gundy eyed the big steer. Bet them horns spread six, maybe seven feet, he thought, but he sure keeps them cows moving right. Gundy also liked the fact that the old longhorn didn't scare easily. Skittish, he might cause a stampede. But if that old steer was like that, he'd be stew meat quicker'n scat.

At the chuck wagon, Gundy filled his plate and poured coffee before he sat by Kelly. "Gonna be spendin' more time scoutin' for water since we turned north. Ain't been over this trail before. Keep the herd strung out. You see Comanches, leave 'em alone an' pull the riders in close to the herd. I'll do what dickerin' we have to." He chewed a chunk of beef, swallowed, and continued. "Big a crew as we got, don't think they'll attack, but they might try some sort o' trick so they can cut out a few head an' be gone 'fore we can hit 'em."

Kelly nodded and kept eating. After cleaning his plate, he looked at Gundy. "I hear those Indians sometimes ask for cows. Claim they're hungry. What you figure to do in that case?"

Gundy gazed at the fire a moment. "Don't know. I might give 'em one head, but no more. And yeah, reckon they probably are hungry in most cases, but the government made 'em that way so let them handle it. They wanted the buffalo killed so as to make the Indian toe the line. Hell, you know why they did it. By killin' them animals they got rid of everything the Indian needed for food, clothin', tools, tipis— even what they used to make fires where they wasn't no trees."

Gundy filled his plate again, looked at the cook, and said, "Good stew, Cookie. Keep cookin' like this and you'll spoil us."

He again sat by Kelly. Even though Kelly was only five years younger, Gundy thought of him as just a kid. Kelly had done some wild things, but he'd never been in many situations where it was kill or be killed. Gundy thought the firefight they'd had down in Mexico might have been the first time Kelly had experienced anything like that. Fights like that one tempered a man. But Kelly still was too inclined to give a man a chance, or warning, when in a tight situation. That could get him killed.

Gundy finished his food, scrubbed his gear, and turned in.

The next morning he was in the saddle before daylight. The cows were beginning to stir when he rode out of camp ahead of the chuck wagon. When he found water and graze close enough for a nooning he'd let Cookie know where to stop.

The country he rode through was rough: mesquite, prickly pear, yucca, and greasewood. Gundy rode with care. This was Lipan Apache country. He could palaver with the Lipans, but there were also Comanches. They raided into Mexico for horses, and brought them up through this part of Texas on the way back to their villages.

Gundy veered off course to a water hole he'd found one time when coming from San Antonio. There wasn't enough water in that hole for his herd. But he'd seen the seep twice before and wanted to make sure it still had water. He might need it someday.

He approached on foot, making no sound. If he knew of water in this country, there was no doubt that both the Lipans and Comanches knew of it. He led his horse over sand, and around bushes that were likely dry and would make noise.

He wanted to picket his horse and go in alone, but a horse left alone was easy pickings for anyone who might have seen him coming. He had a clear view of the small pool from fifty feet out. His gut muscles tightened. His hand clutched the buckskin's reins convulsively. He wasn't the first one there.

A lone Comanche on his hands and knees looked up at him, water running down the sides of his chin.

Gundy signed him to go ahead and drink, that he came in peace. The warrior, not taking his eyes from Gundy's, backed away from the edge of the pool. He came off his hands and slowly straightened, his hand on his knife, and Gundy wanted it that way. Gunshots might bring others.

Gundy pulled his bowie. Without looking, he looped his horse's reins around a low-hanging mesquite branch with his left hand.

The Comanche had not looked to either side, so Gundy

thought—and hoped—he and the warrior were the only ones close by. Energy flowed through him. He came alive, vibrantly alive.

Silently, guardedly, they circled, still not close enough to swing their blades, but looking for an advantage. Gundy moved to his right to make the Comanche turn to face him. Now his foe was only a foot or so from the edge of the pool.

Gundy charged and thrust his knife, thinking the Indian would retreat, hit the edge of the water, and be off balance. Instead the warrior moved with the grace of a dancer to his own right. Now Gundy stood at just about the spot he'd seen the Comanche on his hands and knees. The warrior glanced over Gundy's shoulder, a triumphant gleam in his eyes.

Gundy threw his knife to his left hand in a border shift, dropped flat on his stomach, drew his .44, rolled to his back, and fired at a young warrior who had launched himself, knife drawn, toward Gundy's back. A blue hole appeared in his chest. Gundy rolled again, came to his knees, and fired at the first Comanche. Then, still on his knees, Gundy took deliberate aim and put a head shot into each of them.

He stood and faded into the chaparral, reloading as he went. His horse was still tied to the mesquite, and Gundy went flat on his stomach and lay there, not moving for as long as he thought it would take someone within hearing to seek out the source of the shots. He was about to stand when a large rattlesnake slithered in front of him. Gundy froze, his gut muscles tied in knots, the brassy taste of fear flowing from under his tongue and into his throat. As long as he didn't pose a threat to the snake, maybe it would continue to wherever it was headed. Instead it stopped and lay there— within three feet of his face.

The damned thing lay stretched out. Gundy thought to roll to the side, pull his gun, and fire before the reptile coiled to strike. He decided to wait it out.

He cut his eyes to each side, seeking an avenue of escape, then glanced past the snake—too late to roll from the arrow coming at him. The rattler became secondary. Gundy threw himself to the side, drew his .44, and fired at the same time the feathered shaft buried itself in his shoulder. A hole, fol-

lowed by a red gusher, opened the Comanche's throat.
Rubber-legged, he continued toward Gundy and fell directly
toward the rattler. By Gundy's count, fangs buried themselves
in the warrior twice before the snake slithered off.

Not wasting a move, Gundy gathered the weapons of the
dead Indians, stripped a bone necklace he fancied from one,
spent a few precious moments locating their horses, and
headed back to the trail before trying to do anything about the
arrow imbedded in his shoulder.

He twisted his neck to look at it. The head stuck about two
inches out his back. Pulling it out was impossible. The barbed
head would tear muscle and probably arteries—and it already
bled a steady stream. He could push it farther through and
break it off—if he didn't pass out first—but his hand couldn't
reach far enough behind to pull it out. He had to find the
chuck wagon.

The first numbing pain settled down to a steady throb.
Gundy hoped the Comanche had not dipped the point into a
rotted animal liver or rattlesnake venom, as they were known
to do.

He rode slowly, trying to soften the bounce of the horse so
the arrow would not jiggle, and he held the shaft with his fist
pushed snug against his shoulder.

After about two hours his shoulder hadn't turned black,
and Gundy figured the arrow had been clean. Sometimes a
man got lucky. Another thirty minutes and he heard the jangle
of harness. He'd not found a good place for a nooning, but he
had found the chuck wagon.

"Hey, Gundy, what you got stickin' outta your shoulder?"

"What the hell's it look like. Ain't found a noonin' place,
so pull up and fix the victuals anywhere. Get the cookin'
started, then help me get this damned thing outta my shoulder."

Cookie pulled the wagon to a stop. "I'll cook after I take
care o' you. That arrow needs to come out now."

"Start the grub. Those men're gonna be hungry when they
get here."

Cookie gave him a sour look, climbed down, and went
about starting a fire. He turned to Gundy only after he had

dinner started. "All right. Now can we get that thing outta there?"

Gundy gritted his teeth. The Mescaleros had taught him to not show pain. He was damned if he would let a white man see him show hurt.

"Got any whiskey?"

"Didn't know you was a drinkin' man."

"Ain't, but that hole in my shoulder might like a drink— both sides of it."

Cookie went to the back of the wagon, dug under some staples, and brought out a bottle. It was either crystal-clear pure corn whiskey or tequila. Gundy didn't care which so long as it kept his wound from festering later.

The cook looked at Gundy's back, then looked him in the eye. "Gonna push it through far enough so's I can get ahold of it. Then gotta break it off on this side. Both are gonna hurt."

Gundy deliberately wiped his face clear of expression. "Get it done."

Cookie stood behind him, circled the shaft with his left hand and pressed hard against Gundy's shoulder. Then with his right hand he pulled. The arrow hung for a moment, then slid a few inches through.

Gundy's throat muscles tightened, almost choking him as he tried to stifle the moan pushing at the back of his throat. He controlled his expression—and his tendency to moan— but he couldn't control the rivulets of sweat streaming down his face.

The cook handed Gundy the bottle. "You better take a healthy swig of this. We ain't even started good yet."

Gundy, not more than an occasional drinker, took a pull on that bottle that took his breath away—and drew the level of alcohol in it down about three inches.

Cookie held it up, squinted at it, and grunted. "Damn, shore am glad you ain't a drinkin' man."

It took only a few seconds to break the shaft and pull the remains through, but it seemed the cook moved with agonizing slowness. Gundy thought several times he would embarrass himself. When it was over, with a liberal dousing of alcohol and a clean bandage front and back, Gundy's bones and muscles felt as limp as wet doeskin. He couldn't stand if the entire Comanche Nation rode up.

Cookie stood back and admired his work, then looked at Gundy straight on. "Son, you got more gumption than any man I ever seen. Figured the least you'd do would be to pass out." He shook his head. "Ain't never seen a man what could walk in yore boots."

The cook's words put some of the starch back in him. He was almost glad for the wound. He felt he'd made a friend because of it.

"What's your name, Cookie? I'm mighty beholden to you for what you did."

The old man looked at him out of the corners of his eyes. "I'll exchange names with you. Last one I went by was Thaddeus Brown, but Cookie's good enough. And I may be the only one on this drive what knows who you really are. An' I ain't tellin' nobody long's you don't want it known."

"Some of my crew know about me, Cookie, but I'd just as soon you kept it quiet. I got troubles enough."

Cookie nodded. "That's the way it'll be then."

They talked and drank coffee while the beans and bacon cooked. By the time the point riders came in they'd finished three cups and Gundy felt he could ride again. It was about eleven o'clock. They would let the herd graze until about one o'clock before they again started them down the trail.

When Kelly rode in, he filled his plate, sat down, and started eating. After a while, he said, "Well, you gonna tell me about it? What happened?"

Gundy nodded toward the grub wagon. "They's some trophies in the wagon yonder. Think they'll tell the story better'n me."

When Kelly finished his second plate of food, he walked to the wagon and glanced at the artillery Gundy had brought back. Then he pulled out a finger necklace, studied it a moment, and asked what all the strange-looking little white bones were.

"Them's finger bones. Them what had 'em's got no more use for 'em. The Comanche are good 'bout that. They use any part of a man, woman, or baby to fix themselves up. Even seen one what used a man's ball-bag for his medicine bag."

"Judging by the firearms you brought back, you killed three of them."

Gundy only nodded.

CHAPTER
13

Three weeks later, the Red River was behind them with no loss of cattle, men, or horses, and Gundy sat his horse several miles ahead of the herd. He massaged his shoulder a few moments to ease the pain. It had healed well, but still stiffened overnight and occasionally shot sharp pains through his arm.

Rolling grasslands spread as far as he could see. No man or animal broke the expanse. But he searched anyway. This was Kiowa and Comanche country. Both were mean as hell when they wanted to be, and that was most always. Gundy didn't take the empty land for granted. He'd seen Indians seemingly rise right out of the ground to attack a foe. He had been part of war parties that did.

In deep grass or sand, they would burrow into it until the enemy came close enough for attack. That tactic always brought victory.

Gundy thought he would be coming onto the Canadian River in time to bed the herd for the night. This time of year it shouldn't be flowing, but there would be pools along it, enough water for animals and men.

He topped a land-swell, and not over three miles ahead lay the crooked, sandy riverbed. From where he sat his horse, he could see water in small sumps catching the sunlight and breaking it into beams like those from fine crystal. He nod-

ded, grunted with satisfaction, and reined back toward the
herd.

He came on the chuck wagon first. "Cookie, the Canadian's not far ahead. Cross it an' set up camp the other side.
Gonna get the herd across 'fore we bed 'em." Cookie nodded,
slapped the reins against the team's back, and drove on.

Another hour and a half and Gundy came on the point riders. Then he passed the swing, and then the flankers. He
pulled up and started back when he got to the drag riders.
He'd not ridden far when he saw an Indian top a hill. Then
four more of them followed in single file. There might be
more. Gundy kept his eyes peeled, but after a half hour
the number remained the same.

He alerted each man, then kneed his horse to ride at the
side between the herd and where he'd spotted the Indians.

He held his position until every cow and man crossed the
sandy track of the Canadian. Then he allowed the cattle to
drink and graze before bedding down.

Gundy followed Kelly. "We got trouble. Double the night
riders and keep weapons fully loaded. If them Indians come
to the fire, I'll talk. If they stay out yonder till after dark,
bring the horses in close. We'll all stand watch. I ain't seen
but five, but that don't mean nothin'. Just be ready."

He tied his horse to the wagon's tailgate and poured a cup
of coffee. He sat there, waiting. They would either be
attacked—or visited. He hoped for the latter.

The sun still sat a half hour high when they rode in. Gundy
walked to meet them. The five Indians he'd seen were now
seven—and there might be others behind each hill. There
were many renegades who could not be held on reservations.

The Indians sat their ponies, silently staring at Gundy. The
leader was sitting his horse a few feet ahead of the others.
Gundy had him figured for Kiowa. Then the leader signed
Gundy that they were hungry and wanted something to
eat. Gundy signed back he had only enough for his men.

Then the leader signed that they didn't want white man's
food, they wanted twenty head of cattle, and if they didn't get
them they'd take them all.

Gundy locked eyes with the arrogant Kiowa, stared a moment, then told him that if he and his warriors were hungry he'd give them one, and only one, cow. If they wanted a fight, then bring it to him and there would be much crying and wailing in their tipis.

Five cows, the warrior signed. Gundy tried hard to keep from smiling. He dealt with no more than the seven he looked at. Otherwise the ante wouldn't have come down so quickly.

"You take *one* animal and clear my camp, right now, or you ride with nothing."

"We take."

Gundy said over his shoulder, "Madison, cut them out one old steer; make *sure* it's an old one."

"Okay, Boss."

Gundy studied the warrior while he followed Madison away from the fire, comparing him with the Mescaleros he'd grown up with. *That* Indian didn't come up short on any count. If the odds were different, Gundy figured he'd have real trouble.

Despite the small Kiowa party, he doubled the watch as he'd originally figured to do. He cautioned each rider to do no shooting unless he definitely had an Indian in his sights. One shot might cause a stampede. But luck had been with them so far, and that luck held. They had no visitors that night or for several nights after.

Two weeks later, after crossing the Wolf, North Canadian, and Cimarron Rivers, Gundy bedded the herd about a mile outside of Dodge City. He rode into town to find a cattle buyer, and found the town much changed since his last visit.

Jim Masterson, Bat's brother, was marshal, while a rather dim-witted saloon-keeper, George Hinkel, was sheriff. Hinkel had defeated Bat in the election only the year before. Gundy's first stop was the marshal's office.

Masterson sat with his feet crossed on the desk in front of him.

"That what we taxpayers get for our money?" Gundy said. "The marshal sittin' around loafin' with a wild bunch o' Texans just outside of town?"

Masterson tilted his chair forward and let his feet down.

"Damn, Gundy, figured we got rid of you last time you were here." He walked around the desk and stuck his hand out. "Howdy, boy, how you been doin'? What you doin' back in Dodge?"

Gundy shook hands and, without being invited, went to the coffeepot and poured himself a cup. "Got a herd of 'bout five thousand head outside o' town a piece. Thought maybe you could set me straight on what buyers are here."

Masterson called out a list of nine, then recommended two he thought would give the best prices. "Charly Whitehead and Phil Lambert'll treat you right."

"Done business with both. I'll look 'em up, probably down at the hotel," Gundy replied. Then he changed the subject. "Sorry to hear 'bout your brother Ed gettin' killed. Couple of drunken cowhands done it, from what I heard."

Masterson nodded. "You heard right. Ed was never much of a hand with guns. He always tried to talk people into doing the right thing. The folks here in town loved him because of it, but it didn't work with those two. Ed and Bat killed 'em both, but one of them got lead into Ed before he went down."

Gundy thought about that a moment, then said, "Reckon you done answered my next question. What kind o' gun law you got now?"

Masterson gave Gundy a cold smile. "Yep. You got your answer. No guns within the city limits. And another thing, make sure your hands stay on Front Street. Don't want 'em botherin' the citizens."

Gundy translated that to mean "respectable citizens." That attitude raised the hair on the back of his neck, but he understood the necessity. And if the cattlemen wanted to keep a town open to market their cows, they had to adhere to *that* law in particular. He grinned. "Don't reckon my crew wants anything they can't find in the part of town you spiked out— women, whiskey, an' poker, not in that particular order. All right, Marshal, I'll keep 'em there."

They shook hands again, and Gundy went looking for the cattle buyers. But first he stopped at a couple of saloons to talk with cattlemen who had sold their herd in the last few days. He hit pay dirt at the Longbranch. Now he had some idea what price he could stand fast on. And as he thought, the buyers were at the hotel.

Whitehead said he had all the cattle he could handle from the last herd that came in. Lambert appeared not to care whether he bought or not. That was all part of the game. Gundy knew how to play as well as they did.

"You two are the first I've talked with. Lambert, let's ride out to the herd, you look them over, and if you can't offer a price fair to both of us, I'll talk to some of the others."

Lambert slanted him a look. "You have any trouble on the way up?"

Gundy shook his head. "Not even a little. No high water, no stampede. Lost only one cow. I gave him to a hungry Kiowa. Cows are well fed, and I ain't filled 'em full o' water. You'll get what you pay for."

They spent the afternoon looking at the herd, negotiated a price that satisfied Gundy, and agreed that he'd bring them into the loading pens the next morning for a firm count.

Lambert left, and Gundy told his riders they had one more night nursing cows before they could go into town for a little fun. He got some griping, but not much. Even Senegal's riders accepted him as a fair trail boss. Most of them told him so.

The next morning the sun rose on the five thousand or so beeves moving slowly to the edge of town. Sitting alongside the pens, watching each cow file singly into the loading chutes, Gundy thought how much closer this one step brought him to his goal—and to asking Dee to become his bride.

Kelly, standing at his shoulder, said something, and Gundy turned his head to the side to hide the fact that he could hardly swallow. For some reason his eyes seemed full of water. Damn! But he was happy—and proud. At the same time he felt a degree of guilt for wanting Dee so bad even though he and Kelly hadn't discussed it other than soon after they'd left Alex's home ranch. But hell, he had a lot of time. He thought to sound Paul out on the subject before talking to Alex and Maria, though he had to admit that whatever Paul thought of the idea, it wouldn't change his intentions a bit.

It took most of the day to get a solid count and for Lambert to pay him—in cash. Gundy used his possibles bag to put the money in. Looking at it, he was amazed that there was that much money in the world. Then his gut and chest tightened. His head hurt, and for the first time in his life he got scared of something that wasn't life-threatening. He had to carry all of this money across the Indian Nations and slam across Texas to deliver Senegal his part of it.

Well, he thought, the only way it ain't gonna get there is if I'm dead. He went to his room and counted out in even stacks the money to pay the crew with. Then he licked the end of a pencil and carefully wrote the name of each man and the amount of cash due him in his tally book. Then he knocked on the wall to get the attention of Kelly, who had the room adjacent to his.

Only a few moments later, Kelly tapped on his door. After determining that it was in fact Kelly, Gundy let him in, paid him, got his signature by name in the tally book, and told him to gather the crew—it was payday.

When they trickled into his room in twos and threes, he followed the same procedure he had with Paul. When they had all come in, Gundy asked if any of them were quitting to see what lay over the next hill. Only two hands said they figured to ride on. They wanted to see the Montana country. He wished them luck. "Next time you're in my part of the country and need a job, come see me." Each threw a hand up in farewell and left. He addressed the rest of the riders.

"You Senegal men, you can cut out and get back to your boss any way you want, but I reckon you'd be better off to ride in a bunch, or with my crew." He looked at Kelly. "When you leave, I want you to take our riders back and start working the chaparral west of where we wiped out Yount's bunch. As for me, I'm gonna go back by way of Austin, see what land's empty an' get some of it if I can.

"Cookie, meet me in the mornin' an' we'll stock the grub wagon for the trip. You men what are goin' back with Paul take four days here, get your ashes hauled, get drunk, and the mornin' of the fifth day be ready to head for Texas. Make sure you leave your guns with Masterson if you haven't already."

He'd been sitting on the side of the bed, using the box which served as a nightstand as a desk. He stood. "See you in the Big Bend."

CHAPTER
14

Three weeks later, Gundy rode into San Antonio. He'd left Austin two days before with papers that gave him the right to claim land north of Marfa. He knew he asked for trouble, but he just flat didn't give a damn. He didn't cotton to Ross, or his daughter, Hillary.

The sun slipped slowly below the horizon. It was one of those hot, still days. Dust didn't rise behind his horse. It kicked up and fell in little puffs.

Gundy's throat felt caked with dust. A beer might loosen it up. Then he'd take a bath and get some sleep. He carried his possibles bag slung over his shoulder—in it his whole future.

The first saloon he came to faced the Alamo across the plaza.

He stood at the bar next to a man who was tall and slim and whose blond hair was almost white. Gundy paid him little attention except to comment on the watch fob the man fingered. It was some of the best Zuni silversmithing he'd ever seen. They talked a bit, and then the man finished his drink and left. Gundy left soon after.

He untied his horse and rode to the livery stable. He couldn't find the liveryman, and called a couple of times. Finally, he shrugged, led his horse to a stall, and stripped the gear from him. While patting the buckskin on the rump, Gundy saw a flicker of something from the corner of his eye, and tried to grab at it before it connected with his skull—and the world exploded. In a dark void he crashed into unconsciousness.

Gundy stirred, groaned. Hot, he thought, never seen it so hot. He lay on his side, tried to turn over, and had to struggle. Something musty, smelly covered him. His head ached like a herd of buffalo had stomped him, and he hurt all over. He pushed from under the weight that covered him. Old hides. He should have recognized the stench. He lay in a stable, in the back stall.

He tried to stand—and stopped. His head spun like a dust devil. Touching his head with his fingers, he brought his hand down and gazed through the dim light at his fingers. They were dark, looking almost black in the half-light. Gundy didn't have to be told that it was blood that covered them. He'd seen it many times, his own as well as that of others.

Abruptly, he went cold inside. His possibles bag—the money. He groped around the stable floor, went inside the stall and looked, went back outside and searched again. It was gone.

He couldn't think clearly, couldn't remember where he was or if he'd been with anyone. He stood there a moment, bent over, trying to clear his head. Then he sat on a bale of hay. His head began to clear—and memory slowly returned.

He'd ridden into town, stopped for a beer, and passed a few words with a white-haired man, not old, but white-haired, a man who'd continually fingered a watch fob.

In slow waves anger built in him. His throat muscles tightened, blood rushed to his head, a cold icy knot formed in his stomach and spread. Bile boiled in his throat. The money was gone, and even worse, at least half of that money belonged to an old man who trusted him, an old man he liked and respected. The thin veneer of fourteen years of civilization flaked from him as a snake sheds its skin, only faster. He again felt like an Apache. Thought like an Apache.

Gundy stood, steadied himself, and walked from the stall. His hands searched for his weapons without much hope they'd still be there. But the slim, deadly Mexican throwing knife, the long, heavy bowie knife, and his Colt .44 were all in place. Whoever had done this to him was in such a hurry for the money that he'd hit him, grabbed his possibles bag, and run.

"Where the hell you come from?" an old man asked.

Gundy pinned him with a hard look; he didn't feel like answering any fool questions, but he answered. "Been in that there stall where somebody dumped me after beatin' the hell out o' me—an' robbin' me."

The old man studied every inch of Gundy's tall frame. Then, apparently satisfied, he nodded toward a room in the corner of the stable. "C'mon over here, lad, and let me clean up that gash on your head. Must have happened while I was out eating supper."

Stuffing back a groan, Gundy followed the liveryman into a small room that apparently served as an office and living quarters.

"Sit down. I'll get you a cup of coffee. Got no whiskey. You drink while I take care of your head."

The old man worked in silence while Gundy sipped the strong, black liquid. Finally he stood back and seemed to be admiring his handiwork, then nodded with satisfaction.

"That should do it. It won't stop the pain, but maybe it'll prevent infection from setting in."

Gundy frowned. The old man didn't talk like a stove-up old puncher like most liverymen. But then, you found men of every station in life throughout the West, doing jobs that in no way reflected their background.

"Much obliged, sir." Gundy stood and extended his hand. "Name's Trace Gundy."

The spindly old man gripped Gundy's hand. "Name's Tom." He released his grip and walked around Gundy. His look raked every inch of him. "You're a well-set-up young man. Don't see how you let yourself get suckered like that."

Gundy shook his head and said, his voice rougher than he intended it, "Hell, Tom, didn't figure nobody bein' here but the one what runs the place. Anyhow, I'm beholden to you for fixin' me up."

Abruptly, Tom walked to the pantry next to the stove,

picked something up, and came back to Gundy. Then, holding out his hand, he said, "This belong to you? You might have lost it when they clubbed you."

The old man was holding the Thunderbird watch fob the man in the saloon had worn. It had to be the same. Gundy doubted there were two like it in the entire State of Texas.

He picked it up from Tom's palm, held it to the light, and studied it. "A man in the saloon wore one exactly like this. Where'd you come on it, Tom?"

"C'mon." Tom nodded toward the door. "I'll show you. Way I figure it, you must have had a scuffle when they hit you, and maybe it broke loose from his watch in the scuffle."

"It wasn't no 'they.' " He followed Tom to the stall where he'd started to stable his horse. "But I do remember grabbin' at him."

Tom stopped and pointed to some scuffed-up dirt in front of the stall. "Right there, by golly. Yes, sir, that's the exact spot where I found it."

Gundy looked at Tom straight on. "Reckon I know who took my herd money." He shook his head. "All I gotta do is find 'im." He still held the fob and again looked at it. "Mind if I keep this awhile? Give it back soon's I find the man what owns it. He ain't gonna have no use for it."

Tom gripped Gundy's shoulder. "Keep it, son. It's rightly yours anyway. The only thing you can do is go after him, but be careful. If he'd hit you from behind in the dark, you can bet he'd shoot you the same way."

Gundy headed for the stable door. "See you after I find 'im, Tom. Buy you a drink." He started for the front, changed his mind, and went out the back door.

Night had closed in. Gundy judged it to be about ten o'clock. He must have been unconscious but a short time, because even though it was barely sundown when he rode in, it had been close to eight o'clock. The sun set late these summer evenings.

He hugged the wall as far as the alley, ran to the building next to the stable, crossed in back of it, and went toward the street between it and the next store. Caution was a part of him—and now that he had enemies in this town his care had an edge to it.

When he reached the street, he stood, his shoulders pressed flat against the rough adobe wall. He searched the square, then the store fronts. The battered ruins of the Alamo stood to his right. A few Mexicans sat on the rubble that had once been its walls. His gaze flicked past them. The one who owned the watch fob was Anglo.

Before continuing his search, he sucked air deep into his lungs and pushed it out slowly, trying to rid himself of the anger eating at his brain. He did this several times. Anger could get him killed.

Finally, satisfied the man he looked for wasn't on the street, he walked toward the saloon where he'd had a beer. Nearing the batwing doors, Gundy flicked the leather thong off the hammer of his handgun.

Trouble rode his shoulders. He again fought the cold gnawing anger that threatened him. He liked—wanted—peace, but most times he'd found a man had to fight for even a few moments of it at a time.

Gundy slipped through the doors, slid to the side, and searched the room for his man. Since he'd just come in from the dark, the light of the coal-oil lanterns made the room seem bright. He had no trouble seeing everyone there. The man he looked for was not among them. He started to leave, then turned back toward the bar.

Keeping the wall close to his side, he moved to the end of the polished surface lined with cowboys, Mexican *vaqueros*, bull-whackers, and a smattering of townsfolk. The man next to him turned his way, glanced down at the tied-down holster, and moved to make room for him.

The Mexican bartender asked, "What you have, *señor*?"

"Beer. Cold."

The Mexican drew his beer, sloshed foam off the top, finished filling it, then brought it over and set it in front of him.

"One more thing, *amigo*." Gundy kept his voice low, not wanting others to hear. He held the Thunderbird out in the palm of his hand. "You remember the man what was wearing this?"

The Mexican took it, studied it closely, and handed it back. *"Sí, amigo,* I remember heem, but I do not know heem."

Gundy frowned, feeling hope drain from him. "You got any idea where he might be stayin'?"

"No, señor." The bartender shook his head. "I do not know of thees thing you ask."

"Tell me what he looks like best you can."

"Sí, I weel do thees for you." He walked down the bar, poured one of the customers a drink, and came back. "Thees man ees a little shorter than you and, how do you say eet— sleem? *Sí,* sleem. Hees hair ees *blanco, sí,* almost white, and hees eyes are *muy malo,* very mean."

Gundy reached in his pocket and tossed the Mexican a double eagle. His attacker had not gone through his pockets, so he still had four double eagles and some silver. *"Muchas gracias, amigo.* Buy yourself a drink. Might not come back this way. Always pay what I owe."

A flash of white teeth gave Gundy his thanks.

Gundy went from saloon to saloon seeking information, but found none. Many of those he asked remembered the man who played with his watch fob, but none knew where he might be.

Gundy's head throbbed, and every muscle in his body ached. He'd been in each saloon and store on the square. He swept the area again. The Menger Hotel was the only place he'd not been. He headed for it.

He walked through the doorway, glanced around, and saw only the desk clerk.

"What kind of room you need, mister?"

Gundy shook his head. "Don't need a room. Lookin' for a man what was supposed to meet me here. Rode in earlier than I figured. Thought maybe he'd be stayin' here. Don't remember his name, but said he'd buy some cows from me."

"Well, tell me what he looks like; maybe I'll remember him."

Gundy nodded, squinting thoughtfully. "Might help more if I show you somethin'." He held out the Thunderbird. "He wears a watch fob like this here one."

The clerk glanced at his hand and nodded. "Uh-huh, he stayed here about a week. Then tonight, maybe four or five hours ago, he left. Said he was heading east, to Nacogdoches, on business."

Gundy tipped his hat. "Much obliged. Reckon he decided against my cows." His voice came out flat, not showing the cold anger boiling his guts. He walked out.

To take the trail tonight would be foolhardy. A good night's sleep and an early start in the morning made more sense. He walked slowly toward the stable. Tom wouldn't care if he slept in the haymow.

If he'd just robbed a man of thousands of dollars, he didn't figure he'd be telling anybody where he was heading—unless he wanted to lay a false trail. Gundy frowned into the night. Yep. Bet that's what he was doing, but maybe he's smarter than that. Maybe he'd figure me for thinking it was false.

Gundy leaned against one of the ancient live-oak trees on the plaza. Then he ran all the possibilities through his mind. The thief would probably double back on his thinking a couple of times, but Gundy decided he'd end up heading west.

Satisfied he had it figured, he said aloud, "Yep, if one o' them Comanches out west of here don't get him, or get me first, I'm gonna make him wish they *had* gotten 'im." He pushed away from the old tree and walked quickly toward the stable, his hurts forgotten.

The next morning, Tom seemed surprised to see him climb down from the loft. "Figured you'd be gone by now. Coffee?"

Gundy nodded.

After accepting the granite cup from Tom, he sat at the rough-hewn table sipped his coffee until Tom sat across from him, then told him what he'd found. "Won't do no good to tell the sheriff," he added. "He can't go out of his bailiwick. Besides, I want to get him myself."

"Figure this hombre is pretty cagey. He laid a false trail; then to my way o' thinkin' he doubled back on it a couple of times." Gundy squinted thoughtfully at the old man. "I'd almost bet my saddle he ended up headin' west."

Tom stared into his empty cup, then slanted him a look that said he agreed. "Wouldn't believe it so strongly," Tom said, "except a wagon train left here early yesterday morning, headed for California by way of Fort Stockton. Don't believe any man with much sense would try to cross Apache and Comanche country alone. But if your man could catch up with that train in a day or so, he'd have plenty of company around him." He nodded. "Yeah, I think your saddle would be safe. You wouldn't lose it on that bet."

Gundy stood. "Be gettin' along then."

Tom grinned. "I don't think you're one of them I need tell to be careful. For some reason, I have you pegged as being pretty close acquainted with those red devils."

Gundy let a smile reach his eyes, shook Tom's hand, then on impulse pulled one of the double eagles from his pocket. "Here, Tom, figure I owe you. If I find my man, I ain't gonna need it. This trail's gonna end with one o' us dead. Either way I won't need it." He forked his horse and rode out feeling Tom's friendly gaze on his back.

CHAPTER
15

Gundy forded the San Antonio River and pointed his horse west. If the man he looked for figured on joining up with the wagon train, he could catch it long before it reached Fort Stockton. The wagons might figure to go from Stockton to Del Rio, and from there head upriver to El Paso. It was there Gundy feared he might lose his money for good. Mexico, with the wild life of Juárez, lay just across the Rio Grande, and finding anyone in that town, if they didn't want to be found, was impossible.

He pushed on into the chaparral. The scrubby brush, hard on horses and men, afforded no shade, and water belonged only to those who knew where to find it. Gundy was one of those who knew where to find it. After leaving the Mescaleros, he had traversed this country from east to west and north to south living off the land. Not many had ever done that and lived to tell about it.

Sweat streamed down his face, chest, back. He was barely conscious of the heat. It was something that happened this time of year. If you didn't like it, you left.

The wagon tracks were easy to follow: broken brush, crushed cactus, and litter. Gundy could have followed it in the dark. He wondered about the Comanche, and thought they wouldn't hit a large train, but would hang back and attack stragglers. Of course, there might not be an Indian within miles, but Gundy didn't ever figure on the easy way. If they *were* here, he wanted to see *them* first. This wasn't native Comanche territory, but they raided far and wide. Matter of fact, they went wherever they damned well pleased.

Gundy's eyes were never still. He searched the skyline, hollows, and ravines. Jackrabbits occasionally scurried from under his horse's hooves. Birds flew up close by. It was not these close-in things that bothered him. Had they been flushed into moving while out away from him, then he would worry.

A glance at the ground showed his shadow short, nearly covered by his horse. He grunted, thinking it about time for nooning, and at the same time thinking his horse would have to wait until sundown for water. He kneed the buckskin toward a shallow dry wash.

Reaching it, he climbed down, pulled his Winchester from its scabbard, took jerky from his saddlebag, and squatted in the shade of his horse to eat.

Finished, he poured a little water into the palm of his hand and held it for his horse to wet his mouth. Then, not treating himself any better, he took some more, swished it around in his mouth, and swallowed. Then he again forked the buckskin.

Every hour or so, Gundy cast his eyes back and forth to each side of the trail, reading the ground like most men would read a book. Indians would not ride in the tracks of the train. They would stay off to the side, knowing any riders wanting to catch those ahead would follow in the smoother going of the broken and smashed scrub, and in so doing would miss seeing the pony tracks.

Mid-afternoon, he picked up sign of another horse following the same route. The tracks told him the horse was shod, and it had been less than a day since it had passed this way.

Gundy squelched a triumphant yell. "That's him. That's my man. Don't think I'll catch him 'fore he joins with the wagons, though." He held his horse to a walk. The Apache had taught him patience above all else.

Gundy had been a lad of only six summers when the Mescaleros attacked the wagon train his folks had joined up with.

The Indians took only the young ones prisoner; the rest died. In the years that followed, Trace Gundy became the White Apache, more savage than any warrior among them.

He stayed with them until his eighteenth summer. It was then he counted coup on a grizzly and killed him in the fight that ensued. That gave him his other Indian name, Man Who Fights the Big Bear.

Gundy left the Mescalero soon after, refusing to live on the reservation, and as a result became outlawed by the Territorial Governor. Though he'd left them, the Apache would always count him a brother, and being brother to the Mescaleros made him a natural enemy to the Comanche, who had met him in combat. They knew and respected him. It was they who had given him the name Apache Blanco. And it was *he* who followed the man who had robbed and beaten Trace Gundy.

The afternoon burned its way toward sundown. The brush cast long shadows. Gundy kneed his horse off the trail toward a sinkhole known only to him—and the Comanche.

Still a half mile from water, he rode the buckskin into a draw, dismounted, put on moccasins, tied his horse to a weathered snag of an oak, and taking his rifle, melted into the brush.

He moved more silently than a vagrant breeze, from prickly pear to scrub oak to yucca. The soles of his feet told him what was underfoot before he placed his weight down. The going was slow, but speed might cost him his hair.

A huge prickly pear materialized out of the dark, so close he could touch it. He stopped and searched his surroundings as much as the night would allow. He tested the air. The pungent smell of smoke did not assail his nostrils. The wind had risen, whispering in the sage. No other sound came to him. He was not alone.

There should be the sound of small animals scurrying about, or the ruffling of feathers as birds settled in for the night, but all was still except for the wind.

The sinkhole was close, but others had reached it ahead of him. He needed to think about this. He hunkered next to the prickly pear, and blended with the cactus in the dark against searching enemy eyes.

If there were only one or two of the enemy, he could take care of them. But if there were more, he could end up staring at the morning sun through dead eyes. Finally, he shrugged. He'd take a look-see anyway. He stood and moved toward the water.

Blanco had been silent before, but now as he moved through the night, he left only a hole in the dark.

Every part of him was now the warrior he had been. Even his skin warned him of what was around him. He sensed the cactus and scrub before he saw it. His sense of smell separated dust from brush, animal from fowl. His hearing defined the rustle of wind and pushed it to the back of his awareness.

He stood downwind of the water hole. It was there; he could smell it. But so were the Indians. Their smell was on the wind also.

Shifting his rifle to his left hand, he slid the slim Mexican throwing knife from its sheath. He would use it to slice, stab, or throw. The big bowie at his left side would be held in reserve.

Abruptly he sensed the water just ahead. He stopped, willing his gaze to penetrate the thick motionless dark. He held his look to the side. Side vision was better at night. The Apache had taught him well.

The black separated into shades of gray. Then he saw them—two of them. His horse would have water tonight. He grinned, wondering how many would have caused him to back off.

One of the warriors stood with his back to Gundy. The other knelt to drink. Gundy wanted no shots. They might signal more Indians to the fun. He stooped and carefully placed his rifle on the ground. He'd have no need for it; this would be close work.

He tested the balance of the slim blade in his right hand. Then, in a lightning move, his arm raised, then swung down, sending the slim bit of steel on its way. As soon as the blade left his hand he pulled the bowie and moved toward the Indian bent over the water. He didn't hear the thump of his knife when it entered the first Comanche's back, nor did he look. He knew where it had gone.

The warrior by the water looked up and grabbed for his own knife. Gundy swung in a chopping motion—and missed. A hot, searing streak burned his side. The Comanche had scored, but not well.

The warrior, standing now, guardedly waved his knife back and forth in front of him, like a serpent seeking to strike. He hadn't made a sound. It was the way of the Indian to fight like this. He would die the same way.

Gundy watched for an opening, saw one, and stepped in, slicing. His blade tugged against his hand. He'd gotten a piece of the enemy—but not enough. The Indian stepped back, then moved in, thrusting at Gundy's gut.

Gundy slid to the side. The knife snagged his vest. He swung his own knife—and missed again. The Comanche spun and came at him again. The man was quick.

Gundy stepped out of his path and thrust straight ahead. The big knife sank to the hilt above the warrior's navel. It was a death blow—but a man didn't die right off from that kind of wound.

With Gundy's knife buried at the center of his life the Indian made one last swing. It was almost fatal. The bite of steel entered Gundy's left shoulder. It didn't stop him. He still gripped the handle of his knife. He stepped in close, grabbed the Comanche's knife hand, and held it so he couldn't swing or thrust. Then he wriggled the handle of his bowie from side to side and up and down, knowing the big blade would carve heart, lungs, and liver.

Even in the dark, hatred lanced from the stricken Indian's eyes. Then his look lost fire, turned blank—and he died.

Gundy pulled his bowie free, dragged the corpse away from the water, then went over and pulled his throwing knife from the back of the other Indian. He scoured both in the sand and returned them to their sheaths.

Gundy retrieved his rifle, untied his horse, and led him to water. They both drank their fill.

He gathered the weapons of the warriors. They each had rifles, but they were old and in sorry shape. He took them any-

way. Tomorrow, he would break them and throw them away
when he could see where he threw them. He also took their
knives, then searched the brush for their horses and turned
them loose. They might find their way back to camp, but not
soon enough to harm Gundy. These things done, he sat by the
water hole and chewed a piece of jerky; he dared not build a
fire. He drank again, letting his horse drink at the same time.

Gundy made camp that night well away from the water
hole, and made sure his horse's picket rope was long so he
could forage for the sparse grass offered by the arid land.

Gundy waited until first light to ride out the next morning,
not wanting to miss any sign his quarry might leave. It was
well he did.

The rider ahead of him stuck to the trail of the wagon train
for four or five miles, by Gundy's reckoning. He was certain
now that the tracks he followed were made by the man he
sought. There were no others.

Abruptly, Gundy reined in, frowning. Something was
wrong. Then he knew what it was. He had not seen his quarry's horse tracks for several minutes. He turned his horse and
backtracked, searching the ground every step of the way.
Then the tracks left the beaten trail and headed more south-
westerly.

It didn't make sense. The man hadn't much farther to go
before catching the train. Gundy shrugged. He'd follow until
he knew what the other rider had in mind.

Fort Stockton was still a hard three days' drive for the
wagons. A man on horseback could cover four, maybe five
times the distance in that time. Tracking the single horse was
harder now than when he'd been following the trail left by
the wagon train—and he wasn't gaining ground on his man.

This day was another one when the winds seemed to blow
straight out of hell. He pulled his horse in and pushed his hat
off his forehead, mopped sweat from his brow and neck, then
pulled the floppy-brimmed old relic back in place. A headband would keep sweat soaked up, but wouldn't do a thing to
keep sun out of his eyes. Gundy was bringing his hand down
from his hat when he saw them.

There were eight of them, and they appeared as though

they had come out of the ground. They didn't attack, but
stood silently, weapons trained on him dead center.

Gundy's stomach muscles knotted and every hair on his
head tingled. To reach for his pistol would get him killed
quickly. He studied them while they looked him over. These
were not Comanche, nor were they Karankawa. They looked
to be Apache, but they weren't Mescalero. If none of these,
maybe, just maybe, they were Lipan Apache. He held up his
hand in the universal peace sign.

"I am Apache Blanco, of the Mescalero. I am warrior and
blood brother to them. Greeting, mighty warriors of the Lipan." He held his breath. He didn't know for sure that they
were Lipan, or whether they were friendly with the Mescalero.

They showed no indication his words would cause them to
relax. Arrows were still nocked and pulled tight against bow-
strings. Then the one closest to him stepped forward, released
pressure on his bow, placed it over his shoulder, and extended
his hand palm outward.

Gundy let his pent-up breath escape slowly, not daring to
let them see he'd been anything less than fearless. They respected only bravery. Anything less than that and they gloried
in killing you. They were masters in the art.

"I am White Wing, war chief of the Lipan. All Apache talk
of the great Blanco at their council fires, you who counted
coup on the great bear of the mountains." White Wing turned
to the others. "The Mescalero are not our friends, but we
have no fight with them. We will not make war on one as
brave as this. Lower your weapons. He will walk in peace in
our land."

Gundy nodded, holding his head in what he hoped was a
proud pose, but one intended to show respect for his brothers,
the Lipan. Then he looked into the eyes of the leader. "I seek
to pass through your land in peace. But first, I have an enemy, a white man, I must kill. He too is in your land. I ask
it of you. Leave this man to me. I will kill him in the way of
the Apache."

White Wing looked at the others. "Our brother has spoken.
It will be as he has asked."

When he turned back to Gundy, it was obvious the formalities were over. "Climb down, *amigo*, it will be as you wish. But first I think you must feed your body with fresh venison. We have much and will share with you." His eyes locked on Gundy's blood-soaked sleeve and shirt. "We will wrap your wounds also."

Gundy returned his smile. *"Muchas gracias."* He nodded, swung his leg over his horse's rump, and stepped down. "It will be good to fill my stomach." He was anxious to get on the trail, but his hunger for hot food would have swayed him if courtesy had not. It would be an insult not to share the food and fire of the Lipan. Besides, he thought grinning to himself, they'd be on me like hair on a dog's back if I turned 'em down. He figured he'd have a helluva time trying to whip all eight of them.

He spent the afternoon and night at their fire. Like men everywhere, they sat around the campfire telling stories of past fights or acts of bravery—or women. Gundy contributed by telling them about the two Comanches of the night before.

Before leaving the next morning, he gave them the knives he'd taken, weapons forged by an artist. Gundy figured he'd made some staunch friends. He had their word they would let his enemy alone to pass through their lands until the Great Apache Blanco could deal with them in the fashion of a true Apache.

CHAPTER
16

Gundy kept his horse at a harder gait than before. He had lost a full afternoon and night with the Lipans, but he felt better for having done so. The cut on his head was much better, and the two knife wounds were now no more than scratches.

By mid-morning he had a good idea why the man he tracked had pulled off the trail. It looked like he was circling in order to get ahead of the wagon train. When they caught up with him, it would appear that he'd left San Antonio before them. That way, if accusations were made, he could use them to prove he'd not been in town on the night of the robbery. "Well, old hoss, reckon that there man ahead o' us is right cagey." He nodded. "Yes, sir, we gonna have to remember how smart he is."

When he was only a spindly youth competing with others his age, Gundy had learned that knowing the enemy is to have half the battle won, and that you should never underestimate a man who might one day hold your life in his hands.

The thief who had robbed him had seemed a city-bred man when Gundy spoke to him in the saloon. Now Gundy was certain that even though the man had the clothes and manners of one used to towns, he had spent much time on the plains. His camps were well chosen. Gundy had seen not even a flicker from a campfire. But what clinched it was that the man had ridden to the only other water Gundy knew of this side of Fort Stockton. Gundy shook his head. His enemy was not a city man, and he was not a damned fool. But he'd made one mistake. He'd chosen the Apache Blanco as his target.

Gundy rode slowly now, not forcing the buckskin to undue speed. This heat pulled strength from man and animal alike. Gundy's mind raced ahead, picking the country apart, trying to anticipate the route his prey would take.

There was a trading post several miles ahead, run by a Comanchero by the name of Valdez. Indians left him alone because he sold them whiskey and firearms. Whites hated him, but left him alone because he could bring the wrath of the Comache down on them.

Gundy squinted across the shimmering, sunbaked landscape, and nodded. "Yep. If I was him, that's where I'd head." He lifted his leg and hooked it over the pommel. He liked to ride like this when not in a hurry. It was sort of restful.

He continued talking to himself. "A man could get to Valdez's place, cut the dust out of his gullet with a shot of that tarantula juice he calls whiskey, sit there in the shade of his galleria, and let the sweat run down his face and neck. That is, unless they's some mean cuss what won't leave him to enjoy himself."

Gundy unhooked his leg. "If things happen that way, then reckon a man's gotta do some convincin', an' that can be awful unhealthy for one o' the other." His horse's ears twitched as if he understood all Gundy said. Through thinking, Gundy kneed the buckskin to a faster pace. "Reckon I'll head for Valdez's store."

He glanced at the shadows, not liking to look at the sun. Doing that blinded a man for a short time. In this country a man needed his eyes to see as far and as much as they could all the time. His glance at the shadows told him he had only three more hours of daylight.

Not gonna stop for supper now, he thought, figuring to get a hot meal from Valdez. Then, as though he'd been talking to his horse all the time, he said, "Don't reckon you need a hot meal, hoss, but you'll sure as hell have hay and water tonight. Now let's get on down the trail."

The sun sank below the horizon, a fiery red ball, leaving only a sky of pastels—aqua, orange, pink, and shades of purple—until only a deep blue-black remained. The only light now was a constant flicker of heat lightning on the horizon. Gundy had seen too much of this kind of weather to think it would rain. There had been no wind from the southeast to bring in moisture, and no wind from the north to bring it down on him. His gaze swept further out, looking for a break in the darkness that might spell lamplight.

He had begun to think Valdez had shut down for the night when he finally saw what he looked for. A city man would have missed it, for a lamp casts only a feeble glow, but Gundy's eyes picked out a pinpoint a bit lighter than the surrounding dark.

Shoulda knowed Valdez ain't gonna shut down long's they's a chance to make a copper. Probably some of that ragtag bunch what usually hangs out there, he thought, hoping the bastard he looked for had stopped for the night.

He held his horse to a slow walk. Otherwise the horse could break a leg, or jab one of the deadly Spanish dagger spikes into it, and a man with a crippled horse out here was as good as dead.

At the tie-rail in front of the store, five horses stood three-legged with drooping heads. Gundy looped the reins around the rail and thumbed the thong off the hammer of his Colt.

He hoped he'd not need it, but if he did, then it hung right handy. He didn't figure himself a gunhand, but many others did. Luke Short, up in Forth Worth, had shown him a few things about drawing a side gun and then making sure your shot went where you wanted.

A few years' practice hadn't slowed him any either. One thing he learned by watching others. They were so intent on getting their gun out fast that they usually wasted the first shot into the floor in front of them. Gundy had learned early not to waste shots.

He walked across the galleria. The door stood open to the night air, so Gundy had a clear view of the inside. He located the five he figured owned the horses at the rail. By his reckoning they all had the stamp of Comanchero. The hair on his

neck bristled. Trouble with one of them meant he would have
to whip or kill all of them. The sixth man in the room,
Valdez, stood behind the rough plank that served as a bar.
The man Gundy hunted was not in the room. A tinge of disappointment flicked his nerves. He walked in.

"Take your finger off the trigger of that shotgun you got
under the bar, Valdez. It's only me, an' I didn't come to carve
you up—this time." Gundy smiled, not feeling humor, knowing the smile didn't show any.

"Come on in, Blanco. I'll geeve you a dreenk that'll un-
freeze that cold-assed smile you always geeve to me."

Gundy knew there was nothing he could do or say that
would get him out of here without a fight. If any man in the
room had been white Gundy figured he could avoid it, but
not with these five. There was only one way. If he could es-
tablish the upper hand right from the start, maybe—maybe he
could get out of here.

One of the five stood against the wall where the bar joined
it. Gundy walked to him. "Move," he said, his voice soft.

"Ah, but, *señor*, I have theeze place before you get here."
The Comanchero nodded. "*Sí*, I weel stay here."

Gundy grabbed his shirtfront, spun him around, and
pushed. The hardcase stumbled backward, clawing for his
gun. He never got it out. Gundy's Colt was pointed at him
before he could clear leather. "Don't do it, *amigo*," Gundy
said, feeling some of the tension flow from him. The others
hadn't taken a hand. Maybe they would let it rest.

The hand reaching for the gun dropped limply to the side
of the greasy chaps the man wore.

Gundy turned his gaze on the others. "Don't try to give
him any help. Don't want to have to kill you." He was surprised that he meant it. Must be gettin' soft, he thought.

Of the five, three were Mexican, the other two were
breeds, but they were all Comancheros.

"Ain't takin' on nobody else's fight," the Mexican closest
to Gundy said. "If he cain't take care of his own trouble, to
hell with him."

"Right glad you feel that way. Saves me trouble too."
Gundy holstered his .44 and made a move to turn to Valdez.

He caught a flicker of movement out of the corner of his eye, spun, drew his Colt, and fired. The slug tore half the man's face away. He waded into the middle of the remaining four and swung his pistol like a club. His bowie came easily to his left hand.

The skull of the first opened wide under the weight of his Colt. He swung his left in an arc, shoulder high. The neck his knife sliced through spurted blood over his forearm. One of the bunch, a Mexican, stood about five feet from him. Gundy thumbed back the hammer and put a slug through his brisket. At the same time he jabbed his bowie into the nearest breed. He still worked the handle when he spun toward the bar.

"You touch that shotgun, Valdez, an' I'll cut you in two."

Valdez backed against the wall, his hands shoulder high. "No, Blanco, I do not take sides in theez things. *Madre de Dios*," he said, his voice barely above a whisper. "Now I see why you are called Apache Blanco. A blood Apache is a woman next to you. Their guns never cleared leather."

The Apache within Gundy fought with the white man within. But with men like these, hesitation meant death. "Never mind the talk. I came here for two things." He leaned across the rough plank and pinned Valdez with his gaze. "You lie to me and the buzzards'll be eatin' your eyeballs come daylight. Understand?"

Valdez nodded. *"Sí, señor."*

"First off, they was a skinny hombre come through here in the last day or so. How long's it been an' which way'd he head?"

Again Valdez nodded. *"Sí*, he came about nooning time today, had a drink, and headed east toward Santone. Didn't eat."

Gundy didn't let up. "The second thing I come for is a drink, an' don't give me any o' that swill you give everybody else. The best you got ain't much good, but that's what I want."

Valdez slowly lowered his hands. When Gundy didn't say anything, he reached under the bar and brought out a bottle of cheap bourbon. "Theeze ees the best I got, Blanco," he said, and held the bottle up for him to see.

Gundy wiped the blade of his knife, stowed his weapons, and took the bottle from Valdez's hand. He tilted it, tasting, nodded, and said, "I'll drink it." He frowned. "What did that skinny hombre pay for his drink with?"

"A double eagle, Blanco, why?"

"Reckon he paid for it with my money, but you couldn't know that. I'll pay you for what I drink. Reckon I'll pay you for that steak your woman's gonna cook me too. If she's in bed, get 'er up."

Valdez nodded. "It weel be as you say, Blanco." He yelled over his shoulder, "Feex a steak, frijoles, and some hot tortillas. Theez ees for Blanco; make the steak a beeg one."

Gundy tossed down two glasses of the fiery bourbon, ate, paid Valdez, gathered up the weapons of the five men he'd killed, and walked out. Valdez could bury the garbage on his floor.

He didn't want the weapons, even though they were good ones. He'd trade them for provisions somewhere along the trail. Too, he didn't want to leave them for Valdez. He'd sell them to the Comanches, and Gundy sure as hell didn't want that. He watered the buckskin again, fed him, and rode out. He slept in the brush that night.

The wagon train came into view about high noon. Gundy had not caught up with his quarry. He'd followed the tracks of the horse from the trading post. He knew those tracks as well as those of his own horse. He'd find the thief down there in that group of clustered wagons, apparently circled up for a nooning.

When Gundy rode in among the wagons, the wagon master came to meet him. "Where you heading, stranger?" The wagon boss's voice was guarded, as though he knew who Gundy was.

"Figure for right now this's as far as I'm goin'," Gundy answered. He had looked the area over good when he rode in. He'd not seen the man he hunted, but knew he had to be there. "Lookin' for a man. Slim, almost tall as me, light hair—almost white. You seen 'im?"

Gundy spoke loud enough for those in the wagons to hear.

Rifles pointed at him from each wagon's boot. A chill ran down his spine. He thought about digging heels into the buckskin and getting out of there. Then a cold, controlled fire built in his head. He was damned if he'd run. He had come for his money. He'd get it or bleed to death right where he stood.

"Yeah, we seen 'im." The wagon boss slurred his words, apparently impressed with Gundy's power—and knowing he had the upper hand. "We seen 'im," he repeated. "He told us a killer was on his trail, had been ever since Fort Stockton. I figure you're the man he told us about. Said he was carrying a lot of money and figured that's what you were after."

So he told them he'd been to Stockton, Gundy thought. Don't make no damned difference. Fort Stockton or Santone, I'm gonna tell 'em how it really was. They can take their choice.

The guns sticking out of the wagons had not slacked off. Gundy didn't give a damn. "Mister, that dog has *my* money. He stole it from me in Santone, not Stockton. I'm gonna get it back if I have to whip ever damn one o' you."

The wagon boss drew himself up to his full five feet and about a half. "Don't look like you're in any position to be telling us what you're gonna do." His gaze swept the wagons in an obvious effort to assure himself he didn't stand alone. Then the one Gundy wanted to see most walked from between a couple of wagons.

"I told you he'd have some cock-and-bull story when he came in," the blond thief said. "He's a cool customer, stood right there in the officers' mess at Stockton and wheedled out of me that I carried a right smart poke."

Gundy didn't try to refute his statement, but stared at the bandit until the thief's eyes dropped.

"Mister, you took my money," Gundy stated. "Money I worked and sweated months for, scrounging mavericks out of brush that'd tear a man apart." He nodded. "Yep. I done it. Then drove 'em to Dodge City and sold 'em." He stared at the white-haired punk through slitted eyes. This was about the tightest spot he'd ever been in. All but the bandit had their weapons on him. But he decided right then he'd send a bunch of them to hell ahead of him. Even if their slugs tore him to bits, he would get a few of them. As mad as he was, he just plain didn't give a damn.

"Y'all might kill me." His voice sounded almost like silk, even to his ears. "Yep, you might just do that, but I'll tell you one thing, mister. You an' a whole bunch o' these sodbusters are gonna die with me." Gundy continued staring at the man who'd robbed him. He dropped his hand closer to his Colt.

Every man in the circle of wagons stood frozen. Gundy could smell their fear. These weren't fighting men. They'd fight if they had to, but they would rather hire someone to do it for them. The ring of shod hooves broke the stillness.

"Hey, what's going on here?"

A man Gundy had seen many times rode into his field of vision, but his gaze never left the thief, hoping he'd make his play.

The man who had ridden in scouted for wagon trains across this part of Texas. From the corner of his eyes, Gundy saw him turn his look on him.

"Blanco, what you doin' in this train? Never knowed you to stay this close to people before." Then he apparently became aware for the first time he'd ridden into the middle of a potential explosion. "What the hell's going on?" he asked again.

Gundy, forcing his face into an expressionless mask, his hand close to his gun, said, "Ask that righteous bastard." He nodded toward the wagon master. "Then you gonna be outta a job 'cause I'm killin' 'im."

The scout looked at the wagon master. "Tell me."

"This here *outlaw*"—the little man stressed the word as though Gundy was something you stepped on in a hog wallow—"comes riding in here telling us that a man who rode in a short time before him had robbed him in Santone. What makes him a liar is, they both rode in from the west."

The scout Gundy knew as Jed Balfour pushed his hat off his forehead and wiped sweat from his brow. "If I was you, I'd be mighty careful callin' this man a liar. Knowed 'im to kill men for less than that, an' I also ain't never heard tell he'd steal *or lie*."

Balfour glanced at Gundy. "This here's the Apache Blanco." He grinned. "Blanco's meaner'n hell, but he's honest."

The wagon master relaxed slightly. The guns in the wagons no longer pointed straight at Gundy. The bandit stood taut, his hand splayed close to his side-gun.

Gundy spoke to him. "You start your draw, make damned sure you done spoke to the man up yonder"—Gundy flipped a thumb toward the sky—"'cause you're gonna be dead 'fore anybody can stop me." More hooves sounded in the distance, and they didn't sound as if they were shod.

The wagon master still didn't back down, apparently wanting all the onlookers to know he was still in charge. "Now see here; I think we'll divide up and hold a sort of court. We'll decide who's lying."

"Nope," Gundy said. "You ain't holdin' no court on me. Fact is, you ain't makin' no decision about me at all. Shut the hell up. I've listened to your bleatin' more'n I ever did to anybody."

"You can't talk that way to me," the wagon master squealed.

"Done done it," Gundy said, not caring what the short pompous little man said. His ears were attuned to the approaching horses. Those in the wagons heard them too, for they gazed in the direction of the sound; their rifles again pointed out of the wagons. Gundy didn't look. He knew who the horses belonged to.

Jed raised his hand, palm outward. "Howdy, White Wing."

The Lipans with whom Gundy had shared fire and food rode to his side. "What these people do with my brother, Apache Blanco?"

"They ain't done nothin' yet," Jed answered. "Way I figure it, they ain't enough o' them to do nothin', not against Blanco. They figure your brother and the scrawny rat standin' across there come from Fort Stockton, and that Blanco was gonna rob 'im."

White Wing's stare didn't waver. He looked at the wagon master when he spoke. "My brother, and the rat, as you say it, did not either of them come from Fort Stockton. We know.

We see all that happens in our country. They both ride here from San Antonio, make big circle around wagons, and come in from the way of the setting sun."

"Reckon that leaves it 'tween you an' me, Whitey," Gundy said to the thief. He spoke barely above a whisper.

"Ain't nobody going to believe a greasy Indian," Whitey croaked.

Gundy smiled, humorless, feeling the chill in his eyes. "These Lipans get their feelings hurt awful easy. Reckon when I get through with you I'll let th—"

Whitey grabbed for his gun. Gundy went for his bowie and swung it. The hardcase's hand still gripped his gun—but it lay on the ground. Gundy's slice had severed the hand right above his wrist. The bandit stared with shocked disbelief at the stub. It spurted blood as though trying to shoot the red liquid at Gundy.

"You—you've crippled me," he yelled, and with an insane light in his eyes grabbed for his knife with his other hand.

Gundy caught the bandit's knife on the blade of his bowie a scant inch from his own gut. He didn't want to kill him now—wanted to save that until later. This bastard had stolen his money and almost cost him his life. He would not die easy.

Gundy easily turned the slices and thrusts. By his figuring, loss of blood would soon put his assailant on the ground.

Gundy slipped and glided just beyond his opponent's reach while the knife swings grew wilder, and weaker. Whitey pulled his knife up shoulder high and, in one last desperate lunge to get steel into Gundy, staggered and fell to the ground.

Gundy sheathed his knife, and without so much as a second look at Whitey walked to the remuda, searched the tracks under each horse until he found the one he wanted, stripped the bedroll off it, pulled his possibles bag out, hefted it, and slung it over his shoulder. Then, like the flow of a cool stream, the hate drained from him. He slanted a look at the wagon master, knowing somehow that his look had softened.

"Takin' my money now. Don't try to stop me." A glance at Whitey and he realized he had not finished. He drew his

.44, thumbed the hammer back, and fired—not at the bandit's chest, or head, but at the elbow of his good arm. He looked at White Wing.

"I ask one more thing of my brother. Take him. Make him well. Then turn him loose. He will rob no more forever. He is now good for one thing. He can clean stalls or swamp out saloons."

A flicker of a smile crossed White Wing's face. "It will be as you wish, Great Warrior. Your enemy is no longer a man."

Gundy then went through Whitey's pockets, took what money he had, stuffed it in his own pocket, mounted, and rode out, his possibles bag slung across his shoulder.

CHAPTER
17

Five days later, Gundy rode into Senegal's ranch yard, unpacked his possibles bag, and on invitation went inside.

Senegal handed him a drink. "Saw you ride up. Don't b'lieve I was ever gladder to see a man."

Gundy slanted him a crooked grin. "Figure I run off with your money?"

Senegal stared at him a moment. "Son, not once since you left have I doubted you'd get through and bring me what's mine."

"Aw, I was just joshin' you, Senegal." Gundy shook his head. "I gotta admit, though, they was a few times I had doubts about gettin' back."

"Troubles?"

"There's them what would call it that. Comanche, Comancheros, an' one thief. Caused me to be longer gettin' back than I figured." He took a swallow of the drink Senegal had handed him and felt it burn all the way to his toes. "Took care of 'em, though. Got every penny of your money here in my bag—some gold, but mostly paper money. When you get ready we'll settle up." Gundy toed the bag out into the center of the floor. "Boys get back all right?"

At Senegal's nod, Gundy said, "I paid 'em in Dodge. Figure to pay 'em for the time it took to get back here too. That okay with you?"

"Sounds fair."

"My drovers here at your place?"

"Yeah, I kept 'em close expectin' you back soon. After you see them why don't you stick around a day or two and rest up?"

Gundy had no more reason than usual to be tired, but thought the invitation was more to give Senegal company than anything else. He nodded, grinned, and said, "That's about the slickest invite I ever heered. Figure you need somebody to help you drink a bottle or two of that good tequila you got."

"Hell, can't get away with nothin'," Senegal grumped. "Yeah, son, reckon I want a little company; then you go ahead an' get that ranch started." He peered slit-eyed at Gundy. "You decided where you're gonna set up? You could carve out a pretty good ranch right here on land close by."

"Oh! Heavens to Betsy! I thought you claimed everything south o' the Nations. Now you tellin' me I can come in here an' squat on your land?"

"Aw, Gundy, don't give me that there wide-eyed surprised look. You seen through my bluff right off. Hell, boy, I'd be downright happy to have you for a neighbor." His face cracked in that granite smile. "Fact is, you might keep me from havin' to fight rustlers and cow thieves all by my lonesome. What you think?"

"What I think is, Senegal, I'm figurin' to give that slick neighbor o' yourn a lesson in how greedy and underhanded a man can get. Gonna stake claim to a good-sized passel o' land right in the middle of Ross's range."

For the first time, Senegal's face broke into a real grin, and to Gundy's astonishment, it didn't break into a hundred pieces.

"Well, I'll be damned. Couldn't of come up with a better idea myself, son. You figure it's free range?"

"Stopped by Austin on the way home. Yep, it's mine for the takin', an' I'm sure gonna take."

Senegal slapped his thigh and laughed outright. "Can't wait to see it. You better go out and visit with your men now. When you get through, come on back, and we'll have supper.

After we get done with that, we might even pull the cork on a bottle o' that tequila I been savin' for a special occasion."

"Now that there is a outright bribe if I ever heard one. Be back soon's I talk with the men." The door closed behind him.

Gundy found Paul Kelly, Cale Madison, and his other hands sitting in the shade by the bunkhouse, chewing the fat with Senegal's men and waiting for the gong to sound for supper. He sat by Kelly.

"Have any trouble comin' home?" Gundy pointed the question at Kelly.

"Not any. We saw a few Indians, but they didn't give us any trouble. I think we had too many men for them to tackle."

Gundy nodded. "Figure you're right." He turned to the rest of his men. "Any o' you what wants to quit, I'll pay you off. You got a job with me though, if you want it. Anybody quittin'?"

No one spoke up. Gundy stood. "All right. I got a little job of my own, so till I see you again, Kelly's my *segundo*. Y'all head out in the mornin'. Cut out a area about four hours northeast o' Marfa. Put my brand on any cow you see what ain't already branded. I'll send out more men." He looked at Kelly. "Need to talk with you."

They walked off to the side and Gundy stopped and faced him. "Got somethin' needs sayin'."

"Damn, Gundy, serious as you look it must be bad."

" 'Pends on how you look at it, Kelly." He rubbed his hands down his pants legs to rid them of a sudden sweat. He stoked his pipe and lit it, killing time. He smoked his pipe when he had time. Otherwise he twirled a cigarette. Now he decided to take the bull by the horns. "Kelly, you know I'm 'bout ready to start my ranch."

At Kelly's nod, he said, "All right. Ain't got it started yet but will soon. Fact is, you men'll be gatherin' my herd when you leave here."

"What the hell's wrong with you, Gundy? I've never seen you make less sense than you're making right now. You haven't said a thing I don't already know."

His pipe had gone out, so Gundy rolled a cigarette and put a match to it. Then his gaze locked onto Kelly's. "Reckon what I'm tryin' to say is I ain't got much—yet—but I want to marry Dee, an' I want to know how you feel about it."

"Hell, ask her, don't ask me. I don't have to live with you."

"Oh, dammit, this ain't comin' out right at all. Kelly, I ain't askin' you to marry me. I want Dee, an' if you or your folks figure I ain't good enough I'll just leave be—won't never go back to the Territory." He kicked a pebble at the end of his boot that wasn't doing harm to anything. "Know I ain't much now, but figure to be someday."

Kelly eyed him a moment. "Gundy, most men out here start with a lot less than you have. Since you sold the herd you probably have more hard cash than many see in a lifetime.

"You're a hard man, maybe the hardest I've ever known, but you're fair, you're honest, you're a helluva hard worker, and you have your sights set on a goal." His eyes never leaving Gundy's, he rolled a cigarette and lighted it. "The thing that makes me feel better about you than those things, though, is how soft and gentle you get when around my sis and my mom."

Kelly grinned. "There's one thing wrong with this conversation. The person you ought to be talking to is Dee. If she says yes—and from seeing you two together I think she will—my folks will agree to it. I can't think of anyone I'll feel better about my sister marrying than you."

Gundy stared at him, his mind numb. He'd been ready to have to argue. "What'd you say? You sayin' all I got to do is talk to your folks, an' then convince Dee?"

"That's about it."

Gundy pushed his hat back and scratched his head. "Well, I'll be damned."

Kelly punched him on his shoulder. "Gundy, I think before we left Pa's place, you and Dee were about the only ones on the ranch that didn't know you were going to ask her to marry you—and I really believe Dee already knew."

Gundy looked squint-eyed at Kelly and again said, "Well, I'll be damned."

Gundy went back to the big house, ate supper, helped drink a bottle of Senegal's tequila, settled up with the herd money, asked Senegal to keep his share until he got back, and the next morning rode out.

He headed north, wondering how to find the man in charge of all the Comanchero bands. By mid-morning he had come on a plan that might work.

Reiley's place was closer than Valdez's, and by Gundy's reckoning more convenient to the trails the bandits used on their raids.

He let the buckskin pick his own pace. Gundy's saddle-bags, stuffed with jerky, also had a few airtights of peaches and tomatoes. He thought to eat hot meals until he reached a place to keep an eye on Reiley's post. Once there, he'd have a cold camp. A fire would be too dangerous.

Before the sun reached high noon, Gundy shot a spiked buck. With it, he'd have fresh meat until he figured it might spoil. He'd stock up on Arbuckle's in Van Horn. Until then he had enough coffee to make one pot a day.

He stayed off the beaten paths, not wanting to be seen any-where until he found what he looked for.

He rode deep in the chaparral. Thorns stuck his heavy leather chaps and broke off, flies swarmed to his sweat-soaked neck and shirt, dust pushed into his nostrils, and the blazing sun tried to penetrate his squinted eyelids. None of it broke his thoughts. By his reckoning he should be close to Reiley's place by mid-morning tomorrow. He could probably make it about an hour after dark, but he didn't relish the idea of riding this country when he couldn't see what he rode into.

Before leaving Senegal's, he had written Dee a letter. He'd told her Paul was well, a little about the trail drive, and how he was coming with his ranch. Then, wondering if he was be-ing too brash, he'd told her he missed her. Senegal had prom-ised to mail it in Marfa when he went in for supplies, and had mentioned dryly he was running shy of tequila and would be going into town on the morrow. Gundy thought Dee should be getting the letter soon.

He'd been looking for a campsite for the last hour. Water was out of the question unless he came across a sump that had trapped some of the last rain from three weeks ago. He figured on a dry camp, and this would be the last night he'd have a fire for many nights to come. But a hot meal was something he'd done without more times than he could count.

A small glade opened in the brush. Gundy ground-hitched his horse and circled the area several times looking for sign that others used this spot. He found no tracks and saw no charred sticks to indicate a campfire had burned there. He gathered wood and made camp.

After eating, he lay in his bedroll and stared at the sky, trying to focus on the Comanchero fight that soon would come, but try as he would he thought of Dee instead.

He tried to convinced himself he was building his ranch for her, but he knew better. He was pushing himself to build a life for himself. He had never known a home and wanted one. He had never known his parents, and wanted to be one. He wanted the respect of his fellow men, not fear, and he had seen that on too many faces. But too, he wanted all of this for the woman he loved, and he had no right to ask her to share the hard times ahead. He would not say anything to her until he earned the right.

Many miles away, at the base of the Capitan Mountains, Dee stared into the darkness from her blankets, hugging to her breast the one letter she'd had from Gundy. All of the things he'd refrained from putting on paper she'd read into it. Just the simple words that he missed her told her more than if he'd written ardent words of passion and love. He was a man who would show her his feelings and say them to her only when he could hold her close.

She had to get him safely back to the Territory, get him close to her so he would say and do the things she wanted of him. He wouldn't do any of it until he had something to offer her, when the only thing she wanted him to offer was himself.

Her parents would not stand in the way. She had been fearful her father would block the marriage, but now she knew that what he wanted more than anything was her happiness. She lighted the lantern and read Gundy's letter again—for the tenth time, and she'd only received it that afternoon. Oh, Trace, come back to me, come back soon, she prayed.

Three hours after breaking camp, Gundy squatted on a knoll above Reiley's trading post. He took an old military long-glass he had traded for in Corpus Christi from his bedroll. Through it he studied the store and the area around it. Only Reiley's horse stood in the shed. The woman who had cooked steaks for him and his crew came out the back door and dumped garbage to the hogs that were penned there. She went back in, and Reiley came out and sat on the veranda, scratching under his arms and his chest. Gundy settled down for a long wait.

Soon after the nooning, during which Gundy chewed a strip of jerky, two riders came in, stayed long enough for a beer, and left. A couple hours later, a man rode up on a mule, stayed long enough to eat, and left. Gundy wanted to see a group of at least four or more. He hunkered down to wait it out.

The remainder of that afternoon and the next day no one stopped. The third day he watched two pairs of riders go in and leave. About three o'clock of that day, five riders drew in to the hitch rail. They wore serapes, large-brimmed sombreros, and chaps that almost covered their flare-bottomed trousers. Heavily armed, they wore bandoliers loaded with cartridges. Gundy could see the brass shining in the sunlight. His pulse quickened. He had no doubt these were Comancheros.

He kept his eye glued to the long-glass as he trained it on the door of the store. The sun sank toward the horizon and the five still stayed inside. Damn, he thought, now hoping they would stay the night. Tracking them in the dark would be hard, and chancy. He'd have to cling too close in order not to lose them. He put sleep in the back of his mind for fear they'd take a notion to leave. He watched their horses until well after midnight. He gave it up then and rolled into his blankets, figuring they wouldn't leave until morning.

Long before the hot late summer's sun pushed above the horizon, Gundy packed his bedroll, ate a tin of peaches, and waited for the band of Comancheros to leave. They seemed in no hurry.

At first, a pair of them came out on the veranda and sat to eat breakfast. Then the other three came and sat with their legs dangling off the edge of the porch. Finished eating, they went in and came out with granite cups, steam rising from them. Gundy could almost smell the aroma of coffee. Saliva flowed, and he chewed harder on the stale biscuit he had pulled from his pack.

Nine o'clock came and went before all five came out together, saddled, and left headed east. Gundy thought from that they would attack something along the trail between Fort Stockton and El Paso.

Waiting for distance to lengthen between him and them, he circled Reiley's trading post and searched out their tracks. After studying the hoof marks of each horse and being certain he would know them anywhere, he followed at a distance. The hoofprints didn't indicate they were in much of a hurry, so Gundy kept his buckskin at a walk.

As he'd figured, when they came on the trail to Fort Stockton, they took it, still headed east. If he figured right, they wouldn't get too close to a settlement. They would choose their victims where defense would be impossible, then hit them, take all that had any worth, and head for headquarters.

Gundy could not go to the defense of their victims. That, he knew, would be one of the hardest things he'd ever faced. He had to let them do their dirty work and get away if he was to have any chance at all of finding where they unloaded their spoils.

He lost time before noon trying to stay far enough behind so he could pull off the trail when they ate, but they didn't stop. Shadows grew long and they still rode at the same steady pace.

Gundy wondered how to keep from riding up on them when they stopped for the night. He decided he couldn't. He pondered what to do and, feeling his gut tighten, decided to

continue riding like he had nowhere to go and forever to get
there. When they stopped for the night he would pass them,
probably damned close, and would keep riding unless they
tried to stop him. If that happened he'd have to fight. He
didn't want to, but that might be his only option.

Watching the trail for tracks turning off the beaten path,
while appearing to be just slowly picking his way east, turned
out to be harder than he'd figured. Twilight set in and the
ground blended small irregularities into a smoothness that hid
tracks from the eyes. The harder seeing became, the tighter
Gundy's back muscles got, and the feel of a rifle slung slam-
ming him from the saddle became real.

Tracks were impossible to see now, and he would have
missed where they'd turned off the trail except for the fact
that the white of a broken twig stood out against the dark. He
wanted to stop and look closer, but the knot between his
shoulders and the cold lump in his gut screamed to keep going. He put a couple hundred yards behind him before relax-
ing a little, then another quarter of a mile after that. Only then
did he rein the buckskin into the chaparral and peel his bedroll off. His horse drank from water Gundy poured into his
hat. Then Gundy took a few sips, rinsed his mouth out, and
swallowed, hoping the bandits would find water the next day
and leave enough for him and his horse.

Sunup found him squatted deep in the brush with only a
partial view of the trail, but enough that he could identify the
Comancheros when they came past.

An hour into the new day the sound of several horses came
to him. Gundy had no need for the long-glass now, and as
he'd suspected, the horses he heard were those of the outlaws.

Almost a half hour passed before Gundy took their trail
again. He hung back, thinking gunfire would tell him where
they were. If they hit any target it would have to be today because Fort Stockton was only another day's ride. But the day
drew down to a close before the distant popping of rifles and
six-guns warned him of the outlaws' whereabouts.

Again he went into the brush, coaxing his horse through
the tangle of growth until he was close enough to smell the

acrid bite of gunpowder. He stopped, dismounted, and held his hand over the buckskin's nostrils.

He moved through the thicket until he could see two wagons, with three of the bandits at the head of the first and the other two standing by the second.

Gundy studied the two heavy freight wagons and saw no indication that families were aboard. Four bull-whackers stood at the side of their teams, two to a wagon, their hands help up to the sky. The shots so far had been to stop them, but there would be more slugs thrown soon.

Poor bastards, Gundy thought, they're dead men and they know it. Trash like the Comancheros never let a victim live. He was close enough to hear every word.

"Keep your hands where they are, *gringo*."

One of them made a stab for his handgun, but never made it. The Comancheros opened fire. In a few short seconds four bull-whackers lay on the ground by the wheels of the wagons, and two of the bandits had joined them.

"Take everyteeng they got on 'em and drag 'em into the brush. C'mon. Get it done. We gotta get outta here," one of the bandits yelled.

It was all Gundy could do to rein in his temper and keep from killing the three remaining outlaws. He ground his teeth and watched.

Six corpses bumped across chuckholes into the dense brush, stripped of boots, clothing, and guns. They would lie there, carrion for scavenging animals.

CHAPTER
18

Gundy waited until they tied their horses to the tailgates, took the long bullwhips into their hands, and walked beside the teams of oxen while headed west. Then he gave them another half hour before he led his horse back to the trail.

The wagons carried a heavy load and made deep tracks in the white-gray dust. He dropped farther back. The bandits would make only ten to fifteen miles a day with those heavily laden wagons, and slow though his horse's pace was, he would still catch them.

That night, having followed the tracks until about an hour before sundown, and being fairly certain he could pick up their sign in the morning, Gundy again put the buckskin into the chaparral. He followed an animal trail he had stumbled on once before when crossing this part of the country. A fresh-water spring bubbled only a mile from where he turned off.

His horse smelled water and tried to take the bit in his teeth and make a run for it. Gundy held him back. A couple of hundred yards from the spring Gundy tied his horse to a snag of an oak and proceeded on foot.

The sheen of water slowed him even more until he dropped to his stomach and snaked his way to within rock-throwing distance. He lay there, searching every inch of the surrounding area. No one had camped there ahead of him. But still not satisfied, Gundy circled the small pond and checked the ground for sign. There were deer, javelina, goat, and a myriad of smaller animal tracks, but no horse or man tracks.

He went to the buckskin and led him to the spring. While his horse drank on one side, Gundy filled his canteens and then lowered his face into the water. He drank until he could hold no more. After he and his horse had drunk their fill, he led the gelding far enough away that they could have a fire with little chance of it being seen.

He made camp knowing they would again have water in the morning.

Sitting by the fire, drinking the first coffee he'd had in days, Gundy glanced at the sky. Lightning had drawn his look. It flashed again, pushing great, turbulent thunderheads into sharp relief. Leaning against his saddle, he twisted and untied his extra groundsheet from behind the cantle. With the one on the ground and this one over his blankets, he shouldn't get more than moderately soaked. Then he gathered a couple of armfuls of wood and covered it with the top groundsheet.

Before he finished his next cup of coffee, huge drops of rain fell, widely spaced. The drops got smaller and closer together. Then it began to hail. Gundy pulled the buckskin to the ground next to him—just in time. The stones increased in size to as large as hens' eggs.

Gundy dragged his blankets from under the top groundsheet, bundled them, and covered his horse's head, then lifted his saddle and poked his own head under it.

Lightning crashed as though to spear and seer him in its fury. The hail increased to the size of a fist. He held his horse to the ground, holding the blankets tight to the animal's head. He gasped each time one of the large stones crashed into his body. Brimstone permeated the air, until the air he sucked into his lungs seemed scarcely enough.

He and his horse lay there like primeval creatures, not understanding the forces unleashed on them, and having no way to protect themselves other than what they had at hand.

The hail lasted only minutes, but it seemed like hours. Then it slacked off to an occasional stone and the rain increased in intensity. It fell on them as though thrown from a huge, world-sized bucket. Then Gundy became aware of the wind.

It bent the scrub oak to near the ground. Then it stopped. An eerie stillness gripped the land. The buckskin stirred, tried to get up. Gundy held the horse fast—he'd seen this sort of thing before. If running would do any good, he'd be up and hightailing it, but he couldn't outrun a tornado on horseback.

His best bet was to stay flat. If there had been a dry wash or ravine to crawl into, it still would do no good. Any at hand would be full to the banks with a roaring, roiling wall of water. He kept pressure on the buckskin's head, holding him tight to the ground. Then the roar came.

It sounded to Gundy like the cattle trains he had heard in Dodge City. First the noise, then twisting, tearing wind. In an instant it passed and rumbled off to the southeast, but the rain continued, dwindling from a downpour to a steady soaking.

He stood and pulled his horse to his feet. The buckskin stood there trembling, walleyed. Gundy patted the proud neck and rubbed his hand along the horse's side, soothing the fear from him, feeling him flinch when he rubbed a spot bruised from the pounding hail. Gundy felt helpless. The poor devil had taken a beating he couldn't understand, and stood trusting him to make everything all right.

"Can't do anything 'bout your hurts, old boy." His voice seemed to soothe the animal, so Gundy talked and patted him until he stopped trembling.

The rain now dwindled to an isolated drop here and there. Gundy pulled the top groundsheet back and took out about half the wood he'd gathered. Might as well fix coffee, he thought. Ain't gonna be no sleepin' the rest o' this night, wet blankets an' all.

He sat by the small fire until it burned down to glowing embers. He drank coffee until what was left in the pot was so thick and bitter he tossed it out. His thoughts went to the Comancheros.

Any tracks they'd laid down would be long gone with the soaking the ground had taken. But they'd been only an hour or so ahead of him when he turned off the trail, and he should pick up their new tracks in no more than a couple of hours.

Those heavy wagons might even be bogged down, so he figured to be doubly careful not to ride up on them. He sat there until the sky lightened in the east. Then he saddled the buckskin, packed the soggy bedding, and headed for the main trail.

The day dawned gray and dreary. Gundy hoped the overcast would burn off by mid-morning and dry his clothes, but he'd seen these Texas skies hang onto clouds for days, as though afraid that if they turned them loose there would be no more. He shivered, then chuckled. Might be right about seein' no more for a long time.

As expected, not a track marred the muddy ground. Gundy continued west, and after about a mile crossed a trail leading south to Marfa. He passed long enough to glanced down it, and shook his head. He'd continue on the trail he was on for another hour. If he didn't pick up tracks by then, he'd come back and head south.

About thirty minutes down the trail the mud turned back to dry dust. Not a drop of rain had fallen on it the night before, and not a wagon track showed in the dust. Gundy nodded. Now he knew they had turned south. He headed back.

An hour onto the south trail he came on deep wheel tracks in the mud, and at the same time heard a popping sound, almost like gunfire, but not the sounds a pistol or rifle would make. He was close, too damned close. That cracking noise was bullwhips, and from their sound they were handled by men accustomed to using them.

Gundy again pulled off the trail into the brush. He had to let the wagons get farther ahead, but wanted to take a look to make sure they were the same ones he trailed.

He frowned, thinking. There had been no vehicles coming from the west, and the only ones from the east were the ones he trailed. Those tracks *had* to be the right ones. He decided not to chance getting closer.

This route was almost impossible. If they stayed on course, those teams would have to pull the wagons in the Barrilla Mountains. Most of the peaks were above six thousand feet. In between was country only goats should have to travel.

By noon, although you couldn't tell the time by the sky,

the mud again turned to dust. Several times Gundy wished he had somewhere to leave his horse. He could stay closer to the wagons afoot, and he'd like to have a look at what was in them. He thought about that while sitting in the brush alongside the trail. He'd stopped several times in order to stay well behind.

He thought about waiting until they crawled into their blankets at night, then slipping to the back of the wagon farthest from where the Comancheros had bedded down and taking a first-hand look. With only three bandits left, he'd fight his way out if they caught him. He didn't want to kill them. Those wagons had to get through for him to know where they were going.

The fifth day the sun decided to shine all day. Gundy still hadn't taken a look at what the wagons carried. Fort Davis was only another day's travel when he found a place to camp that was to his liking.

Tonight he'd see what the wagons held. They would be turning off pretty soon to avoid army patrols. They could circle the settlement, or their destination could be off in either direction. He wanted to know what they carried before they got to the big boss to divvy the spoils.

About midnight, he banked his fire, put on moccasins, tethered his horse, and slipped down the trail like a shadow.

Only minutes from his camp the ghostly silhouette of wagon canvas curved against the star-studded sky. Gundy stopped. Standing close to the wall of chaparral, he studied the camp. A faint wisp of woodsmoke came to him, yet he saw no flicker of firelight. He eased farther along.

The wagons stood in the middle of the beaten path. About to pass the second one, he again stood motionless. A more than needful distance separated the wagons. He searched that space and saw embers, almost ashed over. Straining his eyes to penetrate the darkness, he picked out what he thought were the three bandits bedded close to what had been the fire.

Damn! Why hadn't they pulled the wagons close to each other and camped at either end? One wagon-bed length, about fourteen feet, separated him from the guns of men he knew from experience could shoot. He kept looking at the bedding of the outlaws. The one closest to the front wagon grunted and turned over. Gundy's gaze shifted to the other two. They didn't stir. He stood there another few moments, and decided if he wanted to see what the wagons held, he might as well get on with it. First, he located the teams, eight oxen to the wagon. They were hobbled out ahead of camp.

He went to the end of the last wagon and slipped quietly to the closed tailgate. Getting into the big Conestoga without noise was going to be more than he dared hope. His only alternative was to climb over. If he tried lowering the tailgate it would surely creak, or bump. Gundy wouldn't take that chance.

He levered himself up and threw a leg over and into the wagon bed, thankful he had worn moccasins. Boots were more likely to make noise. Now to identify what was in the wagon. He had to do it by feel—or perhaps smell.

To the side were bales of tightly packed cloth—woolen? Yes, he thought, they must be blankets. He was tempted to strip one out of the pack. His were still damp and moldy. He shook his head, giving up the idea.

On the other side were kegs. He tilted one and shook it. Something sloshed inside. Working by feel, he worked his hand around the top, located a bung, placed his nose close to it, and sniffed. Whiskey.

Crawling to the top of the bales, he inched forward. Between the blankets and the front of the wagon were wooden boxes, some long and others much smaller. Measuring each side with the length of his arm, he decided the long boxes held rifles and the smaller ones ammunition. Again sniffing, he thought he detected the odor of Cosmoline. If he was right, they *were* rifles.

Gundy worked his way around so as to face the back of the Conestoga. He had to get out. He was about to crawl to the top of the blanket bales when someone coughed at the side, about next to the rear wheels.

Gundy dropped into the space between the boxes and the blankets. A voice from the front asked, "What the hell you doin' prowlin' round in the dark like that?"

"Cold. Gonna take me one o' them blankets. I'll put it back 'fore we get to the boss."

"Bring me one too. Freeze at night and bake during the day."

Hardly daring to breathe, Gundy lay flat as the space he was in would permit, hoping his legs were out of sight.

A match flared, lighting the whole interior. Gundy thumbed the thong off the hammer of his .44, held the butt firmly in his hand, and waited. Abruptly, the match went out and the Comanchero cursed.

The wagon bed shook. The bandit climbed into the wagon. Gundy held his breath.

Then came the sound of cloth being dragged across cloth and the click of metal. "Damn! These ropes are tight. Gonna have to cut 'em." Then the squeaky sound of metal sawing on something. Gundy figured the squeak was that of a dull knife blade pulled through manila line.

A small pop sounded, like a tightly pulled rope makes when it parts. "Bastard oughta get his own blanket," the bandit grumbled. Then cloth rubbed on cloth twice.

That's two blankets, Gundy thought. Now get the hell out of here.

Steps thumped on the wagon bed, and the big Conestoga shook at about the same time something hit the ground. Gundy let his breath out a little at a time. He was the only one in the wagon.

He lay there until all sounds toward the fire ceased, maybe ten or fifteen minutes. He pulled his legs under him, slowly straightened, and worked his way toward the back. He reached for the top of the tailgate, changed his mind, and reached for the blankets. He took two of them. From their heft he judged them to be Hudson Bay blankets, costly enough that he had never bought one for himself. He eased himself to the ground and melted into the darkness. After taking the blankets, he would have to move camp. They were sure to look for the person who had been in their camp.

CHAPTER
19

Gundy wasted no time breaking camp. He tied his belongings behind the cantle, exchanged moccasins for boots, and made tracks back the way he'd come earlier in the day. Before getting to the mud he turned into the brush.

Working his way through the thorny growth at night was not to his liking. He might lame his horse. He walked, leading the way, pushing his booted feet ahead to avoid leading the buckskin over a Spanish dagger or other such growth. If a rattler was in his path, it would probably slither off. He spent a good thirty minutes finding a place to spend the rest of the night.

If the outlaws tried tracking him he'd hear them long before they found him. But he didn't think they would spend much time trying to find him. They would make sure, though, that he didn't follow them.

The next morning, Gundy heard them scraping through the scrub, cursing and blaming each other for letting a thief get into their camp and steal stuff they would have to account for later.

When they gave up and headed back to the big freighters, he waited for them to get out of smelling and hearing distance, then made breakfast, threw his moldy blankets away, and rolled his new ones. They were Hudson Bay blankets just as he'd thought. After eating, he took their trail.

The tracks led around Fort Davis, hit the main trail to Marfa again, and two days later turned east onto a much-traveled road. Now Gundy kept them in sight, holding to high ground in order to see them, but being careful to stay below the skyline. They must be getting close to headquarters.

They held easterly for one day, then turned back south. Gundy stayed east of the trail they had taken. Late the second day after they had again headed south, a large group of buildings came into sight. Gundy squinted against the afternoon sun, took out his long-glass, and studied what he at first thought was a town, although he'd never heard of one here.

The glass brought the settlement close enough to see a large ranch, with several outbuildings, all encircled by an adobe wall Gundy judged to be about eight feet high. There was one way to enter the grounds. An arch, with heavy wooden gates mounted to it, stood about a hundred yards in front of the sprawling ranch house. The wagons he followed were driving through the gates.

Gundy searched the terrain between the ranch and him. Broken by deep ravines, chaparral, and a couple of high hills, the land looked like there might be cattle there, but he didn't see working cowhands. From where he stood, he could watch the goings-on without danger.

Not about to barge into a setup like that without a damned good plan, he looked for a campsite.

A steep-walled ravine, with a shelf about twenty feet up the side closest to him, looked suitable for camp. The buckskin picked his way down a game trail to the shelf. Gundy stripped the gear off, and led his horse to a small sinkhole with water enough for both of them for a few days.

A glance at his surroundings showed a place hidden from anyone wandering the countryside at night. A good place to hide, but one easy to get trapped in. The only ways out were the open end of the ravine or its steep sides—with a good chance to die climbing them. He shrugged. He figured to be here a few days, and damned if he would gnaw jerky all that time.

Putting his thoughts into action, he built a fire and set the coffee water to boiling.

After a hot meal, Gundy sat next to the fire and thought of the layout he'd looked upon earlier. If anyone recognized him while he was inside he'd be a goner, and he could think of no way to learn who the big boss was without going in and somehow getting inside the big house. After that, getting out would be one hell of a lot of fun. One thing about it, though. From this point on he didn't have to be careful not to kill anyone. Now he knew where the exchange point was, and the only way he could find out what was inside was to go in and see for himself.

A shiver went up his spine. His chances of marrying Dee had slimmed considerably since seeing where the Comanchero boss holed up. But with a price on his head, put there by whoever was in charge down there in that fortress, the possibility of a long and happy marriage was slim at best. And a man did what he had to do.

Daybreak the next morning found him leaning against a rock slab, his long-glass trained on the compound. With the morning sun at his back, he didn't worry about light reflected off the lens being seen by anyone below. He'd have to be careful using the glass in the afternoons, though.

The arch drew most of his attention. Two men stood at each side of the gates and waved riders and wagons through. Guards, he thought, but they didn't look as though they looked for any identification. Maybe they knew those they let inside.

His glass trained on the wall and he shook his head. Along the top, glass shards were imbedded in the adobe. He'd cut his hands to ribbons if he tried going over it. To get in through the gates seemed the only sensible way to go.

Inside the compound as many as twelve wagons were lined up side by side. A crew of no more than four men engaged in unloading them. It looked to Gundy as if it was a case of first in, first out. They unloaded one wagon at a time.

He studied the setup two more days, memorizing every aspect of it: building locations, wagon locations, how long they took to unload, how far they took the loot for storage, and how many men were inside the wall at any given time.

The stables drew much of his attention. The riders who escorted large trains of wagons inside took their horses to the stables, and when they left the stable with bedrolls, they went to what Gundy thought must be the bunkhouse, left their gear, and went to a small building not far from it. There they stayed awhile, and then went to what looked like a saloon. Gundy grunted. That was a regular town inside the wall.

Not being able to think of any use for the smaller building, he figured it must be the office. If that was true, that would be where the head of the operation spent his days. But Gundy didn't figure to do anything during the day. Night was his only ally.

Early and late he watched the big house for traffic to and from it to the office. In the mornings, a man and woman left the house and went to the office. About noon they went back to the house and spent an hour or two, then back to the office, where they stayed until near sundown. This seemed to be routine. The morning of the fourth day, he had a plan. He'd live—or die—with it.

There were now fourteen wagons lined up for unloading. He saddled the buckskin, rode west, crossed the trail, and rode deeper into the hills, into country where an Apache had an advantage over anyone else.

He looked for a particular kind of place, one shielded from the path pursuers on horseback would have to take and suited to someone afoot.

Shadows stretched long when he found the kind of setup he wanted. The chaparral he'd wended his way through all day was bad. Then it got worse. He came on a tangled growth his buckskin couldn't push through. It was like a wall for a couple of miles in each direction. But a man afoot could crawl and make it to the other side if he didn't mind getting stuck, scraped, and stung with prickly-pear needles. Now to get the buckskin to the other side.

He found the only way was to ride around the end. He used care in selecting a place farthest from any route a horse could take. There he made camp—no water, but skimpy forage for his horse. Gundy put the buckskin on a picket rope, cooked supper, and turned in. It had taken him until a couple of hours after sunset, but he felt with a whole lot of luck he might make it back to Senegal and his men.

The next morning the sky had not lightened in the east when he traded boots for moccasins, checked the tether on his horse, left him saddled, and struck out for the trail the wagons took to headquarters.

He thought about trying to make it through the tangled thicket, but decided it would be too risky in the dark on hands and knees. He again went around the end, and by ten o'clock hunkered beside the trail, far enough back in the brush so as to not be seen, but close enough so he could see anyone who passed.

He sat there through the nooning and chewed on a strip of jerky, then waited another four hours before he saw what he wanted. He heard the pop of bullwhips and clank of harness before they came in sight around a bend. Three Conestogas, all pulled by oxen.

The last one passed before he moved. The driver unfurled his whip over the eight plodding beasts. Before the sharp crack of the whip, knowing the bull-whacker would watch until it snapped, Gundy ran into the trail behind the last wagon, grabbed the tailgate, and threw himself inside, hoping he and the cargo were all that occupied the space. He got lucky.

Large bags of flour were stacked high so he hardly had room to squirm over them to the middle of the wagon. There he found gunnysacks of coffee beans. The aroma made him wish for a good hot cup of the eye-opening liquid.

The first part of his plan was taken care of. All he could do now was lie flat and wait until he was inside the compound. Then he'd have to stay still under after dark.

The heavy wagons creaked, swayed, and bumped to the tune of cracking whips. Gundy shifted his position a couple of times for comfort, and still they rolled.

When he began to wonder how far out they were, the wheels stopped turning, and someone Gundy assumed was a gate guard said, "*Alto,* what you got in there, *amigo*?"

"Coffee, flour, and tobacco, *señor.*"

"I take a look."

Damn it! Gundy drew down into a small space. He'd not seen any of the guards get that nosy while he watched the gate. The wagon rocked and he heard a grunt, and then the sound of the guard dropping back to ground. Gundy hadn't realized he'd tensed, but as soon as he heard the guard drop to the ground his muscles relaxed.

"Go ahead, *amigo,* follow those two. Park at the side of the last wagon in that row. Then get some grub."

The wagon jerked when the wheels again turned. Gundy swallowed hard. He was inside the compound—with no way to escape except through the gate.

Only a few more moments of movement and they stopped again. All was quiet until he heard the teams unhitched and led away. Now more waiting—until well after dark.

He lay there, not daring to shift position for fear of making a noise someone would investigate. The low light of sunset passed and the patch of sky Gundy saw from his hiding place darkened.

Mingled odors of chile, beans, tortillas, and coffee wafted past his nose. It was almost enticing enough to draw him from hiding. He'd stay put, though, until the sounds of foot traffic lessened.

Finally—Gundy judged the time as about ten o'clock—most outside noises quieted. He brought his cramped and stiff legs under him. His scalp tingled so much that he'd have bet his hair stood on end. A chill went up his spine and his chest muscles tightened. Scared? Damned right. He'd never deliberately put himself in a situation with little or no hope for getting out alive. He willed himself to relax. It was too late for second thoughts. He searched the contents of the wagon for bales, anything wrapped in wire. He found what he looked for. Several wooden boxes had the lids secured on with wire.

Using his bowie, he pried the staples loose and gathered six lengths of wire about two feet long. He bent and pulled them through a belt loop.

Before leaving the safety of the Conestoga, he brought his eyes level with the edge of the tailgate and searched for anyone afoot. He saw no one. But his area of vision was limited.

He dropped, landed on his feet, and walked to the front of the wagon, trying to make it appear that he was checking it as a guard. Still the compound seemed deserted.

Through all the months spent in the chaparral, Gundy had never thought he would wish for big clumps of the thorny growth, but he did now. Between him and the big house, the ground lay barren of even a blade of grass—nothing to hide behind or to shield his movements.

He headed toward the wall, away from the bunkhouse, and circled to come up in back of the big house. He froze while checking the walls, doors, and windows. Lamplight painted the windows a golden hue, but cast little light onto the grounds. He checked again looking for guards, anyone who would raise the alarm.

At one corner of the house, Gundy finally spotted a man sitting, leaning against the wall. Then he checked the other corner and saw another guard. It was unlikely they were anything other than sentries.

To get in the house he had to get by them—or kill them—and he had no way to slip up on either man. He couldn't figure how he'd gotten this far without being seen—unless they sat there asleep. He studied the situation a moment, and decided if he got to the back of the house, he might be able to get close to its side.

Moving slowly, he again circled until he could no longer see the sentry. Then he ran, silent as a breath of wind, to the house. He came up against the wall and turned toward the corner where he'd spotted the man. Now he moved in slow, fluid motion until he looked down at the top of the guard's head leaning against his folded hat.

Carefully, Gundy pulled one of the lengths of wire from his belt, fashioned a loop in it, dropped it over the man's head to his neck—and pulled tight. Clawing fingers tried to loosen the garrote, scraping deep furrows in neck and cheek. Gundy held the wire until the man kicked, straightened, and lay still. He twisted the wire a couple of times so it wouldn't slip, and walked toward the other guard. This one would be harder. He'd be facing him.

The man tilted his head to look at Gundy. " 'Bout to go to

sleep sittin' over there. Need a smoke—you got a match?"
Gundy said.

The guard reached for his shirt pocket, and Gundy dropped
the looped wire over his head. When the man convulsed and
straightened, Gundy again twisted the wire and walked toward the back door. Any shred of civilization that had remained with Gundy was now gone. He was as much Apache
as any warrior in Geronimo's camp. Pity, compassion—none
of the words white men were taught from birth meant anything now. They were words foreign to the Apache tongue.

The door through which Gundy slipped opened into a darkened hallway. He eased along it until he could see into a large
room. A man sat in a massive chair with his back to Gundy,
and across the room a woman read a book. The man with his
back to Gundy must be Ross, because the woman reading the
book was Hillary. Any degree of satisfaction Gundy had in
identifying the Comanchero leader was now more than doubled. He was not above feeling good about Ross being his
man.

Gundy hadn't counted on a woman being here. He
couldn't, wouldn't kill her. A shot to get rid of Ross would
alert every man in the compound. He shook his head. That
would get him shot to hell faster than a man could blink.
He'd have to wait them out and hope Hillary would head for
bed soon, and that both of them didn't decide to go at the
same time.

A coat rack stood in the hallway corner just inside the
door leading into the sitting room. Gundy slipped behind it.
He could hear, but could not see what went on in the next
room.

He had stood there about an hour when Hillary said, "I'm
going to bed, Father. You need your sleep too. It'll be another
long day tomorrow. We're going to have to go to San
Antonio in a few days. I need clothes, so we'd better get
those wagons inventoried and not let them stack up any
longer."

"Go to bed. I'll turn in as soon as I finish this listing of
things from yesterday's take."

"All right. Kill yourself working, and I'll be the one to

enjoy the results of our work. Good night." Heels clicked on the floor, coming toward the hall in which Gundy hid. He held his breath. She passed and turned in a door across the hall. He still waited. Finally, the light under the crack at the bottom of the door through which she had gone darkened.

A last look at her bedroom door, and then Gundy slipped from behind the rack and peered into the room in time to see Ross pour himself a drink and glance toward the hall.

With that look, Gundy saw recognition flash in Ross's eyes and his mouth open wide. Gundy's hand went to the back of his shirt collar, grabbed his throwing knife, and flashed forward. The knife turned over once while in the air before entering Ross's chest, the blade buried to the hilt.

The yell forming in Ross's throat turned into a sighing moan. Gundy reached him almost as soon as the knife. Not taking the chance the knife had failed to do its work, Gundy pulled another length of wire from the belt and slipped it over Ross's head.

Still alive, Ross stared at him from bulging, terror-filled eyes. Gundy locked eyes with him a moment. "Ross, put the money you put on my scalp back in your pocket. 'Stead o' money, I'm takin' your hair." He pulled the garrote tight, twisted the ends together, pulled his knife free, ran the blade around Ross's head, and peeled his scalp from this head, leaving a white, shiny skull gleaming in the lamplight. He cleaned his knife on Ross's shirt and slipped it into its sheath.

"Father, put out the lamp and come to bed," Hillary's voice said from the hall. Gundy pushed Ross into his chair and sprinted silently to the side of the hall door.

"'Father, come to bed this instant. . . .'" Any other words she might have uttered choked off behind Gundy's hand. He pulled his neck scarf off, tied it around her mouth, pulled out his last two lengths of wire, and wrapped one around her hands and the other around her ankles.

He looked at her lying on the floor at his feet. "Ma'am, you an' your pa once said I didn't know nothin' 'bout nothin'. You was wrong. I know trash when I see it—an' I know how to kill. That's 'bout all anybody ever learned me. Case you get to wonderin' who I am, I'm the man your pa said he'd pay a thousand dollars for. I'm the Apache Blanco." He cast one more look into her hate-filled eyes, and went toward the door.

CHAPTER
20

Gundy reached for the front door and changed his mind. The guards at the back would not cause him trouble unless they'd been discovered, and he'd heard no noise to indicate that was so.

He retraced his steps, went to the cabinet where Ross had poured himself a drink, and poured about three fingers in a water glass. He downed it and again looked at the witch-like eyes of Hillary.

He went out the back door and headed for the stables. To try to breach the gate afoot would be suicide. His plan had not considered that an option.

The stables were dark and, Gundy hoped, deserted. He went in through the back and silently searched for anyone who might be posted there. He found no one.

After inspecting all of the horses, Gundy picked one he figured would be the fastest, and rigged it like he'd seen the Comanches rig theirs.

Leading the horse he'd chosen to ride, he opened the door to every stall, straddled his horse at the back of the stable, and yelled, "Heeeyiiii!"

Horses poured out, some trying to run by him, some running for the front. He turned those headed his way and, leaning low over his horse's neck, continued yelling, driving the pack ahead of him.

Men stumbled out of the bunkhouse in every state of un-
dress, all carrying weapons. By the time they reached the
gates he'd run his horse into the middle of the herd. Bullets
whined by his head. It seemed like the whole world had
trained guns on him. A bullet slammed into him—then another.

He fell to the side and rode like a Comanche, hanging to
the side of his horse, one leg hooked in a rope across the
horse's back. When he went through the arch he was in the
middle of the pack and must have made a poor target, because he took no other hits that he could tell. He didn't know
where he'd taken lead—only knew he had.

Numbness had not started, and there was no pain—yet. He
had to get to the brush barrier before the nausea, numbness,
and pain set in.

About a mile down the road, Gundy slipped off his horse,
letting him run with the pack. He faded into the chaparral at
the side of the trail. In only moments the wolf pack followed,
some afoot, some riding mules, and all cursing and chasing
the horses. He figured the time they would use trying to collect their remuda gave him plenty of time to get to the brush
barrier—if he didn't pass out first. Pain slowly spread down
his left side and leg.

He reached for his bandana, and remembered Hillary had it
in her mouth. He wouldn't put it on a bullet wound anyway
after she'd had it in her mouth, he thought.

Working his way through the chaparral toward the barrier,
Gundy stripped his shirt off, tore it in strips, and plugged the
holes, one below his ribs, and one in his thigh. Both bled
more than he wanted to see. With blood loss, his mouth got
dry and he weakened. He had to make it to the barrier. The
horses would stop running soon, and the bandits would find
he wasn't with them. Then they would spread into the chaparral to hunt him.

Time passed. Gundy didn't try to estimate how long it was
until he reached the thick brush, dizzy, fuzzy-brained, and
hurting like blazes. He heard no sign of pursuit.

Dropping to his hands and knees, he wormed his way into

the thorny mass—sometimes on his stomach, sometimes crawling—never was there room for him to stand.

Without his shirt, thorns raked, stabbed, and scratched his shoulders, back, and chest. He ignored them, and called upon enough of his Apache training to push back the pain from his bullet wounds. But loss of blood took its toll. When he broke free of the brambles he tried standing, and couldn't. But luck still rode with him. He'd gauged almost perfectly where he'd had to come out close to his horse. The buckskin stood not twenty feet away.

Again he tried to stand, putting his hands on his knees and climbing them up his thigh until he stood, wobbly but on his feet. He had left his horse saddled, knowing he'd need him in a hurry if he got back. He went to the end of the tether, pulled the stake, and tugged the buckskin to him.

A glance showed the North Star, and Gundy set his course to the southwest, toward Marfa. He'd see Ben Darcy, the marshal, before heading for Senegal's—if he made it that far.

Far into the night he rode before coming to water. Fever had set in and he drank his canteen dry before finding the brackish sump, but it was wet, and would keep moisture in his body. He took time only to water his horse, fill his canteen, and take a strip of jerky from his saddlebags. By his reckoning he should reach Marfa by noon.

Riding down the main street, Gundy drew a lot of attention. People stared at him, shirtless, bloody, dirty. But he didn't give a damn. They were the best sight he'd seen in days. He headed straight to Darcy's office.

With both hands holding to the saddlehorn, Gundy slid to the side, dropped his feet to the ground, and held onto the horn long enough for his head to clear. It didn't. Dark closed in on him, a swimming, dizzy dark that made him want to vomit. Then all went black.

He came out of it lying on the marshal's desk. Someone worked on his side. Two faces came into focus. The marshal and someone he'd not seen before.

"This boy's lost a lot of blood. Hell, the side of his horse was covered with it. I'm surprised he got into town at all. If this infection doesn't kill him, he'll be all right."

Gundy figured from the way the stranger talked he must be the doctor. The man glanced at Gundy's face. "Awake, huh? Lie still until I get this cleaned out and sewed up. Gonna hurt, so suck up your guts."

The doctor turned his attention back to Gundy's side. When he ran a swab, which he dipped in a bottle of whiskey, through the hole, Gundy knew what he'd meant by "Gonna hurt." He'd bet his toes curled.

His two wounds taken care of, Gundy tried to sit, but the doctor pushed him to his back again. "Hell, Doc, gotta get to Senegal's," he said. "Got men workin' out yonder—gonna do my share."

"You will, like hell, son. You'll be dead before you get to Senegal's place. You're hurt. Hurt bad."

Gundy believed him. He'd almost blacked out again when he tried to sit. "Got no money with me, Doc. Have to pay you next time I get to town."

The old doctor grinned. "Take care of yourself so you *will* get back. Don't worry about it."

Darcy reached in his pocket. "I'll pay and you can pay me, Gundy."

That taken care of, the doctor left. Darcy peered at Gundy. "Now tell me what happened."

"Marshal, you can pass the word to the Rangers. Ross was the head of the Comancheros, and he got in the way o' my throwin' knife. When I got to him to pull it outta his crooked hide, damned if a length o' balin' wire didn't get twisted round his neck."

He winced when pain shot into his shoulder. "Didn't have the guts to kill that there daughter of his. Left her tied an' gagged till I could get away. Wouldn't be surprised if she don't take over the operation. She was with him all the time in the office, so she knows how it's done."

Darcy poured a cup of coffee. "Think you can handle a cup?"

"Marshal, if I can't, just stand over me an' pour it into my mouth. Hell, yes. I'll handle it somehow. Help me to a chair."

With a worried look the marshal said, "Blanco, the doctor said you shouldn't be moving around."

Gundy grinned. "Yeah, but he's used to dealin' with you soft townfolk. He ain't never met nobody like me."

Darcy nodded slowly. "That's the damned truth, Blanco. Not many can say they met a man like you." And under his breath he muttered, "Thank God."

After being helped to a chair, Gundy frowned. "Marshal, reckon you better round up any help you can and get out to Ross's place. They's a lot o' loot out there b'longs to some-body, an' that woman is just as guilty of robbin' and killin' as her pa." He lay there a moment letting the pain wash over him, then said, "Better take a whole bunch o' guns and help. They always got a lot o' fightin' men out there, an' gettin' them wagons back to town's gonna take some doin'."

"You sit still. I'll find a couple of men to help you over to the hotel. You've got to be still long enough for those holes in you to scab over a little." Darcy stood, hitched his gunbelt around where it belonged, and stepped toward the door.

"Got a better idee, Marshal. See if any o' my men or Sen-egal's are in town, rent a buckboard, and have them take me to Senegal's." After he said it, he wondered if it was a smart move. He felt hot all over, and the hurt went all the way to his bones.

Darcy left, and in a short while two of Gundy's own riders, along with Paul, came in. They tried to talk him into staying in town until he could mend, at least a little. He wouldn't lis-ten, but told Paul he wanted another word with Darcy before he left.

When the marshal came back to the room, he muttered something about a "pig-headed fool," and walked to the side of Gundy's chair. "Got a couple of deputies rounding up men to go out to Ross's place. What you want?"

"Just want to say, Marshal, when I was in Austin, I staked claim to all the land surroundin' Ross's hacienda. Now that he ain't gonna need it no more, I'm claimin' that too. So tell the men when they get there to be careful they don't wreck nothin'."

Darcy nodded, and when leaving said, "Yeah, if you live that long."

The ride to Senegal's ranch was pure hell. Gundy passed out more times than he could remember, and when not unconscious he wished he was. Every time the wagon hit a chuckhole, or got crossways in the ruts, new torture washed over him. Twice when he knew what went on around him, Paul was replacing his bandages.

Once, when lucid, he told Paul to get men out to Ross's place and stake claim to the house and all that stood inside the compound, but to wait until the marshal got through with *his* job.

Finally, they pulled into the ranch yard, and Senegal's craggy old face, looking kinder and with more compassion and concern than Gundy thought possible, hovered over him. By the time they got him between clean sheets he'd slipped into a deep coma.

Time ceased to mean anything. The world was thirst, hurt, and fever that dried his flesh as though making jerky of it. Gundy tried to climb to the top of the oven he dreamed he lay in. Climb to the top or crawl out the side. Even though escape was impossible, in his delirium he fought for it. But the dreams, and the oven, lasted until at least he cooled and water, a small amount of it, trickled down his throat. Then he sank into a dreamless sleep.

He awoke slowly. His first awareness was the aroma of food, spicy food, and baking bread, then coffee brewing. And touch. A soft, gentle hand brushed his brow, leaving a scent of soap and the faint fragrance of perfume. The voice he heard saying something to someone in the room sounded like Dee's. But that was impossible. Dee was far away, in the Territory. He opened his eyes. Dee, a worried frown between her eyes, looked down at him.

"Hi." His voice came out a croak. "What am I doin' in New Mexico?"

"Oh, Trace, you're not in New Mexico. You're in Rance's home, where you've been for over a month. Paul sent Emilio and Fernando to bring me to you. We thought you were going to die." She leaned over and kissed him. "Welcome back, my good friend."

"Reckon I'll do it all over again for another kiss."

"Trace Gundy, don't you ever scare me like this again. You can have all the kisses you want, but don't do this to me again, ever."

"Reckon if what you said is true, you sorta feel the same way about me as I do you."

"I thought I made that obvious before you left with Paul. Even if you didn't see it, Mama and Papa did."

He wanted to continue talking, but his throat wouldn't work. Before he could ask for water he went back to sleep.

The next time he awoke, Senegal stood by his bed. "Boy, I thought I'd lost a good drinkin' partner. Sure am glad to see you gettin' better. Don't reckon, though, I better break out a bottle of tequila just yet."

"Not yet, *mi amigo*. We'll tie into one soon's Dee figures I'm ready for it."

"Son, I might as well start teachin' you right now. Ain't no woman ever gonna figure her man's ready for a few belts. He just has to take 'em when he gets the chance. Then he has to suffer while her tongue scalds him into feelin' like a pup."

Gundy wanted to laugh, but it didn't come out as much more than a rasp.

Each new sun saw him improve, slowly at first. Then it seemed he healed in great leaps. He began to ride a little the third week, and by the fifth he was putting in a day's work. Dee talked of her need to go home. She had written at least once a week, but said her parents were looking for her to return soon.

One evening at sundown she and Gundy sat on the corral fence watching night close in. Gundy toyed with a sliver of wood he peeled off the top log.

"Trace, you've been worrying that piece of wood until it's a frazzle. If you're trying to tell me something, say it flat out."

He tossed the sliver into the corral and looked her in the eye. "Dee, reckon you done got to know me pretty well.

Yeah, I got somethin' to say. Reckon I ought to wait'll I talk to your ma an' pa, but I'm gonna tell you anyway right now."

She stared at him with an impish little smile, and before he could say more, she jumped to the ground and held her hand for him to join her. "Well, go on, say it."

"Aw, damn it, Dee, it ain't right for me to tell you like this, but I love you, want to marry you, want them kisses for the rest of my life."

She threw her head back and laughed, a beautiful, deep-throated sound. "That's why I got off that fence. We might have fallen and broken our necks when you kissed me." Then she was in his arms.

As soon as they walked into the sitting room, Senegal looked at them and smiled. Strange, Gundy thought, the old man didn't seem to have trouble smiling anymore. Before he could worry with that thought, Senegal said, "You young folks look like the cat what got into the cream bucket. You done popped the question, Gundy?"

Gundy had been smiling ever since they left the corral—he couldn't stop. "Yep. But we got trouble. Her pa don't want her marryin' no outlaw." He walked to the liquor cabinet. "Mind if I help myself to a drink? Might even pour you one."

"You better pour me one too," Dee said. "I wish Paul was here to hear this."

Gundy glanced at her. "He'll be here tomorrow." Then he said to Senegal, "I'm gonna take Dee home an' talk to her folks. Got a nice home now. I ain't wanted in Texas an' they can come see us here."

Gundy poured them each a drink, then took a swallow and stared into his glass. "Don't feel real good 'bout the way I got that home for you, Dee. Even as rotten as the Rosses were, it just don't seem right I should trade on what happened to them."

He took another drink, rolled a cigarette, and said, "Wonder what happened to that Hillary woman. Ain't heard nothin' since I left her wired tight in that there big sittin' room o' theirs."

Senegal came and put his hand on Gundy's shoulder. "Been wantin' to tell you, boy. She's dead. Shot while firin' at that bunch the marshal took up there to collect the stuff they robbed from ever'body.

"Hell, that posse didn't know there was a woman behind the gun spitting at them from the window. They were just firing back—she got hit. Can't say I'm sorry. She asked for everything she got."

Gundy continued studying his drink. He looked up after a while. "Don't reckon I'm sorry either. Glad I didn't have a hand in it, though. Never could see hurtin' no woman, even when I rode with the Apache." He nodded. "Yep, feel a lot better about how I got that house now that you told me what happened to her."

They had two more drinks and went to bed. Gundy rehearsed arguments late into the night that he would present to Maria and Alex when they got back to New Mexico. None of them seemed any good. He wanted to go to his wedding a free man, and that wasn't likely as long as Lew Wallace was the Territorial Governor. He went to sleep with the thought he'd talk to Paul about it in the morning.

Gundy had breakfast, and was sitting by the stable wall mending a tear in his saddle skirt when the sound of horses caused him to look up. Paul and Fernando stepped from their saddles at the front hitch rack. "Pablo, Fernando, c'mon over here in the shade. Want to talk to you. We'll get a cup of coffee in a minute."

When they hunkered down in front of him, Gundy punched a thong through a hole in the leather and pulled it through before saying, "Gonna take Dee home. Want you to come with me, Paul. Fernando, you stay at the new ranch to run things. First, I'm takin' Dee there to look it over, see what she wants to keep that b'longed to the Rosses. Then I'm goin' in to see Darcy and have him come get anything she don't want. He can use it or sell it, but I want Dee to have the chance to put her own stuff in that there house." He stood. "We leave in the mornin' for the AB Connected headquarters." He hesitated a moment. "Yeah, might as well tell you now, Paul. Dee agreed to marry me, but first we got to get your ma and pa to say it's all right."

CHAPTER
21

Still not convinced his wedding would happen, Gundy left Dee and Paul at the AB Connected and went to Marfa to see Darcy.

When he walked into the marshal's office, Darcy, sitting at his desk looking at a pile of wanted posters, looked up. "Humph, didn't figure them bullets would kill you. What you got on your mind, Blanco?"

Gundy grinned. "You find my picture in them posters you're lookin' at?"

Darcy shook his head. "Nope. Reckon you've gotten away with it so far. Now, what's the visit for?"

"Just wanted to tell you, Marshal, the woman I'm gonna marry is out yonder lookin' the furnishin's over, pickin' what she figures to keep. They's a whole bunch of right nice stuff what ain't gonna have a home to go in. Reckon you an' your missus might like to stock up on it?"

"Sure you folks aren't gonna need them?"

Gundy studied the wall a moment. "Yeah, I'm sure. They's stuff out yonder what's gonna remind her an' me about the Rosses. Want to get rid of all I can so's it'll be *our* home, feel like it really b'longs to us."

Darcy stared at Gundy a moment. "Know how she feels, Blanco. Didn't think *you* had that much feelings, though."

Gundy returned his look and said quietly, "Yeah, Marshal, I got feelin's. Wish I didn't sometimes."

Darcy cleared his throat. "Sorry, Blanco. Didn't mean that the way it sounded."

"That's all right. Reckon I come across to most folks like what they call me, the White Apache. But Marshal, that don't mean I'm a savage. That is, most times I'm not."

Darcy shook his head. "Funny thing, Blanco, you don't come across that way at all. Most folks like you, including me. You ever figure to tote a badge? Rangers would like to have you."

Gundy laughed. "No-no, Marshal. You ain't gettin' me into that game. Hell, it's too dangerous."

Darcy, for some reason, rolled his eyes toward the ceiling.

"Back to what I come in here for. Dee, that's my woman, promised she's gonna put ever'thing she don't want in the middle of the sitting room floor, so get out there when you can and haul it away. Most o' my crew'll be there. I'm takin' Dee to the Territory to see her folks—an' see if they'll let me marry her."

"Thanks, Blanco. Been meanin' to try an' buy some good stuff for the missus for a long time, but somehow a lawman don't never get that much money ahead. This'll be like Christmas to us both."

Gundy had been standing. He turned toward the door. "Goin' over to the waterin' hole for a drink. Buy you one if you'll come."

Darcy said no, and cautioned Gundy there were still vagrant Comancheros around who would like to collect his scalp. Gundy worried the thought around while heading for the saloon. There would be men of the Comanchero stripe around for a long time. He'd have to make sure to leave men at the ranch when they settled in there so Dee would be safe.

With Darcy's words still on his mind, Gundy pushed through the batwings. He'd been thinking about hanging up his guns once he and Dee settled into ranching. Maybe Texas wasn't tame enough for that yet, but the time wasn't too far ahead when change would come about so it would be possible.

He called for a bourbon while thinking about what the marshal said. He never considered that people liked him. A warmth had spread through his chest. It was a nice feeling.

He sipped his drink, liking the taste of it, liking the feel of it warming his insides.

The bartender walked in front of him and said quietly, "Watch your back, Blanco. There's a man back there figures his self a real curly-wolf."

Keeping his back to the room, Gundy said, "Thanks."

At the same time, someone behind him said in a loud voice, "Well, what do you know, folks, we got the big, bad man right here amongst us. Man who took on the Comancheros all by his lonesome."

Gundy went cold and still inside. He didn't come in here for a fight—didn't want one. He tipped his head and drank the rest of his drink, still looking across the bar at the bartender.

"What's the matter, Blanco, you afraid to face me?"

Under his breath, Blanco told the bartender to get out of the line of fire, then thumbed the thong off the hammer of his Colt. He turned slowly, hands moving off the polished surface to hang at his side.

Across the room, facing him, stood a short, thin man, about his own age. Lank, straw-colored hair hung across close-set eyes. He held his right hand splayed at his side. No one stood, or sat behind him. People in the room had moved to the side walls.

Gundy had never seen the man before. "You got somethin' stuck in your craw, somethin' I done to you? Let's talk about it. I don't even know you."

"Don't need to talk. You're the cock-of-the-walk around here, and I don't like big men. 'Sides that, you killed my partner, Nance Yount."

Any reluctance Gundy had about killing the man disappeared. The cold, burning anger sitting in his gut spread to his head. "Well, up to now I hadn't pegged you as trash, but knowing the kind of scum you claim for a partner, you gotta be nothin' but dirt." He had to make this man draw first.

Gundy watched the gunman's eyes, waiting for them to tell him when the draw began.

"Why, damn you. You never seen the day you was the man Yount was."

"Mister, you look old enough to know better, so why don't you leave your gun holstered, turn around, and walk out that door. I'll try to forget I had to breathe the same air as scum like you."

The man's eyes squinted and his hand flashed to his holster. He was fast—real fast. Gundy waited until the gun he faced almost cleared the top of the holster. In a lazy motion he palmed his .44 and fired, then put two more holes in the man's chest beside the one his first slug had made. His glance swept the room. "Him or Yount got any more friends in here?"

The quiet that held the room abruptly shattered. Everyone talked at once. Gundy said to the bartender, "Another bourbon *por favor*."

The man behind the bar poured, and his hand was as steady as Gundy's. "Self-defense, Blanco. Every man in here seen it, if anyone can *say* he seen it. Geez! I always heard how fast you are, but even after seeing it I'm not sure I seen it. This drink's on the house."

Gundy downed his drink and said over his shoulder when he walked toward the door, " 'Preciate you tell the marshal what you told me."

The marshal came through the batwings before Gundy could push them open. He walked back to the bar with Darcy and told him what had happened, and the bartender and several others agreed it had come down that way.

Darcy tipped his hat to Gundy. "See you next time you come to town, Blanco. Be careful."

Gundy looked at him a moment. "Do me a favor, Marshal?"

Darcy nodded. "If I can."

"You can. While riding around the country, wastin' taxpayers' money, why don't you stop in an' visit with Senegal a little, have a drink with him. Bet you'd both enjoy it."

"Bet you're right. I'll do that."

On the ride back to the ranch, Gundy's caution had an edge
to it. The happening in town put emphasis on what Darcy had
told him. Hanging up his guns would have to wait no matter
which way he thought.

Long before he reached headquarters, big rangy longhorns
wearing his brand came under his scrutiny, and there were
many with Ross's Circle HR. He'd have to get that brand reg-
istration changed so he could sell them. Trouble with Texas
law was something he didn't need.

Gundy rode right through his nooning, wanting to get
home, wanting to see Dee. He seemed never to get enough of
just looking at her, and someday he'd be able to look at her
the rest of his life.

When he rode through the gate, she must have been watching, because before he'd gone another fifty yards she
bounded out the front door and ran to meet him.

"Woman, that didn't look like a properly raised *señorita*
what just come runnin' outta that house." Grinning, he
slipped behind the saddle, reached down, and pulled her up to
ride in front of him. "What's your mama an' papa gonna
think I done to you, with you actin' like a young filly what
ain't had no raisin' atall."

"They're going to think exactly what's a fact. Their daughter found her man, and she isn't going to give him a moment's peace for the rest of his life."

"Hmmm, if you mean that for a threat, you just missed the
boat, young lady. Reckon I'm gonna figure them words a
promise, gonna hold you to them."

When they were in the sitting room, Gundy saw that Dee
had been busy. Furniture, quite a pile of it, sat in the middle
of the floor. "Reckon we gonna have to make a trip to El
Paso 'fore long an' buy us some furnishings. You keep anything?"

Dee nodded. "I kept all the furniture in the guest rooms,
and the kitchen stoves, ovens, work tables, and the dining
room furniture, and the piano. Most of what I'm getting rid
of is the things that were more intimate. You know, bedroom
things and other private things." Her face flushed when she

said the last. Gundy pulled her to him and held her close a
moment.

"Soon's we get ready, we'll head for the Territory and hope
no troops or U.S. marshals try to take me in," Gundy said. He
rolled a cigarette and lighted it. "Sorry, we got no comfortable coach to take you in. A light wagon and horseback is the
best we can do right now."

"Trace, as long as we're together, I don't care if I ride an
ox." She stood back, hands on hips. "The packing for the trip
is about done. I would have packed your things but, Trace,
you don't have anything to pack. All you have is two pair of
Levi's and two buckskin shirts. I don't know what I'm going
to do with you. You'll have to have a suit for our wedding."

Gundy studied her for a moment. "Dolores, you talk like
your folks are gonna say yes to our gettin' married. What'll
you do if they won't let us?"

"Get married anyway." She said it so matter-of-factly
Gundy wasn't sure he heard her correctly.

"What'd you say?"

She smiled impishly up at him. "Said I'd get married anyway."

Two days later they pulled out of the gate and headed for
the New Mexico Territory. Paul, Dolores and Gundy, two
other riders, and plenty of extra guns and ammunition. Gundy
hoped they wouldn't need the guns, but the odds were they
would.

Dee started the trip wearing a split skirt. They were coming
in fashion and gave a proper young lady more freedom. Too,
she refused to ride sidesaddle. "I can ride as well as any *vaquero* on Papa's ranch. Why shouldn't I ride like I want to?"

Paul was the one who took exception to her riding astraddle. But Gundy had grown up seeing Apache women ride like
a man, and it seemed foolish to him to ride a horse any other
way. The two of them defeated any argument Paul could offer.

As long as they were in the mountains, Gundy figured to
make camp where they could have a fire. The trip would be
bad enough on Dee as it was, without making a cold camp.
And there wouldn't be a dry camp as long as he could find

water. Once they broke out onto the plains a fire could be seen from a long way off, but there were sometimes slight swales where one could be concealed.

The first day out they passed no one. The second day, getting close to Van Horn, they passed three wagons, and twice a group of riders returning from a spree in town. Gundy felt good about seeing people, and about traveling a well-beaten trail. The other side of Van Horn they'd be breaking their own path. Dee rode alongside him.

"Dee, I fixed the stuff in the wagon so the bedding an' things like that are on each side. If we get in any kind o' trouble, I want you to lie down 'tween them blankets. Don't want no lead huntin' you out."

"If we get in trouble, Trace, I'm going to be in there between those blankets with a rifle in my hands. Every gun will count."

Gundy looked at Paul for support. Paul stared straight ahead, obviously not going to get in an argument he couldn't win. Dolores could be as hardheaded as an old mule.

In Van Horn, Gundy got Dee a hotel room for the night and they had supper and breakfast cooked for them. This was the last break they'd get from the monotony of the trail. At least, Gundy hoped it would be monotonous.

Three days out of Van Horn it started raining, not the typical drenching summer thunderstorm that came and went quickly, but a steady, soaking, dreary rain that made a quagmire of the grasslands.

"Stay in the wagon under the canvas, young lady," Gundy said. "Don't want you takin' a chill."

"I have a slicker, and I'm no more likely to catch cold than you men are." She went to the water barrels strapped to the sides of the prairie schooner, tapped the sides of each, and said, "Soon as we find a water hole that's not very muddy, we better replenish our supply. At least we can let the mules drink."

Gundy nodded absently. The tracks he'd just seen were filled with water, and he couldn't tell whether they'd been made by shod or unshod horses. The horses had riders on them, though, because they traveled in a straight line. If the horses had been wild, they wouldn't move at a steady pace, nor would they remain bunched like these.

He reined close to the others. "Dee, get in the wagon. You men stay close. We may have trouble."

"Trace, I can—"

"Get in the wagon." His voice came out low, but harsh. "Indians, Comancheros, don't make no difference, they like young, pretty white women. Don't want them to see you if they ain't already." He kneed the buckskin alongside Sanchez. "Strip the gear off her horse and put him with the remuda. They see a extra saddled horse they'll know damned well we just hid our woman."

Less than fifteen minutes passed when Gundy said softly, "We got Indians. Don't do nothin'. They may not mean us harm, but keep your rifles pointed at them when they ride up—if they don't start shootin' first."

They rode like that another half hour. The hair on the back of Gundy's neck felt like it stood on end. Rain washed out any smell other than freshness. When he thought he could stand it not a moment longer, a voice he recognized said, "*Hola, Blanco*, what you do way out here, and you have someone with you this time, *sí*?"

"White Wing, good to see you," Gundy lied. An Apache, even though he'd been friendly the last time you saw him, might not be now.

White Wing had four warriors with him. They didn't have their weapons ready for firing. Gundy relaxed a mite, but not enough that he couldn't get his gun in action fast. They had been tracking him long before he saw the hoofprints of their horses, and had in all probability seen Dee, but not close enough to tell she was young and beautiful.

"*Sí*, my friend." He spoke loud enough that Dee and the others could hear. "My wife is not well. I'm taking her to visit her parents in Nuevo Mejico. They have not seen her in four moons."

"Tell her to come out of the wagon. We are friendly. I had not heard you had taken a woman. This is something new for you?"

"Yes, newer than even I can believe, White Wing." He

kneed his horse around so as to keep all five of them in his
sight. Supper was still a couple of hours away, so Gundy
didn't have the problem of asking them to eat. He glanced at
Paul and saw he and the others still had their weapons ready.

White Wing's warriors looked at the horses Gundy's men
rode, and their looks didn't stop there. They checked the remuda closely. They might ride away for now, but they would
be back.

Gundy talked with them another few minutes before White
Wing swung his horse, and said, *"Vamanos, amigos."*

"Keep your guns ready and stay close," Gundy said to his
men. "The first place we find where they's rocks, a deep
wash, if it ain't runnin' bank-full in this rain, any kind o'
place we can defend, we'll make camp. I want the remuda
held close to the wagon tonight. Hobble the horses and put
them on a short tether. Don't want 'em able to run." Over his
shoulder, he said toward the wagon, "Stay where you are,
Dee. I think they've seen you, but in case they haven't, stay
there."

The rain continued, and Gundy stayed as close to the
wagon as he could and still search for a campsite. Every ravine they came to flowed bank-full, and there was no shelf
along the sides for a camp. About to give up and give the order to make camp on flat and level ground, Gundy saw a
small butte ahead. Jutting through the top were several great
slabs of rock. It reminded him of the place he and Paul had
holed up in in Mexico. He grinned, partly in relief. "Kelly,
this place remind you of anything?'

Paul nodded. "If we were in Mexico, I'd think we were in
the same place." His face serious, he continued. "We lucked
out this time, Gundy. I was about to give up finding a place."

"Yeah, I already had my mouth fixed to call a halt. Yep.
We lucked out." Gundy rode ahead, circled the rocks, and
rode into the middle of them and back out. He waved them
in. "Park the wagon in the middle. Put the remuda 'tween the
wagon 'an that big slab yonder. Kelly, want you to sleep in
the wagon with Dee. Ramon, Sanchez, sleep under the
wagon. I'll be around wherever I figure to be useful."

Like most folks traveling in a covered wagon, they had a

hammock slung underneath between the front and back wheels. Whenever they came on a piece of wood of any size they tossed it into the hammock. Because of that, they had a fire to cook over this night, and more than the hot food, Gundy savored the cup of coffee he held with both hands.

Even though it was late summer, the rain had chilled them. Too, they had been on a steady climb from the AB Connected to the foothills where Alejandro had his ranch. They had taken on some altitude, and after the hot Texas summer, even the sunny days would be much cooler. The hot cup felt good in his hands, and the coffee warmed his insides.

He had not told the others, but he intended to stay on watch through the night. Kelly, Ramon, and Sanchez were good men, but they didn't have the benefit of Apache training.

"Who you want on watch tonight, Gundy?" Paul asked.

"I'll take the first watch and wake one o' you when I get tired." If he said which one, that man would most likely wake automatically. Then Gundy would probably hurt the man's feelings by not showing trust in him. This way he could do it his way.

He sat between two boulders where his field of vision was the entire periphery of the knoll on which they camped. He didn't search the ground with quick flicking glances, but slowly scanned the terrain, letting his side vision do its job. He huddled into his slicker with his groundsheet pulled over his head. The fire burned to glowing embers, then ashed over, and finally the last glowing coal cooled. He sat, feeling the dark around him, listening for the suck of mud on a moccasin, or the squeaky rustle of wet leather.

A smoke would be good company, but a good smoke had often been a man's last smoke under similar circumstances.

He didn't move in order to see the area, only twisted to take in what lay behind him. There were no stars to tell time by, but he guessed it to be about three o'clock when he heard an almost inaudible splash to his right.

He shrugged from under his groundsheet and ghosted to the wagon. He touched each man on the shoulder and whis-

pered to get ready for attack. Then he climbed into the wagon
and woke up Paul and Dee.

He eased back onto the ground and, staying low, ran to the
nearest rock slab. He wanted to use his knife if possible so as
to not alert the others in White Wing's party that they were
expected. Gundy had no doubt that they faced the Lipan
Apache party of earlier in the day.

He lay against the slab so as to blend in with the rock, wet
and black in the darkness. He had no more than settled
against it when a warrior slipped alongside him, obviously
unaware that he stood next to the end of his life.

CHAPTER
22

Gundy closed his hand over the Indian's mouth, pulled his bowie across his throat, and let him slip to the wet ground slowly, quietly.

Before he could move from the rock, another Lipan stepped alongside. Gundy didn't have time to cover the Indian's mouth. He stuck his knife straight out, into the warrior's gut, worked the blade a couple of times, and let him drop. A moan and a soggy splash told the others they had been discovered.

Gundy ran for the horses. White Wing's two remaining warriors reached them at the same time. A form materialized beside Gundy. In the dark Gundy thought it was one of the remaining Indians.

He pulled back the hammer of his .44, then eased off on the trigger. The man close to him was Kelly and he was firing. Two went down under his gun.

Gundy searched the dark for White Wing, then heard Dee scream. He raced for the wagon in time to see the dark outline of White Wing framed in the opening of the wagon. Gundy fired, then fired again—and again.

White Wing dropped to the ground and threw a shot toward Gundy. The bullet whined harmlessly past his head. He fired twice into White Wing again, his shots rolling out as one. With each slug, the Indian chief took a step backward,

righted himself, and tried to step toward Gundy. He died trying to eject a cartridge from his old outdated rifle.

Gundy's first thought was for Dee. The only shot he remembered the Indians firing was the one the chief had fired
at him, but things had happened too fast to be sure. He
sprinted to the front of the wagon.

"Dee, say somethin'. You all right?"

"Yes, Trace, I'm all right. You men took care of everything
before I could be sure what to shoot at. Truth is, I don't think
Ramon or Sanchez had a chance to fire either. When that savage climbed to the front of the wagon, I thought it might be
one of you so I held my fire."

"You did well, *mi amor*." He climbed into the wagon and
held her in his arms a moment. "When I saw White Wing in
the wagon's opening, I didn't know whether he was goin' in
or comin' out. Scared me."

He held her a moment longer, then said, "Rain's done
backed off to a thin mist, probably stop 'fore daybreak.
Might's well fix breakfast. Ain't long 'fore we get goin'
again."

"One of you start the fire, and I'll cook," Dee said. Ramon
took the last of the dry wood from the hammock and kindled
a fire.

By the time they finished breakfast, the sky had cleared
and a light rosy dawn colored the east. They cleaned the
camp up, put the Indian ponies in their remuda, covered the
five warriors with boulders, and headed out.

Gundy spent most of the day scouting wide around their
route. Late in the afternoon, Sanchez killed a four-point buck
that Gundy helped him dress before he took it to the wagon.

They traveled a vast and empty land. Gundy spent the days
making sure it stayed that way. He cast back and forth in
front of the wagon, then made wide circles around it. Each
evening before sunset he found a knoll from which he
searched from horizon to horizon.

One such evening, far below and ahead of him, the wagon
and three horseman appeared as miniatures making their way
into the distance. Gundy could not tell from where he sat who
drove the wagon. It made no difference. They were safe.

It seemed they were the only people in the world, the only sound that of the wind singing its lonely song through the grass, bringing with it a delicate scent of pine from far-away mountains.

There were tracks of wild mustangs. A careful study told him they had passed this way several days before.

Gundy watched the wagon and its party until the horsemen stopped, stripped their horses, and built a fire. He gave the land another last, slow look, and satisfied they were the only ones within miles, kneed his horse in the direction of the pin-point firelight.

Almost an hour later he reined in by the remuda, stepped down, and went to the fire. Dee handed him a plate heaping full. The venison steak she served almost covered the plate. He glanced at her. "You leave any for them other hungry men?"

"You're a growing boy, Trace, and besides, I must get used to taking care of you."

"You be there for me at the end of each day, Dee. That's all the care I need, just lookin' at you."

"That's not quite all the care I have in mind, Trace Gundy. As soon as Mama and Papa agree to our getting married, I'm going to stay so close to you you'll wish I was in the next state."

He let a bare suggestion of a smile crinkle the corners of his eyes. "Only if I'm in that state with you, *mi amor*."

Gundy sat, and leaned against a wagon wheel. Dee sat next to him. The others stayed close by the fire several feet away. Even as close as Paul and the others were, it gave Gundy a sense of privacy with Dee. Thinking back to her comment about what she had in mind for him caused him to wonder.

He had no doubt she knew about the relations men and women had with each other. She could not have spent her life on a ranch and not known. Yet when she implied she had much more in store for him, the very thought warmed his loins and heat flushed his face.

Dee must have been watching him eat, for when he finished the plate of food she first handed him, she stood and brought him another, along with a cup of coffee. This time when he finished, she took his hand in hers and sat there holding it.

"Do you ever think about what it'll be like after we're married, Trace?"

He stared at her a moment, memorizing every line of her face, the way her nose tilted slightly, the suggestion of a slant to her eyes, her full sensual lips, the flat planes of her cheeks, the widow's peak her hair formed on her forehead. He'd never thought a woman could be so beautiful.

"Dee, I sometimes believe I think of our life together too much. Out here it ain't healthy to do that."

"When you think of our life, Trace, what things do you think about?"

He chuckled. "Young lady, it wouldn't be proper for me to say, an' you wouldn't want to hear."

"Trace, I do want to hear." He heard her breath catch. "Trace, it might not be proper, but I don't want to be proper with you. I want to be your woman, and I want to know how every part of your body feels." She scooted closer to him. "I'll tell you how I feel, if *you'll* tell *me*."

My God, Gundy thought, doesn't she have any idea how close I am to taking her in my arms and walking off into the darkness with her?

She acts like we're two children who sit and trade naughty secrets. Doesn't she know she's asking about our desire and longing for each other, about the heat we feel in every part of our bodies, about the shortness of breath, the tightening and swelling of muscles?

He took her hand from his and moved farther away. The feel of her, the warmth of her body that close, was more than he could stand. "Dee, you're askin' me to tell you 'bout things I can only show you, an' I ain't got the right to do that yet. When we're married, I'll show you, show you, an' show you again, till you beg me to stop."

She giggled. "Don't you put any hard-earned money on me ever asking you to stop, Trace Gundy." She stood and poured them each another cup of coffee. When she sat, she again closed the gap between their bodies. "For now, just let me be close to you."

When they finished their coffee, Dee cleaned Gundy's gear. Then, standing by the fire where Paul and the others could hear, she held her hand for him and said, "Walk with me, Trace. I want to walk through the grass, hear the wind whisper to it, and see the stars come down to meet us." She glanced at Paul. "I'll be all right as long as I'm with Trace. We won't be gone long."

He nodded, and when Gundy said, "I'll take care of her, Pablo," he nodded again.

"I know, Trace," Paul said.

Her hand in his, they walked beyond the sound of voices, stopped, and stood gazing toward the distant, vague horizon. The only sounds were those of their breathing, the wind singing in the grass, and an occasional rustle of wings as birds settled in for the night. Dee turned to stand in front of him.

"Trace, kiss me, please kiss me and hold me tight. I need to feel you close to me. I have to know you are mine." She stepped closer—and stopped. His hands gripped her arms, holding her away.

"Dee, don't ask me to do that. You know I want to, but it brings on more feelin' than I figure I can handle."

She stared up into his eyes. "I know I'm not being fair. I know how you want me, and I'm just learning how much a woman can want a man. I didn't know it was like this, but my body is waking up. It's telling me things I only had a remote idea about until now. But let's be unfair to each other. Kiss me and we'll turn and walk quickly to the fire before we can change our minds."

Gundy pulled her to him, brushed her lips with his, then hungrily pressed his lips to hers. They strained to get their bodies closer—and before he lost all semblance of sanity, Gundy pushed her from him.

"That's it, Dee. Ain't gonna take a chance on bein' alone with you till after we're married. Don't trust myself." His voice came out hoarse, passion-choked.

Walking toward the fire, he chuckled. "Ain't too sure I trust you neither."

She poked him in the ribs. "You're mean, Trace. I'll bet you get pleasure out of pulling the wings from butterflies."

"Them butterflies couldn't hurt no worse than I do right now. Reckon it hurt both of us. That's why we ain't gonna chance it again. Both o' us wantin' the same thing, ain't much chance we'll know when to stop next time." Dee walked closer to him and hugged his arm to her breast.

"Thanks, Trace. Thanks for letting me have a hint of what we'll have." She looked up at him. "And thanks for being strong enough to stop. I wouldn't have."

He nodded. "I know."

They sat by the fire until its embers died to white coals. Then Dee went to the wagon and Gundy unrolled his blankets.

The next morning they rode away from the sun. Gundy stayed close to the wagon the first hour, then rode ahead. They traveled the Mescalero country now, and if they met any, he wanted to be where he could talk to them before they attacked.

About mid-morning, Gundy rode to the edge of an escarpment about a hundred feet high. Below, only two or three miles out, a strip of dark green wound its way across the lighter green grass.

Trees, there'll be water there, he thought, then looked for a way down the steep slope. Animal trails wouldn't do; the wagon couldn't make it to the bottom over one of them.

After an hour's search, he determined the only way down was around the end where the cliff shortened to a gentle decline, and that would cost them a dry nooning before making it to the stream for the night. He headed toward the wagon.

After setting them on the right course, Gundy changed to one of the Lipan horses. He was covering a lot of territory and couldn't afford to have a tired pony under him. The mustang he rode was small, short-coupled, hammer-headed, but, Gundy judged, a horse that could stay with him all day.

He wanted to scout the creek's bank for others who might have found the precious liquid before him. He rode a goat trail to the bottom of the escarpment. The mountain-bred mustang had no trouble going down it.

At the bottom, he closed in on the stream slowly, warily. Anyone there before him would see him long before he saw them. They had trees and the creek bank to hide them. He had only shallow swales.

He worked his way in, his gaze trying to penetrate the foliage along the bank. Now less than a mile separated him from the trees. He dropped off his horse, holding tight to the reins. The little horse might take it in his head to run for the wild country he'd grown up in.

Gundy went belly down in an old buffalo wallow less than a half mile from the trees, and pulled the mustang down alongside him. His back muscles between his shoulders were knotted and pained. He'd learned long ago not to ignore such warnings.

He lay still, only his head moving, his eyes searching for a tendril of smoke, maybe a movement somewhere close to the ground.

Smoke would probably be thinned out by the trees by the time it got up where he could see it, and if there was anyone there waiting for him, he figured they could be as still as *he* could.

He had as much patience as anyone, but the wagon would be coming and he had to flush out those at the creek ahead of him, and he had no doubt someone had beat him there.

His neck hair bristled at the same time he saw light reflected off metal. He rolled to the side and pulled his head below the land swell ahead of him. Just in time. A bullet kicked dirt where his head had been, followed by the sound of a shot.

He was neatly pinned down. He searched the edges of the wallow, measuring the edges, trying to gauge a way to get out without exposing himself. He faced a good marksman. That shot a moment ago had been accurate.

The wallow's perimeter looked about the same height. He couldn't stay here, couldn't allow the wagon to ride in on a hostile. The chance of there being more than one group in those trees seemed slim. Maybe he could mount and ride the little mustang away from whoever had fired at him and get to the trees farther upstream.

Ain't makin' no money lying here, he thought. Once in the trees, he figured he'd be as good an Indian as any.

Abruptly, he rolled to his knees and pulled on the reins. He and his horse gained their feet at the same time. Gundy threw a leg across the horse's back and, hanging off the side, urged the pony to a dead run. He made about fifty yards before he heard shots, a steady stream of them. Another hundred yards and the mustang stumbled. He'd been hit. Through sheer will, Gundy kept the pony running.

When the horse's knees began to buckle, Gundy pulled his rifle and hit the dirt running, leaving the pony to fall. He was far enough away now that to score a hit his attacker would have to be lucky or a damned good marksman. So far his antagonist seemed to be both.

He headed for the tree line. Dirt kicked up short of him, causing him to angle farther away from where the bullets hit. Then the little eruptions centered around his feet. His enemy had the range, but too late. Gundy ran into the safety of the trees.

Now they would play Indian. Gundy felt a hard smile touch his lips. He enjoyed this game. He cozied close to the trunk of one of the large cottonwoods and stood, thinking. If he was those hunting him, what would they figure him to do? Finally, he nodded.

Instead of getting into the streambed where he had protection from the banks, most of which were at least head-high, and where he thought they would look for him, Gundy searched ahead until sure there was no one in sight, then moved to the next tree that provided cover.

How many men did he face? Only one had fired at him at first, but he had no idea how many were shooting when he'd made a run for it. Too, why would anyone shoot at him before inviting him to ride in and set—unless they knew him? He nodded. Someone in that bunch knew him.

When he'd covered enough distance on foot, from tree to tree, Gundy dropped to his stomach and inched ahead. Every few feet he stopped and listened. Even the slightest sound not of wind or animal would tell him where they searched. Another few yards and he looked for a place to cover his back and wait them out. He realized suddenly he had been thinking he was hunted by more than one.

Safer to figure it that way. Again, he thought they would figure him to hold close to the streambed. Instead he looked for a cutbank close to the edge of the trees, to protect his back and give him full view of the watercourse and its vegetation.

Instead of hearing them, the first indication he had that they were close was a whiff of tobacco smoke. Some damned fool had lighted a cigarette or pipe, but in these trees Gundy couldn't be sure where the wind blew from. He burrowed farther back into the cutbank and waited.

A scraping of brush sounded, but Gundy couldn't see movement. He waited. A twig cracked. He saw one man, a tall thin man he'd last seen in Marfa. He drew a bead but held his fire. If there were others, who were they and where were they? He waited.

His patience paid off. Another man appeared. The redhead Gundy had fought in the saloon, the one Clay Allison had scared off, appeared a few steps behind the first. Gundy made a quick search of the trees behind them, saw no one, and squeezed the trigger of his rifle. A black hole appeared in the center of the first man's chest. Gundy levered a shell into the chamber and fired again. This time his shot went high into the redhead's chest.

The tall slim one fell, blood spreading across the front of his shirt. His breath left him in a moan. Gundy figured him as dead. He swung his rifle to fire again into the second man, who was on his knees, trying to eject a shell from his rifle but apparently lacking the strength to work the lever.

Keeping his rifle centered on the redhead and his eyes focused so he could see them both. Gundy waited another few seconds to see if there were others. Finally, satisfied they were the only ones to worry about, Gundy walked to stand over his saloon brawler, whose wound spurted blood in measured pumps.

Artery, Gundy thought, then said, "Didn't figure you wanted me this bad, Red. Hell, it was just a little saloon fight."

Red tried to push hard against his chest to stop the bleeding. "Wasn't the fight," he wheezed. "Ross paid me to kill you. I took his money, Blanco. Figured I had to earn it even if you done killed 'im." His eyes shifted to his chest. "Reckon whatever he paid wasn't worth dying fer—an' reckon I *am* gettin' out, ain't I, Blanco?"

Gundy stood there a moment, rolled a cigarette, lighted it, and stuck it between Red's lips. He nodded. "Yeah, Red, you're cashin' in your chips. Hope it don't hurt much—won't be long now."

Red looked Gundy in the eye. "Th-thanks, Bla . . ." The cigarette fell against his chin and his eyes opened wide, sightlessly staring at the trees above. Gundy took the cigarette from Red's chin, tossed it in the stream, and walked to the edge of the trees. He'd have to strip his gear from the pony, but he had plenty of time. The wagon probably wouldn't get here until mid-afternoon.

CHAPTER
23

Gundy, without digging tools, pushed the two gunmen under a sharp cutbank and caved dirt over them. He didn't figure to tell Dee or his crew about the gunfight. He'd say the horse stepped in a prairie-dog hole, broke his leg, and he'd shot him.

After stripping the gear from the mustang, Gundy sat leaning against his saddle at the edge of the trees, waiting for the wagon. They were still a half hour away when he gathered wood and started the fire. Won't have so long to wait for supper, he thought.

Long after they'd eaten and crawled into their blankets, Gundy stared at the sky frowning. Now, more than at any other time, he worried about what marriage would bring to Dee.

According to New Mexico, he was an outlaw, and in Texas there were many who wanted him dead. Would she be a widow before they could much more than start life together? Would she catch a bullet meant for him? Would Lew Wallace ever recognize he had not been part of the renegade Apache raids?

He studied the outlaw tag he had. He'd made it a point to stay clear of any suggestion of an Apache raid. Alex had written the governor in his behalf. What could *he* do? One thing he was determined *not* to do, and that was to turn him-

self in. He could rot in some territorial prison, and there
would be many who thought he deserved it. Anger boiled into
his throat. He swallowed hard, pushed it to the back of his
mind, and went to sleep.

The next morning Gundy told them that with El Paso on
the way, it might be well to stop and do some shopping. He
had two pair of Levi's, two buckskin shirts, one pair of
scruffed-up boots, and an old flat-crowned, flat-brimmed
black hat with two bullet holes in it. He wanted Alex and
Maria to see him looking good.

All agreed, ready to see more than mile after mile of scrub
oak, cactus, and grass.

Two days out of El Paso, a dust cloud moved in their direction. When they were close enough, Gundy made a rough
count of eight riders. They might be no more than a ranch
crew heading home, or they might be riffraff from along the
border. He figured to treat them like the latter.

"Dee, get in the wagon and don't show your face until I
tell you it's all right. Paul, place the extra rifles so they poke
through the slots along the wagon side. Make 'em look like
they's somebody behind 'em, then come out here with Ramon
and Sanchez." He flicked a glance at them all. "Hold your rifles across your saddles in front of you."

Dee stepped up to the seat, hoisted a Winchester, jacked a
shell into the chamber, and said, "There'll be one rifle poking
out those slots that *will* have someone behind it."

Gundy's chest swelled with pride. Each man had quietly
done as told, and Dee had done as he knew she would. The
riders approached.

"*Hola, amigo.* Where you headed?"

Gundy didn't feel hospitable, and he showed it. "Why? We
go where we go. Ain't nobody's damned business where or
why."

The one who had led the group in glanced at the wagon.
His eyes held momentarily on the rifle barrels poking out the
sides. Then he looked at those following him. "Hey, *hombres,*
theez man, he talks rough, eh? Maybe we show heem how to
treat visitors."

Without thinking, Gundy palmed his .44 and eased the

hammer back. He'd not thought of drawing—his gun was just there.

Probably as a reflex to Gundy's draw, the one who had done the talking made a move for his pistol, but stopped far short of touching it. "Ah, *mi amigo*, you are very fast, maybe as fast as me."

"Only one way to prove that. Your men drop their weapons, you keep yours." Gundy didn't like their looks. They were dirty, heavily armed, and all with bandoliers crossing their chests. They looked typical of the Comanchero bands he'd encountered in the past.

On a hunch, he said, "You might's well turn around and go back across the border. They's nowhere to sell the stuff you steal over here. Your boss is dead."

"Wat you mean, steal? We don' steal nothin'—an' we got no boss." Their leader poked his finger at his own chest. "I'm the boss."

"What're you called? *Como se llama?*"

"I am Rodrigo Hernandez."

Gundy nodded. "All right, Rodrigo Hernandez, this .44 makes *me* the boss. An' I'm tellin' you an' your Comanchero friends to get the hell gone, an' I mean real quick 'fore I start emptyin' saddles. Make a move to circle back, I'll kill every one of you before you get here."

The leader sneered. "You talk very beeg, *señor*. Who are you? And why you call us Comancheros?"

"Gonna answer your last questions first. I call you Comancheros because I've killed enough of you to know the breed. Your head man, Ross, is dead. I killed him too. As to who am I? Well, I'm called Apache Blanco." Gundy's gaze bored into Hernandez, and as one the entire band backed their horses a step.

"Ah, I 'ave 'ear of Blanco. You don't look so bad to me."

Gundy holstered his hand gun. "All you gotta do to find out is make a move I don't like."

Hernandez's eyes again swept the side of the wagon. Gundy knew he was trying to guess whether the guns had anyone behind them. "Deeleon, shoot the hat off this pig's head." He emphasized the Dee and before he finished the sentence a rifle cracked from within the wagon. Hernandez's hat flew from his head and landed at the feet of the horse in back of him.

The Mexican leader kneed his horse sideways. "You hold the high cards now, *señor*. We'll meet again." He leaned off his horse on the side Gundy could see, picked up his hat, looked at his men, and said, *"Vamanos."*

Gundy watched until they disappeared behind the brow of a hill. "Paul, ride in the wagon with Dee. Ramon, Sanchez, stay on horseback. If anyone comes close, shoot. Gonna follow, see if they decide to come back. I'm thinkin' they gonna try."

Dee spoke up. "Trace, stay here with us. Let us help fight them. You've done enough. I know you had a fight back there at the creek. I saw where two bullets went through your saddle skirts."

Gundy took his hat off and wiped perspiration. "Dee, I gotta do what I think is best. I can handle this. Don't worry. I'll be back a little after dark."

He gave Hernandez and his bunch a half-hour start, then mounted and followed. He was taking a chance. He could ride right into the middle of them.

He expected them to turn back and track the wagon as soon as they were out of sight, so he reined into the brush and rode up the side of the hill behind which they had disappeared.

Tumbled rocks covered the hill. He hunkered behind one, sweat trickling down his back and soaking his shirt. Still in sight was the wagon, now small with distance. Gundy figured the bandits watched it too, and would not follow until the wagon rounded the hill ahead of it.

A quick study of the hillside showed plenty of cover from the bandits' fire. Another glance at the wagon showed its tailgate rounding the hill. The Comancheros would appear soon.

A few moments passed. Gundy tasted brass under his tongue and in the back of his throat. Regardless of how he'd talked to the border scum, and to Dee, eight-to-one odds were not to his liking, but he had little choice. He couldn't let them get close to Dee.

The soft sound of horses' hooves in the deep dust reached his ears first, then Hernandez's voice saying something to his men. Gundy positioned his rifle, aiming at the spot he figured the first bandit would show. He wanted to get off at least three shots before changing his hiding place. If they looked ready for attack, he'd move with his first shot.

Hernandez, at the head of his riders, came into view. Then, closely packed, the remaining seven appeared. Gundy sucked in a deep breath, as much to steady his nerves as to steady his aim. The bead on the front of his rifle barrel centered on Hernandez's chest. Gundy squeezed the trigger. Without looking to see Hernandez fall, he jacked another shell into the chamber and fired at the second man, then another. His shots rolled out as one continuous sound.

Jacking another shell into the chamber, he ran for the cover of another boulder, skidded to a stop, and fired at the first man to come in his sights. He hit him in the back. As one man, the Comancheros had pulled their horses to a rearing stop, turned them on their back legs, and headed back the way they had come. Gundy got one more of them before they rounded the shoulder of the hill.

He darted back from behind the rock from which he'd fired his last shot. He'd fired five times and figured he'd knocked five of them from their saddles. With ten shells left in the magazine, he reloaded.

By his count there were three Comancheros left. He stopped behind each boulder and searched the winding trail. Then he spotted their horses tied to brush at the side of the wagon ruts. They had taken to the rocks. Gundy figured he'd need everything the Apache had taught him against three men with good cover.

From where he crouched, he viewed the boulders along the side of the hill. His eyes were the only thing that moved. They flicked from one boulder to another, from ground to skyline, from scrub brush to cactus. Movement—he needed to see something move.

Time crawled. His muscles held tense, ready to swing his rifle and fire. Then they began to ache. Then they numbed. He held his frozen pose against the tan-colored stone. Something streaked in front of his vision. He clamped his rifle tight, still frozen. A lizard had run down the side of a cactus. Then out of the corner of his eyes, a greasy mop of black hair eased around the edge of a stone slab. Gundy waited. With motion so slow he was barely able to see it himself, he moved his rifle to aim at the man. Finally, the eyes came into his sights. He squeezed off a shot. If the greasy head had not exploded out the back, Gundy would have thought he missed. He'd hit dead center in the man's right eye.

With the kick of his rifle butt against his shoulder, Gundy ran bent to the ground, his neck twisted to see smoke or guns pointed his way. Shots clipped rock fragments and threw them stinging into his face. Twigs fell from brush cut by the bullets. He made it to a boulder he'd already chosen as his next cover. Now he knew where they hid, but they also knew where he was. He studied the ground around him. He couldn't stay here. He had to take a chance.

Banking on them looking only at the rock where he had gone to cover, Gundy dropped to the ground and inched his way toward a low embankment, a swell of earth thrown up by water runoff. His every muscle tensed against the slam of a bullet. He fought the urge to quicken his pace. A fast motion would draw attention.

Just when he thought his life would run out before reaching the earth-swell, he made it, and lifted his head enough to look where he knew them to be.

"Luck, pure damned luck, Gundy," he mumbled. His hiding place gave him a partial look at one man, and a full view of the other. They had their rifles trained on the spot from which he had crawled. Gundy guessed their distance from him, wanting to use his six-gun, then figuring it to be too far.

One against two, and as soon as he fired his position would be exposed. He'd be lucky to get off two shots, and they had better be good.

He dragged his rifle into firing position slowly, fluidly. One of the men glanced toward him. He froze. The gunman raked the area with his gaze, but never appeared to look at the ground. After a moment he looked away. Gundy let his pent-up breath out a bit at a time. Sweat streamed into his eyes. He blinked them hard, trying to squeeze the salt from them. He couldn't put off what had to be done much longer.

He drew in a long, deep breath and let it out, raised to his elbows, and shot into the head of the bandit who was partially hidden. He fired at the second man, and at the same time a numbing blow hit his side. The bandit jerked backward, caught himself, and again brought his rifle up. Gundy had fired too fast. He levered a shell into the chamber and fired again. The gunman frantically pulled his trigger—on an empty chamber. He pulled it a last time as Gundy's bullet tore through his body from side to side.

If the Comanchero had jacked a shell into the chamber, Gundy knew he might be the one torn apart by a .44 slug.

His side and leg felt like a tree had fallen on it. He looked, expecting to find a hole through his hip. Still looking, he shook his head, grinned, and pulled his handgun from the holster. A slug had wrapped itself around the cylinder, wrecking the action. This was one time he wouldn't mind buying a new Colt.

"Sonuvagun—got lucky once more."

He turned his attention from his six-shooter to the bodies strewn about the landscape. He'd been able to shoot them one or two at a time, except for the first three. He went to them first, approaching from the back in case they were alive. After checking them, he went through their pockets, took their guns, and went to the others.

The six-guns and rifles he collected Gundy strung from his rope through the trigger guards and hung from his saddlehorn.

It seemed a long ride back to the wagon. He was tired, and wasn't surprised. Every time he'd come through a gunfight, storm, or other dangerous situation, he'd felt like two days' work without rest lay behind.

He *was* surprised that the sun sank slowly behind the western hills. The day ended after seeming to have hardly started, yet there had been events during the day that had stopped time.

When he climbed from his horse, Dee stood there waiting for him. Her eyes wide and scared, she scoured him from head to toe, then looked at the guns hung from his saddle-horn. A tremulous breath caught in her throat and she walked into his arms. "Trace, oh, Trace, I think I've died a hundred times today. Not knowing how you were, what you were doing, whether you caught those men, and if you did catch them how you could defend yourself, much less attack them." She stood back and again looked him up and down. "Trace, please don't ever do this to me again. No matter the danger to me, take me with you."

Gundy gripped both her arms. "Dee, if you'd been with me today, I couldn't of done what had to be done." He grinned and pulled her to him again. "*Mi querida*, they ain't many hombres sneaky enough to do what I done. Now ain't you ashamed o' me?"

"No woman ever had more reason to be proud of her man than I do. Here, you sit down and I'll fix you a plate of food."

They had supper, and after they ate Gundy looked over the weapons he had taken from the Comancheros. They were all excellent weapons, but one in particular took his eye, an almost-new Colt double-action .45. After testing it for feel and balance he slipped it in his holster.

They slept that night under a clear sky, feeling free of worry. Tomorrow he would lead them on another leg of their journey.

CHAPTER
24

A week later they rode through the gate of Alejandro Kelly's Circle AK ranch. When they were still two hundred yards from the big house, Alex and Maria ran to meet them.

'Bout as much kissin' an' huggin' goin' on as when I brought Pablo back from Mexico, Gundy thought. Again, he got his share of it.

Alex, gripping Gundy's hand, said, "I was beginning to think you were going to keep my little girl and boy over yonder in Texas with you. Glad to see you, son."

"Yes, sir, an' I'm mighty happy to see you an' Maria. I think, though, when you take a long look at your boy, you gonna find he ain't a boy no more. He's been through a few things, and done a few what's changed 'im. He's a man now, Alex. A man I'm mighty proud to call friend."

"Well, c'mon. Let's go in the house, have a drink, then you can get to your rooms and clean up."

Gundy looked at Alex straight on. "Yes, sir. After we get cleaned up, we got a lot to talk about."

Alex returned his look. "Figured as much. But let's have that drink first."

Just as she had done when Gundy and Paul rode off for Texas, Dee made no effort to hide her feelings for Gundy. She not only clung to his arm, but stood as close as propriety permitted. Gundy noticed Maria and Alex didn't miss her possessive actions. And to his puzzlement, they cast a secretive glance at each other and smiled.

The old grandfather clock chimed three o'clock before they again gathered in the sitting room. Gundy wore the first completely new outfit he'd ever owned, from boots to hat, although as a matter of courtesy he didn't wear his hat indoors as many were prone to do.

"Damn, boy, relax. You act like you figure somebody's going to jump out of the closet at you."

"Tell you what, Alex, it's worse'n that. I feel like if I bend, these clothes ain't gonna bend with me—figure they'll break. Range duds feel a whole lot better." He took a gulp of the drink Alex handed him. "Fact is, *you* might do more'n jump outta the closet at me in a minute. I got somethin' to ask you."

Alex and Maria again shared that secretive little look that seemed to say so much. "Well, ask, boy. Don't know of much I'd say no to."

"Better hear what I got to say 'fore you say any more," Dee said, coming over and standing close to his shoulder. He looked at her and saw pure devilment in her eyes. She and Maria grinned at each other as though they shared a secret.

"Well, go on, ask," Alex said. "We'll see how bad it is."

"Ain't bad. Well, reckon depends on what side you're on an' how you feel about it if it's bad or not." Gundy took another swallow of his drink and put the glass on the table by his chair. "Ain't done the right thing by you 'cause me an' Dee done talked 'bout this. Shoulda said somethin' to you first."

Maria and Alex stared at him. They were expressionless, but it looked to Gundy like they wanted him to squirm awhile. Well, dammit, he *was* squirming, but he might as well get it said and out on the table. "I want to marry Dee. Reckon she feels the same 'bout it as me."

Alex frowned, looking awfully serious to Gundy's way of thinking. "Don't know about that, Trace, you being an outlaw and all. Reckon if you hauled Dee off to Texas again, we wouldn't get to see her hardly ever." He glanced at Maria. "How you feel about this, *mi mujer?*"

Damn, Gundy thought, never figured he'd take it like this. Never heard him call Maria his wife before either. Reckon they don't like the idea at all.

Maria opened her mouth to say something, then couldn't stifle the laugh that pushed her words aside. "Oh, Alex, let's stop teasing Trace. He deserves better than this." She giggled again. "Trace, Dee wrote two or three weeks ago. She told us then you were going to ask for her hand in marriage." She frowned and placed her palm to her cheek. "Let's see, how did she phrase it? Oh, yes. She used an old cliche. She said 'come hell or high water' she was marrying you." Maria held her empty glass out to Alex. *"Por favor?"*

When Alex brought her another drink, she again looked at Gundy. "Alex and I talked it over, and since we don't think we could stand hell *or* high water, we decided to say yes—on one condition. We'll have the wedding, a big wedding, here."

"Y'all sayin' we can get married?"

"Trace, when you brought Pablo back from that hellhole in Mexico, and Dee made it so apparent she had chosen you as her man, we knew then we had lost her to you. We decided soon after that when you asked, outlaw or not, we would give her to you." Maria wiped a tear from her cheek. "Yes, Trace, we're agreed. Treat her well, son."

"Ma'am, if you ever have anything to worry you, it ain't gonna be that I won't love Dee, an' I'll treat her as well as I know how." He pulled Dee to the arm of his chair and looked up at her. "Think you can get used to answerin' to 'Mrs. Gundy'?"

She looked him straight in the eyes. "Trace, I've been practicing for months. Yep, think I about have it down pat, but I'll answer to anything *you* call me so long as I know you love me."

Gundy looked at her mother and father. "Your daughter ain't all I'll be takin'. Paul an' I been workin' together on that there ranch; reckon it's his much as mine. Figure he'll go back to Texas with us."

They looked at Paul for his reaction. He nodded. "Yes, reckon I'm a Texan, but that's Gundy's ranch. I'll work for him."

"We'll talk about that later," Gundy said, and turned to Maria. "Ma'am, we'll get married here, but a big wedding might not be good. It'll take a while to fix for it, an' a lot o' people comin' might know who I am. Might spend my wedding night on the way to prison."

Alex spoke up. "Son, no one in the Territory knows the Apache Blanco and Trace Gundy are one and the same. It's been fourteen years since you were actually an Apache. No one will know who you are, including Governor Wallace."

Gundy almost came out of his seat. "You don't figure to invite the governor to the wedding, do you?"

"He'll never know who you are, Gundy. Trust me. I wouldn't put your neck in a noose."

Gundy leaned against the back of his chair. He didn't think Alex would put his neck in a noose intentionally, but territorial prison was worse than getting hung.

They talked more about it, but Alex and Maria won. The wedding, a big wedding, would be held on the Circle AK—and Lew Wallace would be invited.

During the next few weeks, the traffic to and from the ranch was never-ending: dressmakers, milliners, cobblers—a tailor even fitted Gundy for a fancy bolero and flared trousers embroidered in silver. And all the while he lived in fear that someone would recognize him. There were many in Texas who knew he had been the Apache Blanco, but he had been out of the Territory so long, there didn't seem to be any here who suspected who he was.

As the day for his wedding drew near, Gundy found himself avoiding being alone with Dee. He wanted her so badly he hurt low in his stomach. With her help he could hold himself in check, but she didn't help. He found himself taking her hand in his almost as soon as they met in order to keep her from making their meetings more intimate than they should be, or at least more intimate than *he thought* they should be.

About a week before the wedding, a company of state militia rode in and stayed two nights. Alex and Maria entertained the young captain in command. At first, every time

Gundy was close to or in conversation with the officer, his stomach tossed and turned until he thought he'd throw up.

He would not violate the home of Dee's parents, so killing the captain, if he found out Gundy was Blanco, never was an option. But there was no hint the soldier knew.

Two days before the wedding, guests began arriving. Surreys, buggies, buckboards, coaches, every known vehicle parked by the stables. The farther those attending had traveled, the more elaborate the vehicle. Gundy stared in awe. He had never figured there were that many families in the entire Territory of New Mexico.

Alex's house was huge, but Gundy couldn't imagine where all the people would sleep. Well, he thought, reckon Maria had it all figured before she invited them.

When the big day finally arrived, Gundy realized he'd not been nearly as nervous ever before, even when a gunfight had seemed inevitable. Hell, he'd go through three of them, against bigger odds, every day, rather than do this again. His gut tied itself in knots, then untied itself, and did it all over again.

He'd met so many people, and could call none of their names two seconds after meeting them. But only a few minutes before he went to this room to bathe and dress for the ceremony, he met the one man he'd always remember, Governor Lew Wallace.

Wallace searched Gundy's face a moment. "Seems like I should know you, young man. Have we met before?"

Gundy would have given up Dee, his ranch, everything, for a fast horse between his legs at that minute. He swallowed a couple of times. "No, sir. Reckon if I'd ever met the Governor of New Mexico before, I'd remember it."

They made a few casual comments before Maria pulled him away to meet others. She glanced at him from the corners of her eyes, and said in little more than a whisper, "Feel better? See? He didn't know you."

Sweat poured down Gundy's forehead and cheeks. He let out his breath in one long flow. "Maria, don't never do nothin' like that to me again. Reckon if wishin' myself dead woulda done it, I wouldn't be among the livin' right now. Figured I was lookin' at one helluva long stretch in prison."

She smiled. "Trace, I wouldn't have done it if I'd not been sure.

"Now, I know you haven't seen Dee all day, and that's as it should be on your wedding day, but you haven't long to wait now. By the time you get ready it'll be time to claim Dee as your bride—and start your honeymoon."

"Lord, ma'am, you just don't know how hard it's been."

Maria started to giggle, then burst out laughing. Gundy wished to hell he knew what was so funny.

She controlled her laughter and pushed him toward his room. "Go, go get ready, before I lose complete control."

Gundy had no idea what she had laughed at. Puzzled, he headed to his room.

Two hours later, Dee walked down the aisle between the many guests, only a hint of her face showing behind the veil. Gundy's gaze tried to penetrate the gauzy-looking thing to see her better. Despite only the suggestion of eyes, nose, and mouth behind it, he thought her the most beautiful woman in the world, anytime, anywhere.

The ceremony seemed to go on forever. Gundy muddled around in a quagmire of words, songs, fumbling for her ring, and then finally the words he'd wanted to hear: "I now pronounce you man and wife. You may kiss the bride." *That* was the first time during the entire afternoon he knew what he was doing—and he did it soundly.

They walked toward the door. Hands grasped them from each side, words of congratulations slipped into and out of his ears, an occasional pat fell on his shoulders, and through it all, the only thing real to him was Dee's firm grip on his forearm.

When they got to the door, Gundy's heart sank into his boots. The same company of militia lined up on both sides of the walk between him and Alex's coach, the one that was to take them to El Paso for their honeymoon. The same captain was with them.

At some command from the captain, they drew swords and

crossed them in an arch. Gundy wondered when they would surround him and put him in irons.

To hell with them. He straightened his shoulders, threw his head back, and walked between their ranks.

At the other end, the governor waited for them. Reckon he wants to arrest me his own self, Gundy thought. Wallace placed his hand lightly on Gundy's chest. "Just a moment, Mr. Gundy."

Gundy stopped. The governor reached inside his coat and drew out an official-looking document. Reckon them's the papers tellin' me I'm goin' to prison, Gundy thought. Alex's gamble, and mine, sure as hell blew up in our face. Here he stood without a weapon of any kind. And even if he'd had one, he wouldn't use it for fear of hitting Dee or some of the guests.

The governor was reading from the paper. ". . . and be it known to all men, now and henceforth, the Apache Blanco, also known as Trace Gundy, is fully pardoned from any and all crimes for which he has been accused against the peoples of the Territory of New Mexico." Wallace read more words, folded the paper, handed it to Gundy, and said, "Mr. Gundy, along with this pardon goes my most sincere apology for the way you've been treated by your own people. Had it not been for the determined effort of Alejandro Kelly, this injustice might have gone on forever." He held his hand out for Gundy to shake. "I can only say I'm sorry, son."

Gundy groped for the hand extended to him. He had trouble seeing it through the tears.

Maria, Alex, Paul, and Dee somehow all managed to hug him at once. They had known about this all along.

When Gundy could get his mouth clear of all the kisses, he looked at Dee. *Mi amor,* you remember all them things you wanted me to tell you an' I said I could only show you? Well, times done come. Tonight I'm gonna show you."

Dee smiled. "And, my savage friend, don't hold your breath until I tell you to stop."